Injustice For All - A Harper Ross Legal Thriller

Rachel Sinclair

Tobann Publications

Also by Rachel Sinclair

For information about upcoming titles in the *Harper Ross Legal Thriller* series, sign up for my mailing list! You'll be the first to know about new releases and you'll be the first to know about any promotions!!!! http://eepurl.com/hBqhtr

Johnson County Legal Thrillers (Kansas City, Missouri)

Bad Faith

Justice Denied

Hidden Defendant

Injustice for All

LA Defense

The Associate

The Alibi

Reasonable Doubt

The Accused

Secrets and Lies

Until Proven Guilty

Emerson Justice Legal Thrillers (Los Angeles)

Dark Justice

Blind Justice

Southern California Legal Thrillers (San Diego)

Presumption of Guilt

Justice Delayed

By Reason of Insanity

Wrongful Conviction

The Trial

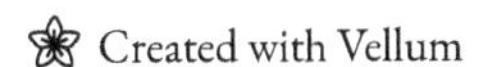
Created with Vellum

One

Darnell Williams was a quiet and studious child. He was one of six children living in a two-bedroom apartment in a run-down house East of Troost. At age 18, he was the oldest child. He was presently working two part-time jobs, in addition to going to school full-time, because he had to save money for college and for his math tutor. Anything he earned, over and above his savings goals and tutor money, went to his mother, Anita, who worked two jobs herself – one job was full-time as a hospital orderly and the other was part-time working as a housekeeper for a local motel. The motel where she worked sometimes charged by the hour and made a Motel 6 look like the Hilton. She never complained, though, and she never took a dollar from the government. Darnell sometimes wished that she would – it would take some of the burden off him.

That night, that fateful night, he was working one of his jobs. He was a fry cook at a Church's Chicken, and he was assigned clean-up duty. Basically, he was tasked with closing the place, which meant that he had to stay after everybody else had already gone home. He didn't really mind it that much – it gave him some rare alone time. Every other minute of his life was filled with people – he shared a bedroom with his four brothers and sisters, so he never got a moment's peace at his place. The rest of the time, he was at school and his two jobs. He never got the chance just to sit in the quiet and hear himself think, so he really enjoyed those nights when he was assigned final clean-up.

"Darnell, now, you know the drill," his night manager, Sally Monroe said to him. She trusted him, more than she trusted any of his co-workers, because Sally knew that Darnell would never take an extra dollar from the cash register. She couldn't necessarily say the same about the other kids who worked there. Not that she blamed any of them for wanting to take an extra dollar here or there - she knew these kids' situations. The best that she could do for any of them was to allow them to take home the chicken that was made but not bought – at least that way she knew that these kids would have something to eat at home. She wanted to give them all a pay raise, but that wasn't her call. "Make sure the floor is mopped, clean the bathrooms spotless, take out the trash, clean out the fryer and make sure all the food is put away."

Sally had, in a leather blue pouch, the day's earnings from the cash register. She was the one who made sure this money found its way to the bank every night. She wanted to have Darnell do the drop sometimes, but she knew that he rode the bus to the restaurant every day, so that would never do. He might get rolled on the bus and then where would she be?

"I know, Ms. Monroe," Darnell said to her. She always asked him to call her "Sally," but he never would. His mama always instructed him to treat his elders with respect. Sally was at least 27 years old, so that made her his elder. He always addressed her as "Ms. Monroe" and "ma'am." No matter how many times Sally chided him, telling him that "Ms. Monroe isn't my name. That's my mama's name. My name is Sally," Darnell persisted in calling her "Ms. Monroe." His own mama drilled that kind of respect into him.

Sally nodded and smiled. She was a chubby woman, with big blonde hair and too much eye shadow. She probably ate too much fried chicken from Church's, as that was her favorite thing to eat.

Darnell liked that she was chubby, because she reminded him of his own mama. His mama was only 33 years old herself, giving birth to Darnell when she was only 15 years old and a sophomore in high school. In her high school, this wasn't exactly an unusual occurrence. A lot of girls in her class were having babies at the same time.

Even so, his mama always told him that he didn't be having babies in his teenage years. She dragged him, when he was only 13 years old, to the local birth control clinic and had the doctor there show him all about condoms and how to use them. He still cringed with embarrassment when he thought about all the times that his mama gave him a condom and had him slip it on a banana while she watched.

No matter, Darnell had no use for condoms yet. He was way too busy with his two jobs and his schoolwork to even notice girls. His math tutor was a girl, a pretty girl named Chantal who wasn't much older than him. But he never even really thought about her that way – she was simply somebody to help him conquer calculus. He had applied to MIT and was determined that he'd go there on a scholarship and go on to study nuclear engineering. That was his dream, anyhow, but he knew that he might have to settle for state university and a degree in electrical engineering. Either way, he knew he'd go on to get a master's degree in some type of engineering. And he was never going to have to share a bedroom again.

Plus, he'd take care of his mama, once he got out into the world and started making six figures. He hated that she had to work so many hours just to keep a roof over everybody's head and food on the table. He wanted her to, someday, be able to relax once in awhile. As far as he knew, she had never, ever, had a vacation. She never even had the chance to go and get a massage or get her nails done or any of that. Every penny she earned was put into groceries, utilities and rent.

All he wanted was for her to be able to slow down. Maybe only have one job, and maybe find a job where she had a paid vacation once a year. Maybe Darnell might be able to give her enough money so that she could actually do something on that paid vacation –

maybe something simple, like take a trip to *The Elms,* which was a tiny resort just north of town. He had seen the website and this looked like just the place for his mama – it offered a full spa and a hot tub and pool and indoor baths that promised a relaxation haven.

Maybe he might even be able to send her to Vegas once in awhile. Not that his mama gambled, but he often caught her watching Cirque de Soleil on television, and he had never seen her face light up so much as when she was watching one of those shows. She also spent her time watching house remodeling shows, and other shows that featured gorgeous high-dollar houses that were for the taking. One such show featured a couple who would look at three different houses and had to pick just one. His mama got mad sometimes that those people on the shows found such faults in such beautiful surroundings – house number one isn't good enough because it doesn't have a pool, and house number three only has four bedrooms, not five, and where are the granite countertops?

"Lordy, Darnell," his mama would say while she watched a couple pick apart a seaside mansion that was situated high on a cliff. "Could you imagine if they came and saw this place?" She'd shake her head. "They'd run screaming from the room, that's what they would do." Then she'd chuckle and speak under her breath.

Darnell always knew that most people in the world had it better than he did. Better than his family. But not anybody he knew. Everyone he knew was in the same boat, some even worse – Darnell always had a lunch to bring to school and his mama always took him clothes shopping before the school year began. Sometimes they went shopping at Goodwill, but, on occasion, his mama would be able to afford to take him clothes shopping at Wal-Mart. A lot of his friends didn't have a mama like his. Some had mamas who were strung out on drugs or were into prostitution. Others had mamas who beat them. Hardly any of his friends had a baby daddy hanging around – most of them had gone to prison or were absent and on the streets.

That was the case with Darnell's mama. He never knew his baby daddy. He wasn't ever around, not even when Darnell was a baby. But that didn't really matter to him – his friends were much the same, so nobody ever felt that they were missing out.

He took his iPhone out, put it on Apple Music, and blasted Drake in his headphones. While he listened to the music, he carefully mopped the floor, taking his time. He enjoyed getting the floor squeaky clean. There was something about seeing a grimy, greasy, oily floor go from being almost black to being sparkling white that fascinated him. He always took his time closing up. Sally had explained that he had to have his work done in one hour, because her general manager would never let him work past that, but Darnell usually took two hours cleaning up. He clocked out after an hour, and then spent another hour, all on his own time, making sure that all the crevices were clean. he'd dust and scrub and get lost in knowing that he was doing the best job that he could do.

It was all worth it when Sally would come in the next day, or Chloe, the morning manager, and they would marvel about how spotless the restaurant was. Not that he cared about getting gold stars and pats on the back or any of that, but he did like it when they noticed that he did a good job. Anybody would, even though too much praise sometimes embarrassed him.

And, truth be told, he was never in a hurry to get home. He reveled in knowing that he was the only person around. He liked that this restaurant, at this time, was his little bit of space in the world. He never had much control around his own house – with six people living there, it was tough to keep up with the dishes in the sink and the spills on the carpet. There was always spoiled milk on the couch, or bits of cereal ground into the rug. One time, his little sister, Alisha, ate a runny egg on the floor, in front of the TV, and that egg yolk hardened into that spot. The place didn't have a dishwasher, and it didn't even have a dining room. Everybody ate on TV trays or on the floor, and there was simply no keeping up with any of it. There also wasn't a washer and dryer in the apartment, nor was there one in the building, so clothes were constantly piling up in both of the bedrooms. Darnell long since forgot what his bedroom's carpet looked like, as it was always covered with clothes, shoes, books and toys.

But, here at the restaurant, he could make the place look just how he wanted it. He could make sure that everything was put back in its place, that there wasn't a crumb of food anywhere and that the floor was so clean that he could eat off of it. There wasn't the chaos in this restaurant, the chaos that he constantly experienced in his home.

He took off his head phones, gathered up the trash and opened the door into the alleyway.

Humming a tune that was in occupying his headspace, he threw the trash into the bin and turned around.

And stopped.

At his feet was a body.

And a gun was right next to it.

Two

I groaned when Pearl came into my office. "You've been assigned a death case," Pearl said. "I know, I know, just what you needed to brighten up your day, right?" She smiled as she handed me the file.

A death case. Another damned death case. I hated these things because I always felt that, if I could talk the prosecutor off the death penalty, I'd plead them out. I never wanted to try a death case if I didn't have to, because there was just too much that could go wrong. I hadn't lost a death case, so far, mainly because I could plead them to life in prison without a chance of parole. That was the best I could usually do with these awful things.

I leaned back in my chair, thinking about Stephen. He was in jail. At first, I wasn't too upset about his being arrested. His bond was only $25,000, so I figured his arrest was only a formality. After all, his identical twin brother, who took his name, was a notorious serial killer responsible for the deaths of 35 local boys and girls in 1972. Stephen was held hostage in the house where his brother was murdering these children, so it was only a matter of time before he'd be brought in for questioning.

I knew when I met him, out in the woods of Oregon, that he was somebody special. That was why I convinced him to come back to civilization after 50+ years of living in isolation in the woods. He didn't want to come out of hiding- he was afraid to be blamed for what his psychotic identical twin brother did all those years ago. He lived in isolation after being released from his involuntary imprisonment. He lived in a time-warp, not knowing about anything that happened in the world since 1972. But he was getting used to all the advancements that had happened since then.

Then something awful happened. The body of a 13-year-old girl, Alaina Morosky, washed up on the shores of the Missouri River. Stephen was arrested for that murder.

Why was he arrested? Stephen had no clue. I had no clue, either. Stephen didn't know this girl, had never come in contact with her, and, besides, he wasn't violent and murderous like his brother. He'd never do something like this.

I spoke with the arresting officer on that case, Officer Cooper, and he gave me no reason why Stephen was arrested, either.

"I can only tell you, Harper, that Mr. Heaney is suspected of being the true culprit in those 35 murders in 1972. He gets into town, and there's immediately a random murder of a young girl. I know there are such things as coincidences in this world, but I don't believe in them. Stephen Heaney is a serial killer who needs to be locked up and have the key thrown away. Or he needs to die with a needle in his arm."

The upshot was that, when the body of the girl was found, and Stephen was charged with her murder, the judge denied him bail.

That broke my heart. I'd grown quite fond of Stephen. He was just a lonely old man trying to get his life together. He worked at a nursery full-time and I'd visited him there. I needed some advice about the garden I was trying to cultivate in my own backyard. He told me how to plant my tomatoes, what to feed them, when to harvest them, and how to fight common diseases.

The saddest thing was, he'd turned a corner right before his arrest. He finally was getting acclimated with society. He was getting used to all the new technology and all the changes that had happened since 1972. He even got his first iPhone, and it was endlessly fascinating to him.

He even met a woman he wanted to spend time with. Her name was Katy MacLeod and they had met on-line. They had gone on a few dates and Stephen was hopeful about seeing her on a regular basis.

Things were going on a smooth track, and then, boom, he answered the door and saw cops standing on the other side. He knew why they were there. He was prepared to see them. He went with them willingly, thinking it was only a matter of time so he might as well get it over with.

But he never thought a girl's body would wash up on shore and the cops would automatically pin that murder on him. He never believed he'd be denied bail.

I never believed it, either. I'd told Stephen I'd take any of his criminal cases *pro bono* and I meant that. Stephen wanted to pay me but I wouldn't hear of it. He wasn't making a ton of money at the nursery and his social security check was tiny – he didn't have much job history, so he didn't have much of a social security check.

No, I wouldn't let him give me a dime. I had to do a certain number of *pro bono* hours anyhow, every year, so Stephen would be my *pro bono* hours for the year.

Of course, I never expected he'd be accused of first degree murder.

And I certainly didn't believe he'd be facing the death penalty for that murder.

Now, with this Darnell Williams case, I'd have not one but two death penalty cases on my plate. One *pro bono* and one assigned.

I looked at Darnell's file, thinking I'd have to plead it. He was only 18 years old, but was facing the death penalty because of the nature of the crime and who the victim was – a 20 -year veteran on the Kansas City police force.

Reading through the file, I realized I'd heard of this case and knew the victim. I'd heard of the case because everybody in town had heard of it. That was what happened when the body of a decorated police veteran was found in the alleyway of a Church's Chicken restaurant. Especially when the accused killer was 18 years old and apparently a known drug dealer.

I shook my head. I hated that this kid was only 18. But, then again, he was caught at the scene with the gun in his hand and a quarter kilo of cocaine on his person. That smelled like a drug deal. I could imagine how it all went down. The officer killed was in plain clothes when he was murdered. Probably what happened was that the kid, Darnell, tried to make the drop with the officer. The officer tried to arrest him and the kid got trigger happy. Happened all the time.

Then, apparently, there was another cop on the scene. It was Officer Cooper, the same guy who arrested Stephen for the Alaina Morosky case. He wasn't the victim's partner but happened on the scene. I was unclear on how that Officer happened on the scene – he stated he was across the street at the 7-11 when he heard the gun shot. He ran to the scene but was too late. Officer Parker was already dead on the ground and Darnell was holding the gun.

Pearl came back in. "So, what's up? What's the story with this new death case?"

I shrugged. "Looks like a dead-dog loser, unfortunately. The kid's only 18. I could probably get the prosecutor off the death penalty just because of the kid's age. I doubt the prosecutor's office wants to court publicity or pressure by seeking death for an 18-year-old. I'll see what I can do about getting Mr. Williams life in prison."

That would get one death case off my desk. I needed that to happen because I needed to focus on Stephen's case. I was determined to prove Stephen didn't kill that girl. I didn't know who did, of course – her body washed up on the Missouri River's shore. There were no clues on who killed her. The best I could do would be look into her background and find out who might've wanted her dead. I hoped like hell she wasn't a prostitute or homeless. If she was, I'd have one helluva time trying to narrow down her killer.

I decided to put Stephen's case aside for the moment and call the prosecutor on the Darnell Williams case. He was initially assigned a Public Defender because his charges hadn't yet been upgraded to the death penalty. As soon as the Prosecutor's office decided to charge Darnell with first degree murder with special circumstances, and announced they would seek the death penalty on his case, Darnell was no longer eligible for a regular Public Defender. All capital cases in Kansas City went to the Capital Crime Division of the Public Defender's system, and, if the attorneys in the Capital Crime Division were swamped and couldn't take anymore cases, the case would be assigned by the State of Missouri to an attorney experienced in taking death cases.

My lucky number was pulled out of a hat so Darnell was my case.

Because Darnell had been through his initial appearance, he was assigned a prosecutor to take his case all the way through trial. The prosecuting attorney's name was Aisha Moran, an African-American woman experienced in death cases. She'd tried at least twenty such cases in her 10-year career at the District Attorney's Office, and, unfortunately, obtained convictions on every case but two. Granted, most of her cases pled out, but her trial conviction rate was astoundingly high. I had no desire to go against her on this Darnell Williams case.

"Aisha Moran," she said when she answered the phone.

"Hey, Aisha," I said to her. "This is Harper Ross. I'm calling you about the Williams case."

She paused on the phone and started to mumble. "The Williams case, the Williams case, uh..." I could hear her humming lightly while she evidently looked for the right file. "Okay, yes, the Williams case. Just a minute, Harper, let me look at the file. I was just assigned this today."

"Take your time."

She hummed some more. "Okay, yes, I'm up to speed. What did you want to ask me about?"

"Well, I wanted to ask you to come down off the death penalty. He's 18 years old. I know your office doesn't like to obtain death convictions against really young guys. Why don't we talk about life in prison? I haven't seen him yet, so I don't know if he'd go for anything at all, but I'd like to come at him with something other than the death penalty. We can probably get rid of this case sooner than you think, but only if you're willing to deal."

"Hmmmm," Aisha said. "You make a good point. We don't like to get death convictions for really young guys. But this one might be a special case. He's accused of killing a plain-clothes police officer. He had a quarter kilo of cocaine on his person when he was arrested. I'm sorry, Harper, but cop killers are a special breed in this office. I don't imagine my boss will let me come off the death penalty."

I sighed. That was the last thing I wanted to hear. "No way, huh?" I asked her. "No chance of getting him LWOP?" LWOP meant "life in prison without parole." "Come on, Aisha, give me something here."

I felt bad for trying so hard to get this kid a deal when I'd yet to visit him. But I was suffering from exhaustion and burnout. I had so many high-pressure, high-profile murder cases in the past few years that I couldn't imagine taking another so soon.

No. I couldn't imagine taking on *two* such cases so soon. Unfortunately, Stephen's case was front page news. Darnell's case was too. Somehow, I was supposed to juggle not one but two death cases at the same time.

It was just too much.

I wanted to go home and pull the covers over my head. Instead, I was looking at working two huge cases at the same time. On top of all that, I had to spend as much time as possible with my two daughters while somehow fitting in time with Axel. Squeezing in an evening or two a week for him was priority, but with two death cases on my plate, both of which probably would go to trial, there was just no way.

"I can't, Harper, I'm sorry. I mean, not at the moment. I'll talk to my boss about an LWOP possibility on this one, but no promises."

I sighed. "I guess that's all that I can ask for, huh?"

"Yeah, I guess. Is there anything else?"

"No."

I hung up the phone and stared at the wall. How could I muster up the energy for these two cases? Death cases took a severe mental, emotional and physical toll. There was always so much to prepare.

I knew one thing – Stephen wouldn't serve a day in prison for the murder of Alaina Morosky. I'd be damned if he went to prison for that murder. I knew he didn't do it.

Darnell, on the other hand...he was a street kid. He was probably in a gang and was a high school dropout. Probably had been dealing for years. It finally caught up with him. It usually did.

Not that I didn't have sympathy for the kid. I did. I knew the available options to street kids like Darnell. They had little opportunity and few resources. His mother was probably a crack-whore, his father was probably in prison, and he probably was left on his own all the time. Gangs were often a substitute for the gang members' absent family. They didn't have a mother or father to speak of but had their "brothers" in the gang. They couldn't make legitimate money to support themselves, so they resorted to dealing drugs and committing crimes.

Darnell was probably just another cog in the school-to- prison-pipeline. That was a sad pipeline and made me sick. Prisons were often"for profit," mainly because they were overcrowded and the state and federal resources to fund them were always being slashed. It didn't help that the past administration reinstituted mandatory minimums for non-violent crimes, such as low-level drug crimes. Darnell would be just another number. He'd be just another tragic story, one I knew all too well.

It was a story of a kid who never had a chance in life, who came into a world of poverty and despair. Who went to schools that didn't know how to teach him and where teachers were suffering from burnout and depression. I'd substitute taught in these schools. I saw how the teachers hated their jobs. The classes were enormous – sometimes 30 kids crammed into one classroom. In that kind of environment, just one trouble-maker would disrupt the entire classroom and make it impossible to teach.

That's what so many people didn't understand. There was such an ethos in this country about personal responsibility and pulling yourself up by your boot-straps. There was such a resentment towards kids like Darnell and towards his parents. Darnell's mother probably received food stamps and welfare, even though she probably worked hard. But when the minimum wage was only $12 per hour, how could she make ends meet? Especially with several mouths to feed.

Yes, Oprah Winfrey came from horrible poverty and violent circumstances. She was raped and molested as a young girl and was now a billionaire. That was inevitably the example used to show how people could easily work their way up from poverty.

That was such a common logical fallacy - *The Exception that Proves the Rule* - where somebody uses an outlier, such as Oprah Winfrey, to generalize about a certain condition, such as poverty. The reasoning goes as follows – Oprah Winfrey came from terrible circumstances and abject poverty and now runs a dynasty. Therefore, any person in poverty can do the same.

No, not everyone in poverty can do the same. They just can't. Oprah was a special case, but Darnell was probably more typical.

I gathered up his file and looked at my watch. I was having dinner with my father that evening. He was finally back from Russia and wanted to speak with me. He'd apparently already taken Albany, Brad and Emma out to dinner to break the news we already knew – he was gay and in a relationship with a man. He wanted to marry Sergei. The whole thing turned my stomach, not because my father was gay, but because he was my father. I was like a little kid who wanted her parents to stay together forever. I didn't want to picture my father with anybody besides my mother.

Yet my mother seemed fine with the whole thing. She would even give my dad away at his wedding to Sergei. That was weird, but, then again, if my mother could be okay with it, how could I judge?

I had a ton of questions for my dad, though. I couldn't be late for our dinner.

"I'll the jail," I said to Pearl. "I'll be gone for the rest of the day. Hold my calls. If there's an emergency, call me on my cell. Otherwise, just tell everybody I'll get back with them tomorrow."

"Of course, girl," Pearl said. "I'll see you tomorrow."

At that, I left the office, intending to see Darnell.

I already wanted to plead that kid. I'd work on convincing him to take something.

Three

I went to the jail and waited for Darnell to come on out. The guards were taking an awfully long time and I looked at my watch. It read 4:15. My dinner reservation with my father was for 6 PM. He was springing for a steak dinner at Eddie V's, my favorite steakhouse on The Country Club Plaza. I could already taste the rare prime rib on my tongue. I could smell the garlic mashed potatoes and the bread with rich butter. I already knew what I'd order – a prime rib with mashed potatoes and a wedge salad.

That was what I always ordered at this place, and, in the past, I usually liked to add a couple of dirty martinis. That was what I missed the most since I quit drinking – ordering dirty martinis with my steak dinners. That particular drink seemed to go with prime rib like peanut butter went with jelly.

As I bounced my pen up and down on the table in front of me, I thought about what kind of drink I'd order with my prime rib. I couldn't have a dirty martini, of course, but maybe I could have something else. Maybe a Virgin Mary. Eddie V's made an amazing Bloody Mary, so they probably made an amazing Virgin Mary.

Yes, okay. A prime rib, a side of garlic mashed potatoes, a wedge salad and an order of steamed veggies. A Virgin Mary on the side.

My mouth started to water as I waited for Darnell to make his appearance.

That was assuming Darnell met me soon. I'd have to leave by 5 PM at the earliest if I wanted to go home and take a shower before dinner. Any later than that and I'd have to head straight to the restaurant. I didn't want to do that. I always needed a chance to decompress before seeing people for dinner.

I found myself daydreaming and looking at the ceiling, so I didn't even notice Darnell was finally coming out. I looked up and saw him.

He was walking slowly, his wrists shackled, as were his ankles. He was African-American and had a very short Afro. He was 18 but looked younger than that, even though he was fairly tall. His eyes were red rimmed and his nose was running. His lips were quivering.

He walked very slowly, his head bowed, his shoulders slumped. He eventually made it to the table with me and sat down.

I sat up straighter as he sat down and got a Kleenex from my purse. I reached over and put the Kleenex on his nose and he blew it. "Thank you, ma'am," he said softly.

I nodded. I noticed his arms were free from tattoos, as was his neck. I couldn't see if he had tattoos anyplace else.

Maybe I was wrong about this kid.

Something about how he walked out made me think he wasn't an East Side gang-banger. I had those gang-bangers as my clients. They usually met me with a swagger and confidence like they owned the place. They usually had a certain look that they'd seen it all before. They usually tried to intimidate me.

But Darnell looked...soft. Scared to death. His hands were shaking, and his head was deeply bowed.

He finally opened his mouth again to address me, and his words were quivering. "Ms. Ross," he said politely. "Thank you very much for seeing me this evening. I very much appreciate your taking the time out."

I nodded. "Of course. I just got the case, but I wanted to visit and let you know I'm your attorney and answer any questions."

"Thank you," he repeated. He paused and then looked up at the ceiling and then back at me. "I was wondering what happens next? I went before the judge a couple of days ago. He told me what I was charged with and denied bail. That's a bad sign, isn't it? Some of the guys in here told me it's a bad sign I don't have bail. I can't post it, of course, because I don't have the money. But I was wondering what you thought about that."

"Well," I began. I wanted to lie to this kid for some odd reason. His brown eyes looked at me with a mixture of hope and dread mixed with absolute despair. I felt oddly motherly towards him. I wanted to say that denying bail wasn't a bad thing when I knew it was.

It was a very bad thing.

He kept looking at me, a question in his eyes. He waited patiently for me to speak, which was also different about this kid. Usually, with my other clients, the drug dealers caught murdering another dealer infringing on their turf, they wouldn't let me get a word in edgewise. They'd ask me a question, and then loudly talk over me when I tried to answer them.

But Darnell sat there, on the other side of the table, quietly waiting for me to finish my sentence.

I cleared my throat. "It's not great," I said. "To be denied bail. But I'll see what I can do about that. I'll try to get you something."

He shook his head. "No, that's okay, Ms. Ross. That's okay. As I told you, I couldn't post any bail, at all. Even if the bail was only $1,000, I couldn't post that. I have savings, but that's all tied up in a college fund."

He looked embarrassed. "I'm 18 but a year behind in school. I just started my senior year this fall. I had some learning problems when I was young, so I started school a year late. My mama thought it best I go to pre-kindergarten when the other kids were starting kindergarten. I guess that was best."

I cocked my head, feeling somewhat charmed that he explained his learning situation in such detail. He apparently felt the need to apologize for being behind in school. He wanted me to know he was graduating later than other kids not because he was held back but because he was a late starter.

I wondered why he felt it so important that I knew that about him.

He looked up at me. "I've been saving, Ms. Ross, since I was 15 years old. I've been working at that Church's Chicken since then and every penny I make goes into my college fund." He shook his head. "Well, that's not entirely true. I have a math tutor, too. I've been having problems in my AP Calculus class. I'm getting a B in that class right now so wanted extra help. And I give my mama money from time to time. She works two jobs but there's not a lot to go around. So I can't make bail."

I swallowed hard. This meeting wasn't shaping up like I thought it would. To say the least.

I mentally kicked myself for prejudging the case. I just read the Statement of Information and automatically assumed Darnell would be like the kids I'd met who were good for their crimes.

I had a feeling Darnell wouldn't fit that mold.

I got out a pad of yellow paper and tapped my pen against the table. "Okay, Darnell, I've read the police report and the Statement of Information. It says you were caught with a quarter kilo of cocaine on your person and you were standing over a plain-clothes police officer. Your hand was on the murder weapon." I nodded.

"Let me get your story."

Darnell shook his head. "I don't know," he said. "I don't know what happened there. It all happened so fast."

I wrote down his words and I looked up at him. "What happened so fast?"

"I was finishing up my shift at Church's. I closed that night, so I was the only one at the restaurant. I always try to make sure the restaurant is really clean. I take pride in what I do. My mama has always instilled that in me – always do an excellent job. I don't like when I come to the restaurant in the morning and the floors are still dirty and there's still trash in the bins. I want to have the floors looking so clean you could eat off them."

He sat up straighter as he was recounting his shift at Church's.

I nodded and wordlessly encouraged him to continue his story.

"I finished my shift and went outside to the trash dumpster. I dumped the trash, turned around and there he was. A man lying on the ground."

Darnell shook his head. "Just lying on the ground, Ms. Ross. I mean, I've seen people lying on the ground before. Where I live, there are always homeless people who sleep on the streets. So, I didn't think anything of it. I stooped down to see if he was okay, but when I turned him over, I could tell he was dead."

He shuddered, but I could see that death was something Darnell was all too familiar with. I could see it in his haunted eyes. He bit his lower lip and lowered his head. Soft tears formed.

"My daddy left when I was just a baby, so I never knew him. But my mama had this one guy around the house for a little while. His name was James and was like a daddy to me. He died of a heart attack in our house. I found him lying on the floor and I called 911 but it was too late. So, this guy looked like James did. His eyes were dead and he was cold, just like James. I knew this guy was dead."

I wrote down his words as he spoke and looked at him. I reflexively put my hand on his arm as a gesture of empathy and concern. This kid looked so young, so innocent, so fresh...it broke my heart to see him behind bars.

"I stooped down to see if I could do something. Just in case I was wrong and he wasn't dead. You know, in school, I took this class on what to do in an emergency. I learned CPR, mouth-to-mouth resuscitation and everything. They have these dummies in school. They wanted us to learn all that because our teachers know most of us will have to revive somebody at some point in our lives. So I knew how to do CPR and mouth to mouth. I tried that but knew right away it wouldn't be any good. This guy had apparently been dead for a minute."

I nodded and kept writing. “So, he was dead when you got there. Did you see anything around the body?”

“Yes.” He looked at his handcuffed hands. “I did. There was a gun next to the body. I was stupid and not thinking. I mean, my mama is always telling me what to do when I come up on a situation like this. She’s always telling me not to touch anything and just call the police. She’s beat that into my head, but you have to understand, Ms. Ross, I was...” He shook his head. “I was in shock. I wasn’t thinking. I saw the gun next to him and picked it up.”

I sighed. I was hoping this kid didn’t pick up the gun. That would’ve been a saving grace. I’d have to explain it away. “Okay, you picked up the gun. Then what happened?”

“I dropped the gun on the ground. All at once, I remembered what my mama told me about picking up guns or things if I found a body. I went back into the restaurant to get my cell phone to call the cops.”

He stared at his hands and bowed his head. More tears came to his eyes.

“I went back to the body and was about to call 911 when a cop rolled up in the parking lot. I thought that was a good thing. I thought he’d be there to help me. Instead, he pulled his gun on me and told me to get up against the wall. He searched me and found this bag of cocaine in my pocket.”

“Were the drugs yours?”

“No, ma’am. That’s the thing, Ms. Ross. I don’t know who those drugs belonged to. I’ve never done or sold drugs in my life.” He sighed. “I did something else not too bright. I put on a jacket one of my co-workers left in the restaurant. I didn’t bring a jacket with me to work. I realized it was kinda cold that night. I didn’t know how long I’d have to wait for the cops to come, so I put on that jacket and went back outside to wait for the cops.”

I tapped my pen against the table. “Whose jacket was it?”

“Another guy who works with me. His name is Antwan. I didn’t think he did drugs, either, but he must’ve. He must’ve left that cocaine in his jacket.”

That didn't make sense to me. I couldn't imagine anybody being so careless. According to the Statement of Information, there was a quarter kilo of coke in this jacket pocket. That was about $18,000 worth of coke. It was possible somebody would be so careless to leave his jacket at the restaurant with that much coke in it, but I seriously doubted that.

"You think this cocaine belonged to Antwan?"

He shrugged. "I guess so, Ms. Ross. It didn't belong to me. I wouldn't know how to get that much coke. Or any coke, for that matter. I don't know any dealers. There are dealers at school but I stay away from them. I've never done illegal drugs. I've never taken a drink, not even a beer. I don't know where to get drugs, Ms. Ross. I don't know where that coke came from. I really don't."

I bit my lower lip. Nothing was adding up. Darnell struck me as a good kid. Respectful, polite, intelligent and articulate. He seemed to be telling the truth. So why was he saying the drugs weren't his? I didn't think Antwan would've left that much cocaine just lying around. There must've been some other explanation for how Darnell had those drugs on his person.

"Okay," I said. "The police patted you down and found these drugs on you. What did they do?"

"They immediately arrested me. Read me my rights in the alleyway. Brought me downtown, booked me, fingerprinted me. You know the drill, Ms. Ross. At first, they charged me with possession with intent to distribute. About an hour after they brought me I found out they were charging me with murdering that man. I guess they processed that gun and found my fingerprints on it."

I nodded. That sounded about right. "Did you confess? Did you say anything to the cops when they brought you in?"

"No. They tried to get me to confess, but I wouldn't. They had me in that room for hours. They brought me a bunch of cokes to drink and then wouldn't let me use the bathroom. They made that room really cold. I mean, really cold. They did all kinds of things to make me confess, but I did nothing, so I wouldn't say I did."

"At what point did you ask for an attorney?"

"After about four hours. Then they put me back into my cell. The next thing I know, I'll court with my public defender and being charged with murdering a cop. Then that public defender told me she couldn't represent me anymore because my charges were upgraded to capital. I know what that means, Ms. Ross. They want to kill me."

He bowed his head and the tears started in earnest. I came over to his side of the table and wiped away his tears and he blew his nose. "My mama's in the hospital," he said. "She has problems with stress. She works night and day. All she does is work. She has to work around the clock to make sure me, my brothers and my sisters have stuff. I work for that, too. I give money to her all the time. She doesn't have money left over for nothing. When she heard I was in here facing the death penalty, she had a stroke."

He sighed. "My brothers and sisters are at home. My auntie is watching them but has kids of her own. I'm scared, Ms. Ross. I'm scared my brothers and sisters will end up in foster care. They'll be broken up. I'm scared my mama will die. You don't understand, Ms. Ross. There's not enough money as it is. With my mama in the hospital, my family will get kicked out of their home."

I put my hand on his hands and looked at him. I wanted, for all the world, to help his family. What would happen if his mom couldn't work for awhile?

"Will your mother be okay?" I asked him. "Will she recover?"

"I think so. My auntie came to see me today and said mama was recovering. But I don't think she can work like she did. She maybe can't work for awhile. I need to be home, Ms. Ross. I need to get back to work. My brothers and sisters are younger than me, Ms. Ross. My oldest brother is 13 and my other brother is 10. I have two sisters, age 7 and 8. None of them can work, Ms. Ross. I'm the only one old enough to work."

I sat up straight. "Let's see what we can do about getting you bond." I sighed, knowing it was a long shot. He was accused of killing a cop and had a quarter kilo of coke on his person when arrested. I didn't think a judge would give him a bond, at all, and if he got a bond, it wouldn't be less than a million.

"That's okay, Ms. Ross. I couldn't afford a bond no-how."

"There must be something I can do," I said. "How much is your rent where you live?"

He shrugged. "It's around $600. It's a two-bedroom apartment on Euclid Ave."

"I'll see what I can do. I'll go to Legal Aid and ask them if they can do something to ensure your family doesn't get kicked out of their apartment."

"Thanks, Ms. Ross," he said. "But what'll happen if my auntie can't watch my brothers and sisters all the time? They'll end up in foster care if my mama can't get out of the hospital soon."

"I'll think of something," I said.

Then I looked at my watch. "I'm so sorry, Darnell, but I'm running late for dinner with my dad." I smiled as I thought about what my dad would say to me. I wasn't the first girl to find her father was gay and I wouldn't be the last. Still, it was odd. I wondered if Sergei would also be there.

Darnell smiled. "That's okay, Ms. Ross," he said politely. "You have a life. I'll see you soon, I hope."

"Of course. I'll start my discovery process and will be visiting you from time to time. I try to see my clients at least once a week. Hopefully more."

"That would be good."

I motioned for the guards to get Darnell and a female guard appeared through the door. She led Darnell out and he smiled at me one last time before going through that metal door.

As I left, I thought about that poor kid. If he was telling the truth, a terrible injustice was perpetrated. He was arrested for something he had nothing to do with. Because he was arrested, his mother ended up in the hospital and his brothers and sisters might end up in foster care. If there was nobody to care for them or his mother couldn't work as much, so she couldn't make rent, they could all end up homeless or in the system.

People in Darnell's situation were always on the edge of the cliff. If everything went right, they could scrape by. But throw in a crisis, such as the oldest child being arrested for something he didn't do, and a subsequent hospital stay for the mother, and it all falls apart.

If there was something I could do to ensure it didn't fall apart for Darnell's family, I'd do it.

Four

"Sorry I'm late, Dad," I said, walking into the restaurant. It was 6:15. I tried to be on time, but parking on The Plaza was notoriously hard to find. I ended up parking about a mile away from the place, and even though I almost sprinted towards the restaurant, I was still a bit late.

Dad stood up and kissed me on the cheek. My dad was a big guy, broad, tall and bespectacled. Like my mom, his hair was dark, but it was receding and greying just a bit around his temples. I never understood where I got my curly red hair, or why my brothers and sisters all had reddish hair as well, considering both our parents were dark-headed with straight hair. He was wearing a suit and tie.

Right next to him was, I'd imagine, Sergei, who was handsome like an older version of Viggo Mortensen. He had a broad face, twinkling blue eyes and a bright smile that reached his eyes. He was taller than my 6'2" father. He was at least 6'4". He shook my hand, his handshake firm and confident.

I sighed. This would be awkward but I was cheered by Sergei's friendly face. "Harper," Dad said, "this is Sergei. Sergei, this is my daughter, Harper."

"Hello," he said, still smiling big. "Your dad told me so much about you. You're his attorney daughter."

"That's me," I said, looking at my dad. "It's good to meet you, Sergei."

All of us sat down. "I ordered an appetizer," dad said. "Crab cakes and oysters."

"Thanks." I took a deep breath, looking at my dad's glass that was filled with his usual neat scotch. Sergei was also drinking a dirty martini, my favorite drink. My mouth watered as I saw these two men drinking. I wanted, for all the world, to join them.

"Can I get you something, Harper? I know how much you love your dirty martinis."

I shook my head. I never told my dad I was an alcoholic. I was embarrassed. I always wanted my father to see me in a good light. I was forever trying to please him. I never wanted him to be disappointed in me, and I knew he would be if he discovered I had an alcohol problem. He could never be proud of me if he knew my weakness.

"No, thanks, Dad," I said. "I..." I licked my lips, wanting to tell him, but thinking it wasn't a good time. Not when I was meeting his new boyfriend. *How weird to even think that in my head. My dad's new boyfriend.*

"You what, Harper?" Dad asked. "Come on, live a little. It's not every day you get to meet your dear old dad's new guy." He winked and I smiled. That was my dad – treating this whole thing like it wasn't a big deal. For that matter, my mom treated it the same way.

"I'll stick with Perrier," I said. "I have an early day tomorrow and I can't get shloshed."

Dad shrugged and flagged down the waiter to order a sparkling water.

"Well, okay," he said. "I wanted to ask you to dinner because I wanted you to meet Sergei, but I also know you have a lot of questions. So, ask away. Don't be shy. Sergei and I have heard it all and have been asked every question you can imagine." He shook his head. "You should've seen us answering Albany's questions. That girl is a pistol, let me tell you. Anything you put to us will be a breeze after that."

"Uh," I said, looking at Sergei shyly. I didn't know this man from Adam, yet I was supposed to ask questions about his relationship with my dad?

"Yes?" Sergei asked. He had a slight accent, almost imperceptible. Some people had a knack for languages – for different inflections and pronunciations. I was always impressed with people who master different languages so well that one could barely tell the person wasn't a native speaker. Sergei seemed to have just that mastery of English. "Go ahead."

"Well, I'd like to get to know my new, uh, stepfather, I guess?" I had no idea what Sergei would end up being to me. He'd be considered my stepfather after he married Dad. That was just too weird to me, too. If Mom married again, I'd end up with two stepfathers at the same time. I wondered if anybody ever experienced that. I was quite sure it was more common than I thought.

Sergei nodded. "I was brought up in Russia and was married for forty years, like your father. Her name is Elena, my ex-wife. I have five children, all living in Russia now. Arthur has met Elena and my children."

"How is Elena with all this?"

Sergei shrugged. "Not good. In Russia, being gay isn't accepted, even though it's not a crime. People there aren't as understanding as here about such things. Elena hasn't told anybody the truth about why we divorced. As far as anybody there knows, I left her to come to America. No other reason."

Sergei took a sip of his dirty martini and smiled at my dad. His smile at my father was no different than a man smiling at his wife. There were the same emotions in his eyes as when I looked at Axel or Axel looked at me.

"How did you guys meet?"

"I came here," Sergei said. "For business. I came into the hotel bar. Your father was there, entertaining clients. I caught his eye, and after your father finished entertaining his clients, he came over to talk. He didn't know I was gay, and didn't know that he was gay, either." He shrugged. "I didn't know I was gay but I knew it when I met Arthur. Something in our interaction told me there was something between us."

I took a sip of my sparkling water and the waiter came by with our crab cakes and oysters. Sergei took an oyster and put it on a cracker. "Bottoms up," he said with a smile as he put the oyster in his mouth.

"Something between you," I said. "How did you guys stay in touch after that?"

"I was here for a month," he said. "My business trip was a month. I was staying in that Marriott Hotel and Arthur visited me a few times. We had dinner, drinks, some laughs, and by the time I went back to Russia, I'd fallen in love. I never loved Elena. After I met Arthur, I finally understood why."

I turned to my dad. "Dad, when did you know you were gay?"

"Harper, I don't use labels like that. I was always attracted to men. Your mother knew about it. But I was very much in love with your mother. I still am. She was my first love. But the passion died down long ago. I love her more as a friend now. She feels the same way about me. I don't have a passion for your mother anymore, and I have that passion for Sergei. But that doesn't mean I'm gay. My therapist told me I'm bisexual."

"I guess that's good," I said. "So you weren't actually living a lie all these years with my mom?"

"No, not at all," he said. "You have to understand, Harper. I grew up in a different time. A different era. I was born in 1950 and used to struggle with my attraction to men. I was also very attracted to women, so I decided it would be easier to live a life with a woman than with a man. I loved her, Harper. I still do. I wasn't living a lie. We really were two crazy kids in love back then. But I decided after I met Sergei to explore the part of me I never allowed myself to explore all those years ago. That's all. That's it."

Bisexual. My dad was bisexual. I knew enough to know there was a prevailing thought that everybody was bisexual to a degree. I just never associated my parents with that prevailing thought.

What about Sergei? Was he bisexual too?

Sergei cleared his throat. "Arthur is bisexual," he said. "But I'm not. I was living a lie with Elena all those years. In Russia, though, it's very hard to live as a gay man. Otherwise, I probably would've been living as a gay man all these years."

The waitress came around and took our order for the rest of our dinners. I ordered a prime rib, mashed potatoes and a wedge salad. My mouth started watered thinking of my dinner to come.

"You still like your prime rib, huh Kitten?" Dad asked me with a smile. "I remember when you were little. You liked prime rib even then. I never knew where you put it." He turned to Sergei. "You should've seen my Harper when she was 10. That piece of meat was bigger than she was, but she ate it all. The baked potato, too, although I guess she likes the garlic mashed potatoes more."

"Good taste," Sergei said with a smile.

"Yeah," was all I thought to say. "So, dad, when's the wedding again?"

"In six months," Dad said, his hand covering Sergei's on the table. "We have to get married for Sergei to stay in the country. That's not the only reason, of course, but that's why we can't wait. By the way, how are things with your new guy. Axel, right?"

"Good," I said. "They're fine." I took my napkin, put it on my lap and took a sip of water. "My job, on the other hand…" I shook my head. "I need a vacation. I can't remember the last time I've taken one. That's sad, huh?"

"I worry about you," he said. "It seems like all you ever do is work. Work, work, work. You really should take up golf. It's very relaxing. Sergei and I love to golf."

"I hate golf," I said, crinkling my nose. "I don't like sports, in general. I like to ride my bike, though. I haven't done that in awhile. I stay in shape by going to the gym and taking long walks."

"Well, you need time off. I hope you can take some."

"Maybe. But I have two death penalty cases on my plate. I hope both don't go to trial." The more I thought about it, the angrier I felt about Stephen's arrest for the murder of that poor girl washed up on the Missouri River's shores. The police had no evidence

Stephen did it. They were only trying to railroad him because they had to pin that murder on somebody and Stephen was convenient. It was a matter of time until I could get those charges dropped for lack of evidence. I would definitely give that case more thought.

As for Darnell...that poor kid. That poor, poor kid.

Dad was laughing with Sergei. "My daughter is..." He looked over at me with a smile. "A bit of a bleeding heart, I'm afraid."

Sergei looked perplexed. "Bleeding heart?" He put his hand to his chest and looked over at me questioningly. "Does that mean she's sick?"

Dad shook his head. "I keep forgetting non-native speakers have problems with colloquialisms. No, my daughter is very soft when it comes to the underprivileged and underdogs. She's always been like that. I can't tell you how many stray dogs she brought home for us to adopt. Most of them went to the shelter, of course, but we adopted a few dogs along the way. She always cried when she saw a hurt animal, too."

"I still do," I said. "I still cry when I see injured animals. That's human. But, yes, I'm drawn to the underdog. I've always been that way. That's why I do what I do. That's why I defend people accused of crimes. Not that I think they're all innocent, of course, but I think they all need a champion. No matter what they did."

Sergei smiled. "A bleeding heart. Okay, thanks for teaching me that saying, Arthur. Don't worry, Harper, my daughter Valentina is the same way. There's a lot of suffering in Russia, much more than here, and my daughter is studying to be a doctor over there. You'd like her, Harper. Hopefully she can come to America one day."

The waitress wordlessly came around and put our dinners in front of us. She refilled all of our waters and my dad ordered another scotch neat for himself, another dirty martini for Sergei and another sparkling water for me.

"I don't understand why you won't have a drink with us," Dad said as he cut into his filet mignon.

"I told you, Dad, I have an early morning tomorrow. I don't drink when I have cases mounting up."

"Okay then," he said.

We talked about various things for the rest of dinner. All the while, my cases were lurking in the back of my mind. I had a good time with my father and my future step-father, but I couldn't let myself go. Not when I had one scared kid and one scared old man relying on me.

My father was right. I *was* a bleeding heart. My heart was bleeding for both Darnell and Stephen. My dad also worried me but not as much – he seemed perfectly happy with Sergei. My mother also seemed fine with it. Who was I to judge? Sergei was handsome, charming, intelligent and seemed to really love my father.

Love was love, after all.

Five

The next day, I had to start investigating Darnell, but I first had to see Stephen in jail. I also had to speak with the prosecutor about dropping Stephen's charges. The prosecutor had nothing to go on aside from prejudice. I needed to tell the prosecutor about how Stephen was held hostage by his identical twin and had nothing to do with the murders of those kids all those years ago.

Before I seeing Stephen I stopped by the prosecutor's office. The prosecutor for Stephen's case was Bill Sanchez, who I'd worked with several times before. I mostly got along with Bill – he was fair and not as much of a show-boater as Vince. I wanted him to drop Stephen's case for lack of evidence.

"Come on in, Harper," Bill said when I got to his office. "What can I do for you?"

"Stephen Heaney," I said as I sat down. "I want to talk about his case. I want to know why he's being charged in this murder."

Bill sighed. "Listen, Harper, I don't have to tell you how much interest Alaina's case has generated. It's been on the news 24/7 since she was found. There's little that gets the general public going like having the body of a pretty young white girl from a decent family washing up on the shore of the Missouri River." He shrugged.

"Your guy is a suspected serial killer from way back. He shows up and so does a body on the river. She's young, she fits the profile of the kids he used to murder and he looks good to the cops. He writes out a confession, and there you go."

"What confession?" I looked at Bill, trying to figure out what the hell he was talking about. "I don't have a confession in my file. I spoke to my client and he said not a damned word about him confessing to anything."

"Well, the cops on the scene added this confession into the file today. It was a clerical error, I'd imagine." Bill looked through the files on his desk and found the right one. "Here," he said, handing me the written statement. "A copy of his confession."

My heart was pounding as I read through it. "When did this turn up?" I asked. "Stephen never gave this confession to the cops. There's nothing in the Statement of Information or police report that indicate he said a damned word."

"It was found in his apartment," Bill said. "That's why it didn't make it into the file until today. But it was found on a piece of paper in his place."

I shook my head. It was a typed confession. Stephen had just bought his very first computer and printer, and I was helping him learn how to work all of that. It was possible he typed this confession on his computer. I didn't know. "This was found at his apartment?" I was confused. Stephen seemed such a nice, gentle man. Nothing but a kind-hearted older man desperately trying to put the past behind him and work towards a bright future. I was instinctual about people and I never got that he had a violent bone in his body.

Now this.

I read the confession carefully while I sat across from Bill:

My name is Stephen Heaney and I am responsible for the death of Alaina Morosky. Alaina is a young girl whose mother worked with me at the Crossroads Plant Exchange. Her mother's name is Olga Morosky. She currently works at the Crossroads. I met Alaina through her mother and I became obsessed with her beauty. I knew she was only 13, but she came into the nursery on a regular basis with her older brother Peter. I fell in love with her and knew I had to have her.

I didn't mean to do it. I met Alaina at her house. I went to visit Olga, but Olga wasn't there, and neither was Peter. Alaina was home alone. I couldn't help myself. I raped her that night and didn't want her to speak to the authorities, so I killed her and dumped her body into the Missouri River.

The reason why I am writing this confession is because I feel the need to unburden myself. I need to confess to my God about the wrong I've done. My sickness from long ago came back to haunt me. I thought I was over my sickness, but it turned out I wasn't cured like I thought.

May God have mercy on my soul.

Six

I shook my head in disbelief. Stephen couldn't have done this. He just couldn't have. Was I wrong about him all along? Was Stephen really the killer all those years ago? Was his story to me, when I saw him in the woods, just covering up that he was the true murderer?

Was I responsible for Alaina's death? If I didn't bring Stephen back into society, he never would've been in the position to kill her. Maybe I should've left well enough alone.

Bill was looking at me as I studied the confession. "This was, uh, where was this found?"

"On his desk, but there was a copy on his hard drive. The police department got a search warrant for his computer and found it in his documents folder." Bill was reading the file as he was talking to me. "I guess he did one of those things when something's bothering you. You know, write a letter you'll never send. Something like that. Guess he was feeling guilty about doing that to poor Alaina."

I swallowed hard and shook my head. Oh, God, was this happening again? Did I unwittingly leash another murderer on the streets?

I felt a little bit sick. "Okay," I finally said, putting on my lawyer hat. "The police never had probable cause to arrest him much less search his apartment. This confession is fruit from the poisonous tree. Cops can't just go into his house, willy nilly, and search his computer. They can't just arrest him just because he's a suspect in murders that happened long ago. There has to be something else, some other kind of evidence, that made the cops suspect him in the first place. That's the angle I'm taking. I'll get this confession suppressed on that basis, and hopefully get this case thrown out before it sees the light of day."

Bill sighed. "Good luck with that. Of course, the case will go to the Grand Jury, so you know he'll be indicted. Everyone's indicted."

"Yes, but that Grand Jury prosecutor can't use this confession as proof for the Grand Jury. Not if I have a say."

"Well, then, file your motion to have the confession suppressed as fruit of the poisonous tree. I'll object and the judge can sort it out."

"Come on, Bill, seriously. Seriously. You and I both know there was nothing tying Stephen to Alaina's murder."

"There's plenty of circumstantial evidence. Stephen worked with Alaina's mother, so he came in contact with her. The cops obtained a search warrant for the house where he lived in the 1970s. His fingerprints were everywhere."

"Yes, but you know the real killer was found dead in that house. Stephen's identical twin brother killed all those children. My client is innocent of everything."

"I know. You've told me that outlandish story. I know Stephen's identical twin was killed in that house and the police identified that man as Stephen Heaney. You told me the guy killed was actually Robert Heaney, but there's never been a record of a Robert Heaney. The police had a right to search that house where Stephen lived in the 1970s. They found his fingerprints in that house which gave them reason to arrest him for murdering those boys and girls in the early 1970s. You don't dispute that arrest was proper, do you?"

"Yes, I dispute the properness of that arrest. You're damned right. So, his fingerprints were in that house - so what? And pinning him for the murder of Alaina Morosky when there's nothing to go on is neither proper or legal. His fingerprints in that house doesn't give the police probable cause for anything. This confession will go bye-bye and the murder case will do the same."

I continued on my rant. "The cops have zero evidence Stephen was responsible for the murders in 1970s. I mean, really. Everybody is flying blind here. Everybody in this case is prejudiced against Stephen for something his brother did. I smell a lawsuit against the police force for violating my client's civil rights. Stephen will end up very wealthy when all is said and done."

"Think what you want," Bill said. "But we have a confession."

"An illegally obtained confession."

I'd have to ask Stephen about this confession. I didn't know what to think about it. I always believed his story about how he was nothing but a victim and a dupe for his brother. I bought it without question.

Now Alaina turns up dead, Stephen allegedly confessed and I didn't know what to think.

I stood up. "Well, I have to see my client," I said. "So, I'll leave. I'll be in touch shortly."

I left and went to the jail.

I had to look Stephen in the eye and ask him some serious questions. Hopefully he'd answer them truthfully.

Seven

"Harper," Stephen said when I got to the jail. "I don't know what you're talking about. I never wrote out a confession. Never. I never met that girl. I knew her mother Olga who worked with me at the Crossroads Plant Exchange. A nice woman. But, no, Harper, I never met Alaina."

"The prosecutor said he got that confession off your computer. The cops did, anyhow. Your arresting cop obtained the search warrant, got your computer and found it."

Stephen's blue eyes were watery, much like Darnell's. Stephen, like Darnell, had evidently been crying. I tried hard not to let Stephen's tears affect my judgment, but I always had a problem when people cried. Especially boys and men – watching them cry usually ripped my heart out. I saw hardened criminals cry - men who I knew were good for their cases and men who had a rap sheet longer than my arm. Inevitably, the second they cried, my heart melted for them, no matter what they did.

How a sucker like me ended up in criminal defense was something I questioned every single day of my life.

"Stephen," I said. "I can get you out of jail and have your confession suppressed. This whole thing can be thrown out. The cops never had probable cause to arrest so I'll file a motion to suppress and also file a writ of habeas corpus."

"What's a writ of habeas corpus?"

"Your arrest was unlawful so detaining you is also unlawful. I probably will need Uncle Jack to testify you were completely innocent, but, as you know, he's in intensive therapy at the moment."

Stephen nodded his head. "How is Jack? I worry about him every day."

"Well, he's been working with the DID specialist in New York City. I've been in touch with my brother Jason, who said the specialist is making progress with Jack, but it's been touch and go. His alters are strong and don't want to give up. And Jack still can't face what happened to him as a boy in that house. He still can't face that he was kidnapped, held hostage, raped and tortured for months on end. The therapist is doing his best but Jack will probably have to see him for years." I sighed. "And because of that, I don't know if I can make him testify about what happened in that house. I don't know."

Stephen blinked and blankly looked at the wall. "If you can't get Jack to testify, you can't get him to testify. I was living a dream that ended sooner than I thought. When you brought me back into society, I thought I'd live the rest of my life happy. I met Katy, found that job and was learning about computers, DVD players, cable television, social media, YouTube, Tik Tok and GrubHub." He smiled. "GrubHub. One of my favorite inventions. Katy and I would go to my house and watch something on HBO and order from GrubHub. I never thought it would be possible to have food brought right to the house. Back in the day, we had Chinese food delivered, but I never thought I could look at a menu of different food places and just order."

I smiled, thinking about how Stephen was so grateful for the smallest things. Things I took for granted, like GrubHub and other food delivery services. Things like sitting on a couch, relaxing with the person you loved, ordering food and watching shows on HBO. He lived so much of his life isolated...the sad thing was, he might end up isolated again. Isolated and in prison for the rest of his life.

"Now, tell me about Alaina," I said. "You didn't know her at all? Is that right?"

"Right. I didn't know Alaina. I knew Olga, her mother. I met her brother, Peter, because he works as a busboy at the restaurant down the street from the nursery, Jack's Stack. He gave Olga a ride to and from the nursery from time to time when he needed to borrow the car for something. But Alaina never came in with Peter. I don't know how I could confess to something I didn't do, and I wouldn't confess to actually knowing Alaina when I didn't."

"I'll try to figure this out."

"You believe me, don't you?" Stephen was anxious. His anxiety showed in his haunted blue eyes and stooped posture. He looked defeated yet hopeful at the same time. It was a weird combination of emotions I'd seen in many of my clients. They were usually defeated because they'd been arrested and had been broken down by the cops and jail. But they were also hopeful because they thought I was their savior. It broke my heart that I couldn't save them all, but I knew most of my clients were good for their crimes so I shouldn't feel sorry for them. But I did. No matter what my client did, I usually had sympathy for them.

But could I have sympathy for Stephen if he was guilty of this heinous murder? If he lied to me all along and actually killed those boys and girls back in the day? And I let loose a caged animal by bringing him back to society? No. I wouldn't feel sympathy for him. I'd feel nothing but contempt.

I looked in his eyes, seeing nothing but kindness in them, and nodded. "Yes, I believe you," I said. "I do. I just need to find a way out of this for you. Unfortunately, I'm working another capital case and it's a little much. Plus, this case with Alaina has gotten out of hand in the papers. They're sensationalizing everything about this case, especially the angle that the long-ago murderer of those children was thought to be dead and nobody had a clue an identical twin escaped. It's practically made for *Dateline.* It's just..." I shook my head. “I need a vacation after I get past yours and Darnell's cases, which, unfortunately, is another media-ready case because it involved the murder of a plain-clothes policeman.”

“Well, I hate to be a bother,” Stephen said softly. “I really do.”

“You’re not a bother,” I said. “Trust me, you’re not a bother.” I looked down at my file. “I’ll file some motions to get you out of jail and get your case thrown out, but I won’t promise a thing. I wish I could but if I promised you something, I might fall down on my word. That’s the last thing that I want. I need you to trust me, which will be difficult because I can’t trust myself.”

I wondered about my own judgment. I wanted to think it was sterling. I wanted to believe I couldn’t be played by Stephen or anybody else.

Was that the case, though?

Was I naïve about Stephen?

Eight

I was exhausted when I got home. Mentally and physically drained. I didn't know how I'd do it – work two capital cases while mothering 12-year-old twin daughters. Thank goodness Rina was finally coming out of her hating-me-every-other-day phase, or else I probably would've went bonkers.

"Mom," Rina said, coming over to me that evening after dinner. I was sitting in the leather recliner, the remote control in my hand, and was staring at the television. Just...staring. I couldn't even focus on what was on TV. I looked down at my hand and saw it shaking.

"What Buttercup?" I asked her.

She furrowed her brows. "Ladybug. She's Buttercup," she said, pointing to Abby. "I'm Rina, that's Abby over there. Or did you already forget how to tell us apart?"

I smiled. "Jessica and Elizabeth," I said, thinking of the twins on *Sweet Valley High.* That was a series I used to read when I was a young girl. They were easy-to-read capers about two blonde twins in Southern California. Jessica was somewhat devilish - gossipy, a bit nasty, a bit of a mean girl, and a bit spoiled. She meant well, though, and I don't think she ever did anything wrong like take drugs, sleep with boys or any of that. She was a just big flirt and gossiper. And

Elizabeth was her sweet, shy, studious sister. The bad girl and the good girl who looked exactly the same.

One book introduced cocaine into the storyline, but a deaf girl was involved with it. A deaf girl named Regina who was the first love of the arrogant jock named Bruce Patman. She tried cocaine one time and died. That book made me afraid to try cocaine because it apparently could kill you the first time out.

Rina rolled her eyes. "Whatever. Anyhow, Mom, I need you to help me write this essay for my class. I mean, it's a book report. On *A Tale of Two Cities.*"

I smiled. "Oh, yes, yes. The French Revolution. You can compare that book to what's happening now in this country. How we're heading for a violent revolution if our politicians don't get their act together and stop legislating on behalf of the billionaires and start thinking of solutions for the people. Why don't you write about it that way?"

"Because I haven't even read the book. The report is due tomorrow. I don't know what it's about, except there's this chick in there named Vengeance or something like that. Who names their kid Vengeance, anyhow?"

"I'm sure she wasn't given that name, but took it as her name anyhow." I couldn't get off that leather chair. I couldn't give Rina the brain power to help her with her report. I felt like an absolute failure of a mother. What I was thinking when I took these two girls into my home? How did I ever think I could give them the proper care they needed? I could function some days. On other days, my job's stress drained all my energy.

"Whatever," Rina said impatiently. "You have to help me, Mom. I know you read this book."

"In junior high," I said. "I can't remember it any better than you can."

Finally, Abby came and put her arm around Rina. "Here," she said, giving Rina the Cliff's Notes for the book. "I got this in the library. You can look at it and do your report that way."

I smiled at little Rina. "You got this, Buttercup," I said softly as I continued to zone out in front of the television. "Don't forget to bring modern America into the conversation. I'm telling you, we'll soon have a revolution. There'll soon be guns in the streets if our legislatures don't get their damned acts together."

Rina gave Abby a weird look and Abby shrugged. "Write that book report based on these Cliff's Notes, and if you have any questions, I can help you. That's one of my favorite books."

"What's wrong with her?" Rina whispered to Abby.

"I don't know."

"I heard that," I said to the two girls. They were standing right in back of my chair, after all. "I'm sorry, Rina, I was assigned a death penalty case and I have another one as well. I have these two enormous cases and reporters are calling me about both. I have people from national magazines trying to get the story on Alaina Morosky and I need a vacation. Just really need a vacation."

Abby came and sat on the floor in front of me. "You're working the Alaina Morosky case?" she asked me shyly. "I know about that case. That girl, she was our age." She shook her head. "Our age. Who do you think did it, Mom?"

"I have no clue," I said. "I'd like to think Stephen didn't do it."

"Stephen?" Rina asked. "What do you mean, Stephen? He was arrested for murdering that young girl?"

Rina had grown rather fond of Stephen. He'd been over to the house a few times and entertained her with magic tricks. He was on her wavelength. Rina liked him right away and was always bugging me about bringing him around more often.

"Yes, Ladybug," I said, finally calling the right girl by the right nickname. "Stephen was arrested for her murder."

Rina crossed her arms. "I want to talk to him. I know he didn't do that. He couldn't do that. You better get him off that murder charge, Mom, you better." She stomped her right foot. "You just better."

Then she ran out of the room and I heard her bedroom door slam.

"Did he do it?" Abby asked.

"No," I said. "He didn't."

But I didn't know if that was true or not. I thought it was. I prayed it was.

Realistically, however, it might not have been true at all.

Stephen might be a murderer after all.

Nine

I'd have to buck up and work these two enormous cases. I'd even meet with reporters. I couldn't talk to them about the case, of course, but I could tell them about how I met Stephen in the woods. That was a good human interest story, anyhow. I wanted good publicity so the media would humanize him prior to his trial.

You could've knocked me over with a feather when I saw the dismissal come in the mail. The police had elected to drop the charges against Stephen regarding the 1972 murders. I was going to file a motion to dismiss because of lack of evidence, but apparently they were ahead of me on that.

"Here, Harper," Pearl said when I came into my office. "This came for you." The envelope indicated this was correspondence from the prosecutor's office, so I eagerly tore into it. Inside was a dismissal of all charges.

The dismissal was short and sweet. It simply said that, because the prosecutor's office had found a lack of evidence that Stephen was involved in the murders of the children in 1972 and before, they were dismissing all charges.

But that still left the problem of Alaina's murder. That was apparently still pending.

This dismissal was very good news. It made defending Stephen much less complicated. I didn't want to go through all the evidence relating to those long-ago murders. I wanted to focus on Alaina's murder, so this dismissal was a gift.

"Call Heather," I said to Pearl. "I need to speak with her. I need her help with this."

Heather had been doing legal research and was getting better all the time. I wanted to train her on a few other things so I had her come to the office at least three days a week. Like Rina and everyone who knew him, Heather was very fond of Stephen. If I asked her to do some work on Stephen's case, she'd be eager to get the ball rolling.

Heather had worked hard on finding cases for Michael Reynold's motion for ineffective assistance of counsel. The motion had been argued in front of the appeals court the month before. He lost, thank God, and elected not to take it further. I also managed to keep my law license, even though he and Kayla Stone filed Bar Complaints against me. I hired counsel to try that case in front of the Bar and won. However, I was put on probation – if I had anymore incidents for another year, my law license would be suspended for six months. So, Michael, Kayla and that whole mess was behind me but I paid a price. Michael had no other recourse so he'd spend the rest of his life in prison.

I pictured him being the bitch of some guy and that thought brought me the first real smile of the day.

Heather got to my office about a half-hour later. "Hey, Harper," she said. "What you got for me?"

"Sit down," I said. "I need a few things. I'll be leaning on you to get some things out of the way. I have two death penalty cases I got slammed with at the same time and I haven't started working on poor Darnell Williams' case. But Stephen is in jail for Alaina Morosky's murder."

Heather nodded. "I saw that in the paper." She shook her head. "That guy didn't murder nobody. He's a really good dude."

"I know. I know. Anyhow, here's his file. I've read through it, time and again, and still can't see where the police had probable cause to arrest Stephen for anything. They confiscated his laptop and found a confession. I need you to prepare a writ of habeas corpus and a motion to suppress the computer. I'll keep trying to get the prosecutor to drop the charges based on lack of probable cause, but that's going nowhere at the moment. Prepare a motion to dismiss, a motion to suppress and a writ of habeas corpus. We can get the case thrown out."

I handed her the file and she nodded. "I can do that," she said. "When do you need all this by?"

"As soon as possible," I said. "The trial judge has already been assigned, but it hasn't gone through the Grand Jury yet. If I can get that computer suppressed so the prosecutors can't use it as evidence in the Grand Jury, they might play ball and dismiss."

Heather gathered the file and stood up. "I'll work around the clock to get this for you," she said. "I'll have it for you by Monday."

"Thanks," I said. "That will free me up to figure out what's going on with poor Darnell. That kid has so many things going. His mom is in the hospital, he has four brothers and sisters at home, and they're all living hand to mouth. The kids might get kicked out of the apartment and might end up in foster care if the mom doesn't get out of the hospital soon. I need to help him figure all that out."

Darnell had extraneous things going, but I'd have to focus on his case.

I'd have to call Axel on this. He was a detective, after all, but I never asked him to get involved with my cases because I didn't want him free-lancing. I didn't want to get him into trouble, which he would if he stepped on other cops' turf by helping me out with my cases. So, if I got him involved it would have to be on the down-low.

It would be all hands on deck if I wanted to get through these next few months.

TEN

The next day, I talked to the cops for Darnell's case. Officer Jake Parker was the plain-clothes murdered officer. Officer Morgan Cooper arrested Darnell. That was always my first place to start – find out what the cops saw, what they were thinking, etc. That didn't always translate on police reports, which were nothing but the facts on the ground. I didn't get much thinking, emotions and what went through the cops' brains when they arrested the kid.

I made an appointment to see Officer Cooper, and he saw me that same day. "Hello, Ms. Ross," he said politely when I went to his office. "Have a seat."

I sat down, pen and paper at the ready. "I need to speak with you about Darnell Williams," I said.

"Shoot," he said. "Ask away. I've got nothing to hide."

Nothing to hide. That was an odd expression for a cop to use, but I let it go. "I didn't think you had anything to hide," I said. "But I wanted a rundown on what happened. How you came up on Darnell and what you did when you saw him."

"It's all there in the police report," he said, pointing to the report in my possession. "But I'll go ahead and run it down with you anyhow."

"Okay," I said. "What caused you to go into that parking lot?"

"I was across the street from the Church's Chicken at the 7-11 when I heard the gunshot at 12:50 A.M. I ran over to the parking lot to check out what happened."

"And you came up and found Darnell with that body?"

"Yes. That's what happened. He was holding the gun. I pointed my gun at him. He put up his hands and I spread him against the wall and frisked him. I found the drugs on him then."

Seemed cut and dry. "Have you ever encountered Darnell before?"

"You mean, have I ever spoken with him or arrested him before this incident?"

"Yes, that's what I'm asking."

He shook his head. "No, I've never seen him before this. No, I haven't." He shrugged. "That doesn't mean he's not a known drug dealer. Maybe he was good at it prior to this, so I haven't had cause to harass him. But trust me, Ms. Ross, that kid is just like all those other kids living in those projects. They deal drugs, gang bang, kill each other all the time." He shook his head. "Black lives matter. If their lives matter so goddamned much, why do they kill each other all the time? From where I sit, I don't think their lives matter much to them at all."

"Is that really necessary? To give me the whole 'All Lives Matter' nonsense?"

"Hey. All lives *do* matter, and that means blue lives too. I risk my life every goddamned day running down punks like Darnell Williams. Every goddamned day. I can't tell you how many times I've had a gun pointed at me. I've seen things you could never imagine, so don't you go telling me this liberal bullshit about black lives mattering. They matter, yeah, but our lives, which are on the line every day, matter too. People forget that."

I bit my tongue. I wouldn't get into it with him, because it wasn't worth it. He was right, black murders usually were perpetrated by other black kids. But that didn't change the facts on Darnell's case. Darnell wasn't a gang-banger. He was a good kid. Yet this cop apparently saw him as just another East Side gang-banger. That wasn't right and it wasn't fair.

"But Darnell has never been arrested. That much is clear. Why did you automatically assume he was responsible for Officer Parker's murder?"

"Because he had drugs on him and his fingerprints were on the murder weapon. Officer Parker probably tried to make the drop. Darnell figured out he was a plain-clothes cop and iced him."

"Officer Cooper, with all due respect, Darnell was at his place of employment at the time. Do you really think he'd do something like that at his workplace?"

"What time does that restaurant close?"

"11 PM."

"And it was almost 1 AM when I found the body. What does that tell you? I tell you what it says. It says the kid was up to no good after hours. It doesn't take two entire hours to close down a chicken store. It doesn't. If you tell me it does, I have some swamp-land in Florida to sell you."

It *did* seem weird that Darnell was hanging around the store two hours after it closed. There was probably an explanation for it, however. "Just because he was there on the premises two hours after the restaurant closed doesn't mean he was guilty of murder."

"What did Mr. Williams tell you about why it was he was still there? What did he tell you he was doing when he went into that alleyway?"

"He was taking out the trash."

"Taking out the trash. Taking out the trash. The kid clocked out at midnight, a full hour before I arrived. Take a look at his time card. Yet he was taking out the trash." He shook his head. "Do you let all your clients do a snow job or just this one?"

He clocked out a full hour before. A full hour before. This wasn't looking good.

It wasn't looking good at all.

"So, yeah, I think your client probably did drug deals all the time in that parking lot. And why wouldn't he? He closes up the restaurant, it's 1 AM, there's nobody around, because all the other businesses around are closed. He goes out there with his quarter kilo of coke worth seventeen grand and tries to sell it to Officer Parker. Officer Parker attempts to arrest him and the kid ices him. End of story."

"Just like that, huh? Just like that? He just ices him, even though he's never been in trouble with the law? How many times do you see that? A kid without a record icing an undercover police officer? I mean, really? How many times do you see something like that happen?"

"Enough." He looked at his desk, which had some papers on it. "Now, if you don't mind, I have some reports to finish. If you have any other questions, please don't hesitate to call."

"I won't."

I left his office, thinking I needed to take a shower.

But I also knew I'd have to speak with Darnell. Officer Cooper made me think – what was Darnell doing hanging around the chicken place long after his shift was finished?

Eleven

I never made it to the jail that day, however. Well, I made it to *a* jail, but not that one.

I was driving home from my office when I got pulled over. "Miss, can I please see your license and registration?" the officer asked me.

I got out my driver's license and car registration and gave it to him. "I hope you can do this quickly," I said. "I have to get home to my two daughters. I try to get home as quickly as possible so they can have supper with me. I'm late as it is."

"Well, this will only take a moment," he said, looking at my driver's license. "By the way, you seem nervous. Why would you be nervous?"

You've been tailing me for blocks, of course I'm nervous. I absolutely hated when cops did that little cat and mouse routine - when they follow closely behind you for blocks and blocks, not doing anything, yet freaking you out all the same. You knew it was a matter of time before they pulled you over for *something.* I would never forget the time when I passed by a cop at 3 AM back in my drinking days. I was the only one on the road, and, when he whipped out and followed me, I knew I was toast. That time, I'd carefully creeped along at just under the speed limit, but he pulled me over anyhow – for driving too close to the shoulder.

The weirdest thing was the cop in that case never gave me a ticket. He never even ran my driver's license. If he looked carefully at me he would've seen I was three sheets to the wind. I thank my lucky stars I didn't get a DWI that night.

"I'm nervous?" I asked him. "Why do you say that?"

"You just look nervous." He narrowed his eyes and leaned into the car. "Hey, why don't you step out of the car? I need to do a field sobriety test on you."

I groaned. "Okay."

I got out of the car and stood next to it. Other cars were whizzing past. I could just imagine what they were thinking as they passed by me. Probably the same things I thought about people standing outside their cars, surrounded by cops – *poor bastard. Poor, poor bastard.* Well, that's what I thought back in the day before I became a defense attorney. After I became a defense attorney, I'd see people by their cars talking to cops and wonder if they'd end up in my office.

The officer pointed to the ground. "Walk a straight line," he said.

I took a deep breath, feeling my heart pounding. I had nothing to hide. But this still was a nerve-wracking experience. I wondered how many people flunked these tests when they were stone-cold sober, just because they were nervous.

Ironic - I probably could've flown right by these tests when I was a drunk. I was always a very functioning drunk, at least I was when I just had a few. And I was always relaxed when drinking. Passing a field sobriety test would be a piece of cake when I was slightly buzzed.

I looked at the horizon, put both my arms out and slowly walked in a perfectly straight line. Towards the end, however, I stumbled slightly before regaining my balance. I looked over at the Officer, making notes, and shrugged my shoulders. "Oops."

He was sitting there, shaking his head and making notes.

"Okay," he said. "Look at me and follow my pen. Don't shake your head from side to side, simply watch the pen with your eyes."

I looked right at his pen and my eyes followed it from one side to the other.

"Touch your forefinger to your nose four times."

I complied.

"Recite the alphabet backwards."

You've got to be kidding me. I shook my head. "Z, Y, X," I began, and then, suddenly, my mind was a blank. What letter came before the letter X? "Z, Y, X, W," I said unsurely. "V, U, T, R..." I shook my head again. This was harder than I thought it would be.

The officer shook his head. "Blow into this breathalyzer," he said, taking the device out and handing it to me.

I blew into it, and it registered a 0.00.

"May I search your car?" he asked me.

What the hell? "May I ask why you would like to search my car?"

"Because you're acting nervous, and I'd like to know why."

"To be honest with you, I was nervous because you were following me for so long before pulling me over. Now I'm nervous because I was just asked to do the field sobriety test, which I apparently failed. That's why I'm nervous, not because I have something to hide."

"May I search your car, miss?"

I groaned. I had to get home to Rina and Abby, and if I refused, this jackass would get a search warrant, which would take forever. "You may."

The officer went around to the back of my SUV, and lifted up the cover on my spare tire. "Uh, huh," he said. "Just as I thought."

"What? What's just as you thought?"

He came around to my window. "What is this?"

He was holding a bag that appeared to contain a large quantity of marijuana. In Missouri, you could possess up to three ounces legally, but that bag contained more than that. I had no idea how it got there. "I don't know."

"You don't know? This is your car, isn't it? You showed me your registration, so I assume it's your car."

"It is, of course it is, but I honestly have no clue where those drugs came from. No clue."

The cop continued to search the rest of my car before coming back around. "Miss, please step out of the car," he said.

I did and he put the handcuffs on me. "You have the right to remain silent…."

"Listen, there's been some mistake. I've never smoked pot. There's been some mistake."

"Tell that to the judge," he said, putting me in the back of his car."You're going downtown with us."

Great. Just great. As if I didn't have enough on my plate. Now I was being falsely accused of drug possession.

"Can I call somebody please?"

"No."

"These handcuffs are cutting into my skin. Can you loosen them please?"

"Those handcuffs aren't supposed to be comfortable."

What was going on? I shouldn't have been arrested, period, for anything, yet here I was, in the back of the cop car, going downtown, all while being treated like I was Public Enemy Number One. "Officer, I did nothing wrong. You never told me why you pulled me over in the first place."

"I pulled you over because you were driving erratically. You were hugging the shoulder and you weaved within your lane."

I bit my lower lip. What he said was bullshit. Of course he chose a bullshit reason for stopping me, the one thing difficult to prove false in court – the infamous weaving charge. I knew the game all too well – when a cop wants to stop you pretextually he will always say he pulled you over for something vague, like weaving or hugging the shoulder. He knows if he claims he pulled you over for speeding, it would be easy to prove false. It would also be easy to prove running a red light was a false charge because you can gather witnesses who could testify you didn't do it. But weaving was just "he said she said."

I wasn't weaving. Maybe I hugged the shoulder a bit, but that was how I drove. I was pulled over pretextually, and, somehow, a bag of coke was found in my car.

I shifted uncomfortably in my seat. I'd been arrested once before, when I "kidnapped" Rina and Abby from their abusive foster home. Then I spent several days in jail intentionally so I could get a witness to testify for Heather. I knew I'd be okay in jail. I also knew I'd be getting out of there as soon as possible.

But I couldn't, for the life of me, understand why these cops were treating me this way.

We arrived at the station, where I was finger-printed, mug-shot and tossed into a cell to await further processing. The worst part of being in a jail cell was the smell – there was a tiny toilet in the corner of the cell and it always smelled like urine, Lysol and excrement. I felt like gagging.

I lay down on the cot, trying to calm my thoughts. I couldn't seem to, though – they were racing. I felt more than a little nauseated, along with being frightened, bewildered, and just plain pissed off.

"Hey," I said to the guard who came to bring me my dinner. It consisted of cold scrambled eggs, evidently left over from breakfast, a piece of dry toast and a rotting red apple. "When will I get my phone call to get out of here?"

"Wait your turn," he said. He was a heavy-set guy with a bald head and a pair of glasses. "There's about five people ahead of you."

I heard somebody shouting about wanting to get out and I sighed. I worried about Rina and Abby. I didn't have Sophia come over and baby-sit them after school. I relied on her less because the girls were getting old enough to watch themselves. Yet I knew they would freak out when I didn't come home. They were somewhat used to me coming home after 6 PM, but if I had a long evening away, I usually got Sophia to make them dinner and make sure they did their homework. On the days when I didn't get Sophia to watch them, the girls pretty much expected me home right at 6.

"I really need to make a phone call," I said. "Just to my baby-sitter. My girls are home alone."

"How old are they?"

"13."

"They'll be okay." He started to move onto the next cell, and I called after him.

"You don't understand. They don't have a sitter. They need their dinner. I don't trust either of them to cook by themselves."

"They'll figure something out." The guard was terse and impatient. "I'm sorry. Just because you're an attorney doesn't entitle you to special treatment. If you wanted to get home to your girls, you should've thought of that before possessing drugs in your car. Just a thought."

My anger finally started to bubble to the surface. I felt it move from my core up through my chest and finally out through my mouth. "Listen, you stupid piece of shit. I did nothing wrong. I don't know what's going on, but I didn't possess drugs, and my being kept here is the very definition of false imprisonment. If you don't want me to name you personally in a lawsuit for violating my civil rights, I suggest you bring me my cell phone and let me call my sitter. If anything happens to those two girls because of this, I will be legally holding you and the entire police department liable for it. I'm an attorney. You don't want to mess with me."

The guard came right back over. "No. You listen to me. You broke the law. I can't help that. Go ahead and sue. You're a criminal defense attorney. You know you're not entitled to a phone call until the administrator of this jail says you are. Nobody's civil rights are being violated here. Nobody is falsely imprisoning nobody. I told you earlier there are five people ahead of you. Now there's ten." He narrowed his eyes. "You want to make it 20?"

No. No, I didn't want to make it 20. I bit my tongue to keep from lashing out again. I sat down on the cot, crossed my arms and tried my hardest not to say anything to him.

"I thought so," he said, and he moved on down the line to the next inmate.

I couldn't eat, of course – that food was unappetizing, and, besides, I was absolutely burning with rage at this point. I had some time to think and realized, for some unknown reason, I was being railroaded.

I thought of all my clients with claims of being railroaded. Treated horribly by the system. It was true – the system was a cold, cruel, heartless beast. You get arrested and nobody cares about you. Nobody cares about two little girls frightened at home, wondering where their mother is. Nobody cares you were unjustly arrested and falsely imprisoned, because you knew you did nothing wrong.

I was immediately plotting my revenge on all of these people. I'd file a Section 1983 lawsuit so fast their heads would swim. They were messing with the wrong person.

A Section 1983 lawsuit was known as a "color of law," lawsuit. Basically, when somebody, such as a police officer, violates your civil rights and deprives you of rights, privileges and immunities secured by the Constitution, you could bring a lawsuit against them. Damages could be quite high in these lawsuits. Ordinarily, you couldn't sue a police department because they enjoyed sovereign immunity. But, since they were clearly violating my civil rights, I'd sue.

At some point, after I'd been in that cell for hours, they brought somebody to share the cell. She was about 25 and dressed in a tiny dress – cut high in the thigh and low in the cleavage. She had blonde hair, wore a ton of makeup and also wore thigh-high boots. The first thing I thought of when I saw her was Vivian from *Pretty Woman* right before she met Edward. The only thing missing was the little hat.

"Hey," she said. "Name's Ginger. What's yours?"

"Harper. Harper Ross. What are you in for?"

"Whaddaya think?" She rolled her eyes. "Third time this year, too. I don't know why those pigs just won't let us working girls alone. Especially that pig, Officer Cooper. He's the worst. The fucking worst."

"Oh? What makes him so much worse than everyone else?"

"Man, he fucking harasses us, mainly because a lot of us girls won't give it to him for free no more. I mean, I gave it to him for free enough times. I gotta eat, you know? I can't be giving freebies all the time just to keep the pigs off my ass. So I told him I ain't gonna give it to you no more for free, and, lo and behold, he's been working my corner and bringing in me and the other girls like every other day it seems."

"That sucks."

"What do you do for a living?" She looked me up and down. I was dressed as usual – grey pantsuit with a colorful scarf, black leather pumps and a light blue button down underneath. "You look kinda classy. I wouldn't expect to see someone like you in here."

"I'm an attorney."

"An attorney?" She smiled. "Man, I thought you attorneys knew how to get out of these joints. Why haven't they allowed you to make bail yet?"

"Good question." I paused. "I pissed off the guard who brought my food. I called him a stupid piece of shit. Guess he didn't like that so much."

At that, Ginger started to laugh. She put her hand out and I slapped it in a high-five. "That's awesome," she said. "Wish I could get away with that. I call Cooper that all the time behind his back, but I don't call him that to his face." She lowered her voice. "Just between you and me, I don't know about Cooper. Some of the girls have warned me about him. Some of the girls tell me I should feel lucky if all he does is arrest me. Some of the girls say he takes it from them when they don't want to give it. Some of the girls say he beats on them." She nodded her head. "That's just what some of the girls say."

I cocked my head. "Really?"

"Yeah, really." She drew a breath and let it out. "I don't know. He's weird and gives me the creeps. I even heard he watches kiddy porn with some of the girls. He has them come over and makes them do stuff to him while he watches little girls getting it from their daddies."

My ears perked up. "Really. Huh."

"Yeah. Well, I shouldn't repeat that, 'cause it's gossip and all, but I'm telling you, I probably need to watch my back. He's so weird."

Just then, a different guard came to my cell. "Harper Ross," he said. "You're free to make your phone call and post your bail."

"Thanks," I said. Then I turned to Ginger and I put my hand on her shoulder. "Listen, I'm an attorney. Please look me up. Please don't forget my name – Harper Ross. I'd like to represent you."

"Would you?"

"Yeah. I would."

"That would be great. I need a girl attorney. I'm tired of those guy attorneys. They're always thinking they can get a little something extra from me. I really need somebody who can get me out of jams."

"Look no further," I said. "Seriously. I'd like to speak with you. Please don't forget my name."

"Harper Ross," she said.

I turned and left the cell, and heard her chanting, over and over, *Harper Ross, Harper Ross, Harper Ross, Harper Ross.* I knew what she was doing, because I did the same thing when making sure I remembered something – repetition made you remember things much better.

I groaned as I looked at the clock. It was 2 AM. "Thanks," I said, as I was led to a pay phone. "I'll call Axel. I hope he's not working."

The guard stood right next to me as I dialed Axel's phone number. He picked up on the third ring. "Hello?" he asked uncertainly.

I felt bad for calling him in the middle of the night. He didn't recognize the phone number, of course, so I thought he might be freaking. "Axel, it's me. Harper. I'm in jail. I need you to post my bond. It's $1500."

"In jail? Harper, why-"

"Please don't ask. I hate to do this to you, but can you come and get me?"

"I'll be there as soon as I can."

After the phone call, I was led into a different cell, where I looked at the ceiling and prayed Axel could get here as quickly as possible. I didn't know what to think everything. What I knew was that Officer Cooper was apparently a rapist, a pedophile and an overall creep.

He was also the arresting officer in both Darnell and Stephen's cases.

Was that significant? I had no idea. Could be a coincidence.

But I'd long since learned that, in life, there was no such thing as a coincidence.

Twelve

Axel finally got there about a half hour later and posted my bail. I was given my purse and personal effects, including my jewelry. "Thanks," I said wearily as I was given my purse by the uniformed police officer standing by the metal detectors.

"Now, do you mind telling me, lass, why you were arrested?" Axel asked as we walked to his car.

"I still don't know. I was driving along, minding my business. I just saw Darnell in jail. I also wanted to sneak in a jail visit to Stephen, just to see how things were going, and wanted to tell him about some motions I'll file on his behalf. I got pulled over for weaving, or something, and the cop made me walk the line. I flunked the field sobriety test and he made me blow. I blew a 0.00, but he searched my car and found a bag of coke." I shook my head. "I mean, what the hell? I've never done coke in my life."

"Well, that shouldn't be too difficult to beat, can it?"

"I don't know. It's hard to challenge these things. The best I can hope for is challenging the stop's legitimacy. God forbid I don't beat this, though – I already have a record. I mean, not a conviction record, but I was arrested twice before, for kidnapping and for that firearms violation when I took your gun. Plus, I'm on probation with the Missouri Bar."

Axel gave me a look. "Get in," he said, motioning to the car door, which he was holding open for me. "And tell me exactly why you're on probation with the Missouri Bar."

I sat down and buckled my seat. I'd never told Axel the truth about Michael Reynolds. I never told him how I deliberately threw Michael's case because I wanted revenge. For some odd reason, I was nervous to tell him. I always had a hard time with confessing my failures, and this was definitely a failure.

"Well, I..." I bowed my head. "I threw a case. Michael Reynolds. My murder case a year or so ago."

"Michael Reynolds, Michael Reynolds..." He shook his head. "Name doesn't ring a bell."

"It was a murder case I tried."

"Oh, right, right. He murdered that judge, right?"

"Right. He did. He was my client, and I did everything in my power to make sure he was convicted. I crossed the line more than once. I did all sorts of things which weren't kosher, including interviewing his co-conspirator and implying I could get her a deal. When I went to court for him, I was terrible. Deliberately awful. I wanted to make sure he was convicted. He saw right through me and filed a motion for a new trial based upon ineffective assistance of counsel and also filed a Bar Complaint against me. So did Kayla Stone, the girlfriend who rightfully thought I'd try to get her a deal." I took a deep breath. "So, yeah, that's what I did. I had to go in front of the Bar to answer for that. They ended up slapping me on the wrist but put me on probation for a year. If I have any other incidents, which would include not only serious Bar complaint charges but any criminal convictions, I could have my license suspended for six months."

"Well, you certainly got yourself into a pickle, didn't you, mate?" Axel shook his head. "Might I ask why you threw this bloke's case?"

"He raped me in college."

Just then, Axel's face changed. "Oh, right. Right. Now I remember. I wanted to kill that bloke with my bare hands. You did the right thing, Harper, in making sure he fried."

"Yeah, but it came at a price, didn't it?"

I looked at my phone, wanting to call the girls, but not wanting to wake them. Besides, my battery was dead.

"Do Rina and Abby know about you going to jail?"

"No." I felt the anger bubble up again. "They don't. That bastard Officer wouldn't let me call them from the squad car. Then that fat-ass bastard guard wouldn't let me call them from my cell. Oh, well, the only good thing that came out of this whole sorry situation is I got a new client out of it. Ginger. She's a prostitute."

Axel was looking at me and not saying anything. He kept looking at me, opening his mouth, and then shutting it again.

"What? You're obviously dying to say something to me. Go ahead, lay it on me. Tell me about what an idiot I am for getting arrested. Tell me you don't believe that coke wasn't mine." I crossed my arms. "Tell me all about how disappointed you are in me. Believe me, I've heard it all before from my mom."

"Why are you laying into me, mate?" Axel said. "I have something to say to you but it has nothing to do with thinking any of those dastardly things you just accused me of thinking."

"Okay," I said. I still felt rankled and didn't know why. "Go ahead. Tell me what's on your mind. Something obviously is."

He tapped his fingers on the steering wheel as he drove along. I looked out the window and saw it had started to sleet. The weather was always so weird in Kansas City, especially during this time of the year – late fall. In October, the saying was always *if you don't like the weather, wait a minute. It will change.* And, indeed, it did – it was sunny and warm earlier in the day and now it was freezing. Literally, because it was sleeting.

"Harper, I don't know how to tell you this. So, I'll just tell you."

"Tell me what."

"It's Stephen." He paused and I felt my heart sink.

"What about him? He's in jail, but I'll get him out. I sent Heather out to prepare some motions to get him out of jail. I know what he's being accused of, and I know he didn't do it."

Axel shook his head. "Harper, Stephen's dead."

Thirteen

"Dead?" I shook my head. "No, you're wrong. I just saw him yesterday. He was doing okay. He was just getting into life. Getting back into society. He was happy." I bit my lip. "He's not dead. He can't be. He just can't be. He lived so many years in that cabin in the woods and was so excited to get a chance to live. He never had that chance, you know. Never. His brother took all that away."

It was then that I felt the tears. We were finally at my house and the sleet was turning into a gentle snow. I could see it in the street-lights and it was making a light dusting on the ground.

"Harper," Axel said, putting his arms around me. "Let me stay with you tonight."

"No," I said. I could feel Stephen's spirit around me somehow and I finally knew what Axel told me was true. "No, that's okay. I need to be alone. Thank you, though, for coming to get me. That's a true boyfriend thing to do, you know."

"Harper, I'm very sorry."

"It's okay," I said. "Really."

As I walked into my house, turning the key to my door, I realized something. It wasn't okay. It wouldn't be okay for awhile.

I didn't know Stephen for that long, but he'd impressed me

more than anybody I'd ever known. He was so...not bitter. He, of all people in the world, had reason to be bitter. He really did. His brother held him hostage, his mother abused him, and he forced himself to live in the woods for years because of what his brother did. Away from society. Lonely.

And Stella...Stella, the beautiful golden retriever, was staying with Katy, Stephen's girlfriend. But she couldn't keep her forever. Stella was very attached to Stephen. Of course she was – she was his only companion these past few years, and he hers.

The first thing I did was go upstairs and check on the girls. Rina was soundly sleeping, but, when I opened Abby's door, she sat straight up.

"Mom?" she asked. There was fear in her voice.

"Buttercup," I said softly.

"Oh my God, Mom," Abby said, bounding out of bed. She threw her arms around my waist. "I was so afraid. You didn't come home and didn't call, and I thought you were dead. Rina kept telling me that if something happened, a cop would visit us, but I didn't know. I was just on the internet, looking to see if any accidents had happened."

Abby started to cry and I was crying, too. She was crying because she was so relieved to see me, and I was crying for Stephen.

Life wasn't fair for some people. It was downright cruel. Why must one person suffer his whole life, only to end up dying in jail for something he didn't do?

He didn't do it, did he?

I hated that I didn't know. I might never know. The computer with that confession seemed to damn him, but I refused to accept that as the final answer.

"Buttercup," I said to her. "I'm okay. I really am. I..." I didn't know what to say to her. I didn't know what to say to anybody about these strange 24 hours. "I'm okay."

"You won't do that again, will you?"

"You mean not come home for hours? Not come home until 2 AM? No, Abby, I won't."

"You promise?" She was wailing now, so loudly that Rina finally awakened, because she was standing in Abby's doorway.

"Hey Mom," she said sleepily. "I told you, Abby, she'd make it home eventually." She gave me the stink eye. "But I won't even ask where you've been all this time."

"Thanks," I said. "For not asking me."

She continued to give me the stink eye. "Where've you been all this time?"

"You just said you wouldn't ask me."

"I lied."

How could I tell Rina I was arrested for drug possession and expect her to believe my arrest was a mistake? She'd never believe me. She'd assume I did it. That was the exact wrong message to give to her.

"It's late," I finally said. "And 7 AM comes really early. In fact, 7 AM is just in four more hours."

"And I'm up," she said.

"You'll end up falling asleep in class. Now, please, go back to bed. I'm here, I'm safe and that's all that matters, right?"

"No, not right." Rina was still glaring at me. "You remember our real mom, don't you? She disappeared, too, one night. Only she didn't come back home. I can't believe you'd do something like that – just disappear and not even call. Abby was completely freaked out the whole time. She wanted to call the police. So did I. I finally decided to go to bed and hope you showed up, but Abby was awake the whole time. Awake and crying. I could hear her through the door."

My fingers fluttered to my throat and I grabbed my necklace thoughtlessly. Rina was absolutely right – their mother disappeared one night and never made it home. She was murdered by my client, John Robinson.

"Rina, I'll tell you tomorrow."

"It *is* tomorrow."

"Then I'll tell you later. Right now, you need to go to bed."

Rina just stood there glaring at me, her arms crossed in front of her. "Mom," she whined. "Seriously, you need to tell us."

I sat at Abby's desk and Abby sat down on the bed. Rina sat down next to her, and I faced two identical sets of eyes. Two identical faces were staring at me, willing me to speak. Speaking was the last thing I wanted to do, but I owed these girls an explanation.

"Well, okay," I began. Why didn't I think of what to tell the girls before I came home? They shouldn't know I was arrested for drug possession. It wasn't true in the slightest but they wouldn't know that. They'd assume I did it, and why shouldn't they?

I cleared my throat. "I was at the jail," I began and the story just starting tumbling out. "I was at the jail, visiting my clients, and, out of nowhere, they went into lockdown. I've never experienced that before. One of the inmates was trying to escape, so they wouldn't let anybody out of the building."

I was proud of the lie I came up with on the fly. "Yes, and I wanted to call, I really did, but my phone died. I forgot to charge it up."

I smiled, knowing this was a good story. It was a story Rina and Abby would have no problems buying. That was the only thing that mattered.

"Why didn't you tell us that earlier?" Rina demanded.

"Well, the whole thing frightened me and I thought it might frighten you two as well. I didn't want you to be frightened so I didn't tell you. I'm very sorry about that."

Rina looked skeptical, but Abby looked happy. "That's not a big deal, Mom," she said. "My phone dies all the time, too. That's exciting. An inmate escaping. Did they catch the guy?"

"Sure, sure," I said, looking down at the floor. I was the world's worst liar. I might've been a good enough liar to pull a fast one on a kid, but any adult would know I was telling a straight-up lie. "Now, girls, would you both please go to bed?"

Rina groaned but went back into her bedroom.

I got up and tucked Abby into her bed. "Good night, Buttercup," I said, kissing her forehead. "I'll see you when I get you up for school."

Abby nodded and closed her eyes. In a matter of minutes, I could hear her breathing heavily.

I tiptoed out of the room, feeling awful that I lied to my girls.

All the while I was wondering how I'd break it to them their friend Stephen was dead.

Fourteen

I had my initial appearance for my drug charge that next day. I was seething by the time I arrived at the courthouse. Once again, I'd be humiliated in front of my peers. At least this time I wouldn't be in a baby-blue jumpsuit. I was wearing my own clothes, but that didn't matter. I was already the talk of the Kansas City Division of the Missouri Bar. Between my kidnapping charge over a year ago, plus my landing in jail by taking Axel's firearm, my peers already thought I was a wild rebel. Add to that the gossip that swirled around my Bar Complaint brought by Kayla and Michael, and the fact that most of them knew my license had been placed on probationary status – everybody was talking about me.

I didn't actually hear the gossip first hand. I never did. But I knew what people were saying. It would be the same thing I'd be saying if somebody else was getting into all this trouble. I was ashamed to admit, even to myself, that I had a bad habit of gossiping. Or, at the very least, listening to gossip and not shutting it down. I'd try hard, in the future, not to indulge in such trivialities.

"Harper," the prosecutor for the initial appearances, Tom Houston, said as I walked through the door of the courtroom. "You just keep coming up on these criminal dockets. What's up with that?"

"Listen, I'm not good for this," I said. "I don't know what happened, but I was pulled over and coke was found in my car. I have no clue how it got there."

Tom started to laugh. "I'm sorry," he said, trying to stifle himself. "You sound like all the other criminal defendants who come in here. The people you defend."

"Ha ha," I said. "Listen, you can laugh all you want, but I'm telling you, I didn't do it. I was framed."

"Okay." He continued to stifle himself. "I'm sorry. Well, I suppose you want to know the offer. I'm sure you can guess that we're offering you Drug Court. I'd take that, Harper, even if you aren't good for the crime. You have to remember, you're on probation with the Missouri Bar. If you get a conviction for this, you'll lose your license."

"Tom, don't you think I'll lose my license even if I get Drug Court? Seriously. A guilty plea of any kind will be enough for my license to be suspended at this point. Sorry, but I have to take my chances with this one."

"Harper, you're making a big mistake." He leaned over and whispered. "Just between you and me, planting drugs is something that happens a lot. But it's impossible to prove the drugs are planted. That's always the problem. You're going against cops and it becomes a 'he said she said' situation. The cops always win in these situations."

"I think I can beat it," I said. "I'll start by challenging the pretextual arrest, and go on through the pretextual search. That cop never had reasonable suspicion to stop me. He never had any cause to search."

I drew a breath as I remembered that I let that Officer search my car. I mentally kicked myself for that. That was one thing I always impressed upon my clients – never give permission to search. Always make the cop get a search warrant. Yet I let Officer Campbell search my car. I had nothing to hide. I never dreamed he'd plant something.

"Harper, you allowed him to search. Maybe you can do something about the pretextual stop, but all he needs is reasonable suspicion. That pretty much means anything."

I rolled my eyes. "Thank you for lawsplaining and mansplaining. I took Constitutional Law, the same as you. I even did well in it."

Tom was right. It would be difficult to beat my drug charge. Cops were given wide deference, and this particular cop, Officer Campbell, was straight-up. I didn't see myself beating this charge, either.

"All rise," the bailiff hollered. "Division 33 is now in session, the Honorable Judge Jackson presiding."

"Please be seated," Judge Jackson said as he sat down at the bench. "The state calls the State of Missouri v. Ross."

I was the first one on the docket, which was one good thing. I had to take my tiny victories where I found them.

I went to the bench. "Hello, Ms. Ross," Judge Jackson said pleasantly. "To the count of possession of a controlled substance, how do you plead?"

"Not guilty."

Judge Jackson nodded. "Okay, this case will be set for trial on December 11."

"Thank you, your honor."

He nodded and called the next case.

I walked out of the courtroom, feeling the snickers and stares as I exited through the double doors.

Fifteen

The next day, I went to Darnell's home to check on how things were going. I specifically wanted to speak with the Aunt watching his brothers and sisters. I wanted to ask her what she knew about Darnell's mother and Darnell himself.

After that, I'd visit Darnell and also ask around about Stephen. Axel had little information about how Stephen died, so I'd have to find that out.

I got to the apartment at 9. I'd called Darnell's aunt, whose name was Violetta, before I came. She told me the kids were in school so it was a good time to talk.

I pulled up to Darnell's apartment building. It was one of three dark red structures bounded by fences. Walking through the parking lot, I saw a basketball court with three kids playing a pickup game. I wondered why they weren't in school. I crunched through broken beer bottles and I reflexively picked up the trash around the building – there was a fast-food bag with a half-eaten hamburger inside and several empty bags that once held Doritos. I gingerly made my way down the sidewalk and into the building.

Climbing the stairs, I got a whiff of old urine and Lysol. The same combination of smells that made me sick in the jail hit my nose like a freight train. The stair case was old and there was graffiti on the walls – gang graffiti. I recognized the symbols because I went to a continuing legal education class on the topic of graffiti and gangs.

The apartment was on the fourth floor, and, as I walked down the hall, I heard loud music coming from one of the apartments. From several other apartments I heard other sounds – in one of the apartments, there was loud sex sounds coming from within. In another, I just heard a lot of screaming and yelling.

I finally got to Darnell's place and knocked on the door.

Violetta opened the door. She was a pretty lady, couldn't be much older than her late thirties. She wore her hair in braids and her nails were long and hot pink. She was dressed in a sweater and jeans and her smile could have lit up a dark room.

"You must be Ms. Ross," she said, holding out her hand. "Come on in."

"Thank you," I said.

The apartment was extremely small but it looked like Violetta had attempted to keep order around the place. Other than a basketball tucked in the corner, the place was neat and tidy. The sofa was covered in an afghan that looked hand-knitted. In front of the sofa was a wooden coffee table. An indoor plant was in another corner of the room and an ancient television was on a stand at the front of the room. Other than that, there wasn't a lot of furniture. There didn't seem to be room for much more.

"Can I get you a glass of water or a cup of tea?" she asked.

"Yes, please," I said.

She went into the kitchen, which was attached to the rest of the apartment and wasn't much of a kitchen at all and came back out with a glass of water. "Here," she said, sitting down next to me on the couch.

"Thanks."

She nodded. "You're welcome. I guess you need to talk to me about Darnell, right?"

"Yes. But I also wanted to ask you about his mother, Anita. Is she still in the hospital?"

"She is. I've been asking after her every day. She's recovering, but it'll be a long haul." She shook her head. "I don't know what will happen. I have two kids of my own. My husband has been watching them but he works nights. My kids are 10 and 11, so they have to stay in their beds with no adults around them. It scares me so I don't know what to do. I don't want these kids to go into foster care."

"How are the bills being paid?"

She snorted a little. "They're not. That's another thing. Anita worked practically around the clock. She depended on her two jobs to keep this place afloat. Darnell helped her out a little with his job and her second oldest son, Jamal, watched the younger kids when Anita and Darnell both were working. It all worked out, but now that Anita is in the hospital and Darnell is behind bars, I don't know what will happen."

"This family has been living on the edge of a coin," she said. "Have you ever seen a coin on its edge? It's very fragile. Any little thing will push it over. Anita getting sick and Darnell going to jail has pushed this family over. I don't know what to do."

"Did you try Legal Aid?"

"I did. I made an appointment with them. They couldn't even see me for two weeks, and then when I finally got in to see a Legal Aid attorney, I was told there wasn't much they could do for me. She pointed me in the direction of a few resources I could tap but it won't be enough to keep the bills afloat."

I was afraid of that. The family was on the edge. I knew that. That was how it was with the poor – it all worked as long as nothing went wrong. Once something went wrong, it all unraveled.

"Well," she said. "I know you're here to talk about Darnell." She shook her head. "I don't understand it. I really don't. Darnell is the last kid I'd dream would be into drugs. And he's the last kid I'd dream would kill a police officer. Or kill anyone for that matter. Truly, Ms. Ross. You don't know Darnell, but he really..." She shook her head again. "He really couldn't have done this. That's all."

"I know," I said. "I don't think he did it. What can you tell me about him?"

"He's a hard worker. Lordy, that boy works all the time. If he's not at school, he's doing homework. If he's not doing homework or at school, he's working his job at Church's. He works at Church's twenty hours a week while going to school and getting straight A's at Lincoln Prep. He's in some AP courses and acing them, too. Plus he works another job at a printing shop. He's a smart boy. A good boy. He wouldn't do something like this."

"Are you certain he didn't deal drugs? According to the police report, it seemed Darnell killed Officer Parker because Officer Parker was a plain clothes policeman. The theory is that when Officer Parker tried to arrest Darnell, Darnell shot him."

"Did you trace the weapon back to anybody?"

"I did. It was reported stolen by a Leonard Jefferson. That unfortunately tells me nothing."

"Did you have the cocaine tested in a lab?"

"Yes," I said. "It was tested and was pure cocaine."

"How about any witnesses?"

"None were listed on the police report. I'll have go to the chicken place and see if I can get anything that might've picked up on the murder. I don't know if they have a surveillance camera, but I also want to figure out if something was picked up by the microphone on the drive-through board. There might also be somebody who hangs around the place a lot. Fast food garbage cans can be a magnet for homeless people who hope to go through the trash and see if they can find food."

Violetta got up, went back into the kitchen and poured a cup of tea for her and one for me. "You might talk to Sally. She's the night manager at Church's. She could tell you if she catches dumpster divers. You're right, dumpster divers are a problem for just about every restaurant. I don't think Church's is any different in that way."

"Thanks," I said. "Is there anything else I need to know about Darnell?"

"No. Just that he's never in trouble. Ever. He does his best to stay out of trouble. This is really an injustice, Ms. Ross. Really an injustice."

I left, intending to go to Church's. And then onto the jail. I'd see Darnell and I was determined that to find out more about Stephen's death. There was something not setting right with me about Stephen. I still didn't believe he'd have confessed to murdering Alaina.

Something was nagging me. There was just a small piece of the story that would connect the dots.

The only problem was, I wasn't quite sure what dots I was trying to connect.

Sixteen

I ended up skipping the chicken place in favor of going straight to jail to see Darnell and find out about Stephen.

Stephen's case was first.

"I need to speak with the person in charge of the Stephen Heaney death," I said when I went into the jail. "I need to find out what happened to him."

"Just one second," the lady behind the window said. "I'll call him."

I went to the waiting room and sat down. I'd never done something like this, surprisingly enough. I'd never had to come to jail to inquire about a client death.

I looked down at my hands and saw they were shaking wildly. I put my head in my hands and the tears started to come. I didn't want to ask this person about Stephen. I didn't want to relive his last terrified moments. I didn't want to think about how everything was finally coming together for him right before this happened.

I didn't want to do any of these things, yet I knew I'd have to. I'd have to face it because if I didn't I wouldn't be doing my job.

After about fifteen minutes, a slender man, about 6'3", appeared. He shook my hand. "Hello, Ms. Ross," he said pleasantly.

"My name is Mac Crawford. I'm the administrator. I understand you're inquiring about the death of one of your clients."

"Yes," I said, standing up and shaking his hand. "I need to speak with you about that."

"Come back to my office," he said. "And I'll tell you anything you need to know."

I followed him back to his office and took a seat across from his desk. "Thank you for meeting with me," I said, feeling my voice break. "Stephen was my client but also my friend. This is very difficult for me."

"I'm very sorry for your loss," he said. "Were you close with Mr. Heaney?"

"Yes," I said. "He helped me with a previous case and I helped him in return. We became pretty close over these past few months."

"Well, he was accused of a very heinous crime," he said. "Innocent until proven guilty, I know, but the death of that poor, poor girl..." He shook his head. "I don't know what gets into men who do things like that. I really don't."

"I know. I have two daughters her age."

"I know you're doing your job in defending him. Innocent until proven guilty. What would you like to know?"

"What happened?"

"He was stabbed in the shower by another inmate, Jock Tucker. He's a member of the Aryan Brotherhood on his way back to prison. He caught a case while serving a life sentence in Leavenworth and was brought to the Jackson County jail to await his trial, which is happening next week. Needless to say, this is just one more case for him. I suppose that would be why he did it – he had nothing to lose."

"Was he put up to it by anybody?"

Mac shrugged his shoulders. "I really don't know. I've opened up an inquest about it. I've been interviewing some of the inmates who knew Jock and Stephen. It seems Jock had a problem with Stephen's crime. That happens, you know. Child predators and child killers are the lowest of the low in any jail. Most of these inmates have children of their own. Most of them were abused as children themselves. They don't take kindly to people who prey on children."

"My client was innocent," I said. "And I'll prove it. It might not matter anymore to anybody but me, but it matters to me. What else can you tell me about this Jock Tucker? Did he have an ongoing problem with Stephen?"

"As far as I know, nobody reported any previous interactions between the two men that seemed out of the ordinary. What else would you like to know about Jock?"

"What's his background?"

"He's a member of the Aryan Brotherhood," he said. "And his sister was arrested for intent to distribute. She was facing 10 years in prison. But that case seems to have gone away."

My ears perked up. "Really? What does that mean? What is her name? I need to know the sister's name."

"Ariel Tucker," he said. "Would you like her address? I can supply that to you if you need to speak with her."

"Yes, please. I need to know her address. I need to speak with her. And what do you mean, the case has gone away?"

"The prosecutor's office is declining to prosecute. That's all I know about that."

"Declining to prosecute. For an offense worth 10 years?" That was weird. To say the least. "Who's the prosecutor on the Ariel Tucker case?"

Mac got on his computer and looked it up. "Looks like the prosecutor for that case is Ellie McCoy."

"Thanks," I said, writing down her name. I knew Ellie. She was an upstanding person. She wouldn't drop a case unless there was reason for it.

"Is there anything else I can do for you?"

"Yes. Ariel's address. Thank you." I didn't know what I was looking for. But my spidey-sense was on high alert about this whole situation.

Mac gave me the address.

"Thanks," I said, after getting the address. "I appreciate that. Is there anything else you can tell me about this Jock Tucker guy?"

"No. Just that he's a piece of work. As I said, though, him killing Stephen was something that wouldn't affect his life one way or the other. He's already serving several life sentences. I guess he figures why not add one more?"

I nodded. Something about this whole situation wasn't sitting right with me.

Again, there were dots to connect, but I just couldn't figure out exactly what they were.

But I was determined to find out.

Seventeen

After I spoke with Mac, I saw Darnell. I didn't have anything to tell him, really, but I wanted to see him and reassure him I was hot on the case. I was diverted by Stephen's case because I was determined to get to the bottom of it. I knew Stephen was innocent of Alaina's murder. I'd prove it for Stephen's sake and for my own. I didn't want to think I showed poor judgment in bringing a pedophile and murderer to town. I didn't want to believe that my actions led to Alaina's death.

I couldn't have that on my conscience. So my proving Stephen's innocence was mostly to clear his name but partly to clear my mind.

Darnell came out about fifteen minutes after I got to the waiting room for him. He shuffled slowly along, his head down. Once again, I saw he had been crying and my heart went out to him.

"Hello, Ms. Ross," he said, sitting down. "Thank you for coming to see me again."

"Hi, Darnell," I said, my hand reflexively touching his arm. "I wanted to see how you are."

"I'm okay, I guess," he said. "But I'm really frustrated I'm here. My brother Jamal came to see me yesterday. He's really scared of going into foster care. He wants to stay with my other brother and two sisters, but he knows they can't stay together if they go into the system. They'll go into foster care if they can't pay their rent. That's overdue already and they're about to shut off the utilities." He shook his head. "I'm already a year behind in school, Ms. Ross. Now it looks like I can't graduate with my class so I'll be further behind."

My heart went out to him. He obviously wasn't thinking he might be convicted of this murder. He was naïve in the manner children his age usually were – he was innocent, so no way he'd end up in prison.

I knew differently. I knew kids were railroaded all the time. This wouldn't happen, not on my watch – at least that was my hope. I hoped and prayed I could prove Darnell innocent but didn't know how to go about it. His fingerprints were on the gun, the drugs were on his person, and there were no witnesses to the murder. At least no witnesses that had come forth. It also didn't look good that he was still on the premises of Church's a full hour after he clocked out.

The odds were stacked against him but all I could do was try my hardest to find an angle. Try like hell to make the jury buy my client's story. Maybe I could find a break in the case somehow but that was always a long-shot.

"Darnell," I said. "I don't want you to look ahead right now to college. Let's get you past this case and then you can worry about scholarships, graduating and all that."

His face fell and he looked down at the table. "You..." He squeezed his eyes shut, but I could see tears coming down his cheeks. "You think I might be convicted?" He shook his head and put it on the table.

My hand was still on his arm. "I don't know," I said softly. "Things don't look so good. I wish somebody around that chicken place saw what happened. I'll have to go over to the scene and see if the murder was recorded somehow. I know your chicken place doesn't have surveillance cameras, but maybe there was surveillance around there."

"No," he said. "I don't know what kind of surveillance there would be." He started to look hopeless. "If I go to prison, what will happen to my mama, my brothers and my sisters? Mama can't take care of them if I'm not around. I chip in as much money as I can to my mama, and if she's trying to get better from her stroke, she can't work like she did." His tears started in earnest again. "I don't know what will happen to my family."

I could do something, short term, for Darnell's family – I could make sure their rent was paid and utilities caught up. I didn't mind paying for that myself. But Darnell was right – long-term, it would be dicey. "Darnell," I said. "I'll pay the rent on that apartment and catch up the utilities. That won't be much. Hopefully I can catch a break on this case and you won't be convicted. If that happens, and you get out of jail, do you think your family can recover long-term?"

"You'd do that?" Darnell asked. "I don't want you to do that. It's not right. It's not your problem."

"I know it's not my problem," I said. "But I want to help."

Darnell started to cry again. "I'll repay you," he said. "When I get out of here. I'll repay you."

"Maybe you will and maybe you won't," I said. "I won't worry about it."

"But I will." He nodded his head. "I will. Thank you Ms. Ross."

"If it can keep your family in your home, it'll be worth it to me. I just hope your Aunt Violetta can keep caring for your siblings."

"Me too," he said. I could see a tiny bit of relief on his face and he smiled. "She does a good job but I hope mama can get home soon."

"And I hope you can, too," I said. "I'll turn over every rock. I'll try to run down Officer Parker's cases to see if there's anything I can glean from that. I'll ask your boss Sally if anybody who is a regular at the chicken place who might've seen what happened. I'm determined to catch a break in this case and you'll go free."

He lifted his face and smiled again. "Thank you, Ms. Ross. You're giving me hope I might walk this case down after all."

I gathered my files, as I needed to leave. "I'll be in touch," I said.

"I'll make sure to keep you apprised about everything going on in this case. And I'll visit you at least once a week even if I don't have new news to tell you. I care, Darnell. I hope you know that."

"I do, Ms. Ross. I do."

Eighteen

"What can you tell me about Officer Parker?" I asked Axel when he came over for dinner that evening. I had a ton to do both to prove Stephen's innocence and prove Darnell's innocence as well, but, just for the night, I'd relax with my guy and my girls.

"Jake Parker?" he asked.

"Yeah, Jake Parker. Officer Jake Parker. What can you tell me about him?"

"What do you want to know?"

We were sitting in the sun room in the big leather chair. It was just roomy enough for the both of us if we cuddled up closely together. Axel had a glass of scotch and we were covered up by a blanket, enjoying the fire. I loved being here with Axel – it was so intimate, so right. It just felt so safe.

"Well, I need to figure out if anybody might've had it in for him. It's a needle in a haystack, but maybe I can try to figure something out by looking at his cases."

"He was a good mate," he said. "A good bloke. It's terrible what happened to him."

I wished Axel could help me with my cases. I always wished that. But he couldn't free-lance. He had to be assigned to a case to work it and was never assigned to my cases. If I could use him he could be a valuable asset, but I never wanted to do anything that would jeopardize his position at the KCPD, so I never asked for his help.

But he could give me a run-down on Officer Parker. That wouldn't be much to ask.

"What kind of cases was he working on?" I asked.

"He's been in the drug unit but has been transitioning into sex crimes," Axel said. "He's been working a few sex crime cases and that was the division he was to be transferred to within the next six months."

"So, he's been working both drugs and sex?"

"And rock and roll, mate," Axel said with a smile. "Sorry, bad joke. But, yeah, he's been working in the drug unit for the past six years, but the transition to the sex crimes unit was coming up. Guess Jake got burned-out working the drug unit for so long."

"And the sex crimes unit will be so much less stressful," I said sarcastically. "But I know what you mean. I wouldn't imagine either job would be like a day in the park."

"So, what are you thinking?"

"Nothing yet. It's just a kernel. I usually try to find out the victim's background when trying to figure out who else might've done the crime. That's important when working a SODDI defense." I pulled the blanket around us tighter and I lay my head on his chest. I worked my fingers through one of the hairs on his chest and could feel his heart beating beneath my skin.

"Do you think it's important?"

"Everything's important. When you have nothing to go on, everything's important. I suppose the fact that Officer Parker was about to transition into sex crimes is as important a fact as any other."

I interlaced my fingers with his and he kissed my forehead lightly. "What do you think we go upstairs?" he asked with a smile.

"I thought you'd never ask."

That Saturday was Stephen's memorial service. Rina insisted she'd go to it.

She was very distressed when I told her about Stephen dying. I didn't give her the details of what happened to him. I thought that was better left unsaid.

She and Abby, who also insisted on going, even though she didn't know Stephen all that well, were silently sitting in the back of my SUV. That was unusual for Rina – that girl could talk more than anybody I knew.

Axel was with me in the car. He wanted to support me but he also really liked Stephen. I looked in the rear-view mirror and saw Rina staring out the window and Abby crying. I wondered if they were thinking of the last time they went to a memorial service – their mother's funeral. I thought about the wisdom of bringing them to Stephen's service for just that reason.

Abby finally spoke. "Are you going to say something, Mom?" she asked.

"I am," I said. "I'm the only one who really knew him and even I didn't get the chance to know him all that well."

I'd paid for this service, as I'd paid for Darnell's apartment and utilities. I was also busy trying to find a nanny for the kids so Violetta could return home. I was determined that Darnell would beat his charge and he had to have a home to return to.

I drove to The Peanut, a Downtown Bar where I decided to hold the memorial service for Stephen. I'd rented out the upstairs room and included an open bar. I also got permission from the owner to bring the girls in. He graciously allowed that.

Why did I hold the service in a bar? I felt Stephen would've wanted it that way. Or maybe I wanted it that way. I didn't want to feel sad, although I did. I felt very sad. Mainly because I felt his whole life was a waste and he never truly got the chance to turn it all around.

I got to the bar, went upstairs and arranged flowers on the all the tables, along with candles for everyone to light. About a half hour later, people started to arrive.

I smiled as the crowd grew to around 50 people. There were his co-workers at the nursery. Anna also made it, because she really was fond of Stephen. Heather came as well. But there were other people I didn't know. Every person came in to greet me and shake my hand, and, one by one, each person told me who they were and how they knew Stephen.

"I met Stephen at the homeless shelter," one lady told me. "He volunteered there every Saturday and Sunday and always had a smile and a kind word and joke for me."

There were several more who had stories like that, including people who volunteered with him.

Another guy came in and explained that he was a GrubHub delivery driver. "He was a good dude," he said. "I worked his area all the time so I delivered there a few times a week. He always tipped me awesome and was one of my nicest customers. I'm gonna miss that dude."

A young girl explained she was Stephen's neighbor. "He always fed my cat when I was away," she said. "I could trust him not to disturb anything. He also fixed my sink when the landlord wouldn't. He never asked for a single thing."

His girlfriend, Katy, showed up with flowers and tears. She was younger than him – she looked to be in her late fifties – and small and petite with dyed red hair and glasses. I hugged her reflexively, and she hugged me back, sobbing.

Other neighbors came in with similar stories.

The upshot was that everyone who Stephen came in contact with seemed to love him. When your neighbors come to your service that means you were a good neighbor. People don't take time out of their day to pay tribute to somebody they either didn't know or didn't like.

I became more and more convinced that Stephen was framed. But who framed him and why was clearly an open question.

The more I thought about him being framed, the angrier I got. He went to jail, where he was killed. He shouldn't have been in jail in the first goddamned place. He should still be alive, still touching people's lives and doing good works. He should still be fixing sinks, watching cats, working homeless shelters and tipping GrubHub drivers. Goddamn it, it wasn't fair.

It was the most unjust thing I could ever imagine.

By the time everybody came in and had a seat and a drink, and I'd addressed everyone, my anger was building to a crescendo. I'd find out who framed Stephen if it was the last thing I did.

I stood at the front of the bar and clinked my glass. Everyone got quiet and I began my speech.

"Hello, everyone. Thank you for coming. I'm really happy to see such a great turnout. Stephen moved to this city in the last six months, but, wow, he really managed to touch a lot of people. Not that this surprises me, because when I first met him, he treated me like an old friend. I guess that means Stephen didn't know strangers – everyone who came in contact with him became a friend."

I could feel a lump forming in my throat as I bowed my head.

"Um, Stephen didn't have an easy life. Not in the slightest. He suffered tragedy after tragedy yet was never hardened. Never hardened. When I met him, he was living in the woods of Oregon, all by himself. He was forced out there by a series of events that made him feel he couldn't live in society. I convinced him he could, so he came out here to live. He hadn't lived in society for over 50 years, yet he came to town and really blossomed. He never complained about the hard life he had, but, rather, always looked towards the future and the promise it would bring for him. He was excited for the future. The painful past was put where it belonged, and the future was nothing but bright for him."

I bowed my head and my hand went to my throat. "He was a victim of injustice. The most powerful injustice that can ever be perpetrated on anyone. The legal system is sometimes unfeeling, uncaring and unjust. It's unjust to the least of us, the people who are marginalized and powerless. Stephen was an innocent man accused of a heinous crime. And I'll find out who caused him to go to jail. It was in the Jackson County Jail that he met his fate. An inmate serving several life sentences killed him. He shouldn't have been in that jail. He should've been allowed to live the rest of his life in peace. He earned that and somebody took that away from him. The person who took that away from him wasn't Jock Tucker, the violent inmate who took Stephen's life. The person who took that away from him was the person who railroaded him into jail. And I'll find that person. I won't stop until I do."

I realized that I was saying things I never planned to say. Things that were probably inappropriate for a eulogy, but things that were at the forefront of my brain. They were words I couldn't help but say. I couldn't have stopped my mouth from saying them if I tried.

I finally just shook my head, embarrassed I'd said too much. "Thank you."

I sat down and Katy got up to talk about her feelings for Stephen. After she spoke, several more people spoke. At the end of the speeches, everybody lit their candles and we all sang Leonard Cohen's *Halleleujah* as the lyrics played across the television in the corner.

On the way home, Axel held my hand. "You going to be okay, lass?"

I shook my head. There was a burning sense of injustice in my chest. "No," I finally said. "I'm not. And I won't be until I figure out the bastard who did this to him."

"We know who did this to him, Harper," Axel said. "It was Jock Tucker."

"I know that," I said, feeling exasperated. "I understand it was Jock Tucker. I need to know who is responsible for Stephen going to jail in the first place. I need to know who railroaded him and who put that goddamned confession on his computer. That's who I want to kill right now." I shook my head. "He was an old man trying to live his life. You heard all those people – the guy was as close to a saint as you can get. It's not fair that he'd have to die like that. It's not fair at all. I'll get the person who did this to him and I'll make him pay."

Axel was quiet and, for some odd reason, his silence made me more angry. "What?" I finally said. "Go ahead, tell me what's on your mind, because something is."

"Harper, I always wondered about Stephen. He gave you a likely story about how he was innocent of wrong-doing, but how do you know that? How do you know? I know his identical twin brother was killed in that house and that Stephen claimed he was completely innocent but you don't know that for sure. He could've been just as guilty as his brother."

It was my turn to get quiet. I was stewing. The anger that was building up in me as I thought about how unjust this whole thing was was still there, but it was combined with anger at Axel. He heard those speeches. How dare he question me? How dare he question my judgment? If I told him Stephen was innocent, he needed to take that to the bank.

We arrived at my house and I got out of the car without a word. I opened the front door and the two girls bounded out and ran towards the house. I walked rapidly towards my door, leaving Axel lagging behind. He made it to the top step and put his right foot on my porch when I turned around. "Um, I'm sorry, Axel, I need to go upstairs and take some aspirin and try to get some sleep."

He dug his hands into his pocket and nodded. "I'll see you, Harper," he said, and then turned on his heels and walked away.

I didn't reply, but just walked into my house and slammed the door behind me.

Nineteen

The first thing I did on Monday was see Jock Tucker in jail. If he didn't talk, I'd see his sister, Ariel. I'd get to the bottom of why Jock would stab Stephen. I couldn't help but think somebody put him up to it.

I got to the jail and waited for Jock to come out.

He walked out some fifteen minutes later. He walked slowly with a huge swagger. He had a shaved head, fierce blue eyes and his entire neck and forearms were filled with tattoos. With his high cheekbones and pillowy lips, he looked like he could've been a male model if he didn't choose to become a murderer for the Aryan Nation.

He sat down at the table. "S'up," he said, looking me up and down. He nodded his head. "Harper, right?"

"Yes," I said. "My name is Harper Ross."

He nodded again. "Jock," he said. "Jock Tucker." He looked me up and down again and smiled. "You pretty cute," he said. "How you doin'?"

I didn't smile back. "Mr. Tucker, I need to ask you some questions."

"You wanna know why I iced that pervert, don't you?"

"That pervert, as you called him, was my client. He wasn't a pervert. He did nothing wrong."

"Right," he said with a smile. His head was bobbing up and down while he stared at me. "Sure. We all innocent in here, Ms. Harper. All of us are innocent." Then he started to laugh. "Whatever. Listen, I don't let no perverts live. Not if I can help it."

"He didn't-"

"Save it," he said. "I know guys like Stephen. I know them. When I was five years old I was filmed giving a blow job to an old man who looked just like him. That old man made me sick then and makes me sick now."

I was surprised Jock was a victim of child porn, but not really. It was always my experience that these hardened criminals have some kind of horrendous abuse in their backgrounds. "Is that why you killed him?" I asked. "Because he reminded you of the man you were filmed with when you were five?"

"Yeah. That's why."

"Is that the only reason why?"

"Yeah. Listen, Ms. Harper, I'm serving five life sentences for icing some dudes in prison. I started out with one life sentence for jacking some pervert on the East Side fucking my girl. I caught several more cases while in the joint. I might as well keep on keeping on – I got nothing to lose, so I might as well rid the world of scum while I can. The whole world will thank me for getting rid of as many of these kiddy diddlers I can." He smiled. "Drain the swamp, man, drain the fucking swamp."

"So, you made yourself judge, jury and executioner," I said. "Avenging angel? *Death Wish?*"

"Yeah, man, Death Wish, man. That Bronson was a good dude. He knew the score, man. You kill 'em before they get a chance to kill you."

"Tell me about your sister, Ariel."

He looked at me and then looked away. "This meeting is done, man. Done. I ain't talking about Ariel, man. Not talking."

"Oh? She was facing prison for possession and now she suddenly had her charges dropped. You explain that to me."

"So what? What does that have to do with the price of tea in China, man?"

"You're telling me that your sister is suddenly getting off her drug charge is just a coincidence?"

"Yeah, man. I killed Stephen because he was a damned pervert, man. No other reason." He crossed his arms in front of him, his steely blue eyes suddenly looking cold and dead. I could see the murderer lurking in those eyes. Those were the eyes of a guy who had been hurt his entire life and had a hardened shell because of it. They were the eyes of a guy who would kill anybody for any reason. He probably found killing fun by now. Killing for him would be a catharsis, a way of exorcising his own psychic pain. It was probably a high for him, almost orgasmic, with the inevitable let-down that happened after. I wondered if it was almost an addiction.

At any rate, I saw in his eyes that he didn't have a problem with killing. He enjoyed it.

"Is this meeting over?" he asked. "I gotta get back to my cell, man."

"So, that's your story?" I asked. "Your sister's charges being dropped have nothing to do with you murdering Stephen?"

"I don't even see where you're making the connection, man." He shook his head. "Thanks for coming down, Ms. Harper, but I really am calling this done." He motioned to the guard, who came right out. "Later, dude," he said, his hand making a gang signal.

I sighed as I walked him swagger back into the jail.

This wasn't the most fruitful meeting.

Maybe my meeting with Ariel would be better.

I got to Ariel's house on the East Side. It was a tiny house, bounded by a fence. It had a new paint job that was a pretty sky blue with white shutters. The lawn was trimmed and the painted porch had a bed of flowers on the railing. There was also a small garden on the front lawn where squash and pumpkins were growing. The house was in a not-nice neighborhood, but looked like the person who owned it was trying to make the house as pretty as possible.

I knocked on the door and a willowy brunette opened the door. Like her brother, she had piercing blue eyes, full lips and high cheekbones. Like her brother, she was tall and thin and looked like she belonged on the cover of a magazine. She wasn't wearing a stitch of makeup yet she was more beautiful than any woman I'd ever seen.

She was wearing blue jeans and a t-shirt that showed her surprisingly healthy chest, considering the rest of her was bone-thin. She cocked her head and smiled at me broadly as I stood on the other side of the door. "Harper Ross?" she asked.

"Harper Ross."

"Come on in." She gestured to the inside of the house.

I walked in, and, like the outside of the house, the inside looked new. New floors, new furniture and new throw rugs. It was a small house, tiny in fact, but the space was utilized to where it didn't seem all that cramped. "I'd ask you to have a seat at a dining room table, but, as you can see, I don't really have a dining room. But you can sit at my kitchen table."

I followed her into the kitchen. It was a cute kitchen with granite countertops and a new chrome side-by-side refrigerator and matching chrome stove. "Can I get you something? A pop, a beer, a glass of wine?"

"Water would be great," I said.

She poured a glass of water and brought it over, along with some cheese and crackers. "My mom would kill me if I had a guest over and didn't offer them stuff," she said with a smile.

"Thank you," I said, taking a cracker and putting a piece of cheddar cheese on it.

She nodded. "What did you want to ask me?"

I cleared my throat. "I understand you're Jock's sister."

"Yeah," she said. "Jock." She sighed. "Jock is a troubled guy. Always has been. I guess he had some issues when he was a kid. I don't really know."

"What kind of issues?"

"Well, our family adopted him when he was 8 years old. He was in foster care. His parents, his mom, really, his dad was nowhere to be found, but his mom sold him into the porn industry when he was five years old. Sold him for drugs." She shuddered. "He did that from the age 5 until when he was finally taken out of the house at age 8. My mom and dad tried for years to give him a normal life, but there was no going back with him. The damage was done."

I was slightly surprised that Jock was adopted, because I saw a resemblance between Ariel and Jock physically. But that was just superficial. And, after her story, I felt for Jock, even though he did that horrible thing to Stephen. I didn't blame Jock for the murder nearly as much as the person who railroaded Stephen into jail in the first place. Jock apparently never had a chance, much like most of my clients. But the person who railroaded Stephen probably didn't have that same excuse. I didn't know for sure, but I had a feeling about that.

I leaned back in my chair. "Ariel," I said. "I'd like to ask you something. I'd like to ask about your drug charge."

She nodded her head. "My bogus drug charge, you mean?"

"What do you mean?"

She sighed. "Let me explain. The cops were called to my house one night. It was about 2 AM, and I had a lousy boyfriend beating on me. I didn't call the cops, though. Somebody else did. Probably a neighbor. But they showed up, questioned my boyfriend, whose name was Lucas, and left."

I nibbled on the cheese and crackers and listened while she talked.

"Then about three weeks later they came back to my house. I have no idea why. They came in the middle of the night, walked into the house and left. They didn't explain why they were there. I talked to my next-door neighbor and she said she'd called the police. I just thought that the cops came to the wrong house and thought nothing of it."

She sighed. "Then about three weeks after that, the cops came back again. They said they had an anonymous tip that I was dealing drugs out of my house. I started to laugh. I mean, I'm the last person who would deal drugs. I'm a nurse. I don't make a ton of money, which is why I'm living in this neighborhood, but I've made enough to buy this house free and clear. It's not much, but it's the most I could afford." She nodded her head. "My parents always taught me to steer clear of debt. They ingrained that in my brain. They used to sit me down and show me how much extra I'd have to pay over the life of a loan, even when the rates are super low. So, I wanted to buy a house I could pay cash for."

She smiled. "Sorry, I digressed. It's just that this whole case has made me so damned angry that I don't like to talk about it."

"I understand," I said. "I've been witnessing a lot of unjust things myself recently. I've been feeling a sense of outrage myself."

"Yes," she said. "Well, anyhow, the cops came back again, saying they were acting on an anonymous tip about my dealing drugs. I started to laugh out loud. They asked if they could search the house, and I said 'have at it, hoss.' You know, I thought there was no way they'd find anything."

I somehow knew what was coming. "And let me guess. They found something."

"Oh, yeah. Yeah, they did. They lifted up the cushion of my couch and found a bag of coke." She shook her head. "I have no clue how it got there. The first thing I thought was my loser boyfriend probably did it. He probably put that damned coke in my sofa and called the cops."

She bit her lower lip and sipped her glass of water. She got up and went in the other room and found a sweater. "I'm very sorry, it's kinda cold in here. Would you like a sweater?"

"No, thanks," I said, smiling.

She sat back down. "So, yeah, they found a bag of coke in the sofa cushions. They arrested me, took me downtown, threw me in jail. God, that was the most humiliating moment of my life. I'm a nurse at Truman. I don't know if you've ever been to Truman, but there are people who come in to that hospital all the time. I mean, frequent flyers, we call them. They show up at the ER constantly, looking for pain meds, usually. Drug addicts. But I treat them all the time, and, when I went to jail, I saw two of them." She shook her head. "So embarrassing. You know? I'm the nurse, they're the patients, and they're seeing me booked and hustled into a cell."

That would be embarrassing. It was embarrassing enough to be arrested and put into jail. But to see people you know down there, especially if you're a professional – that would be the height of humiliation. I was just lucky I didn't run into someone I knew when I was put into jail. If I'd have seen one of my clients there, I probably would've hid my head in shame.

"But the charges are being dropped. Why are the charges being dropped?"

She shrugged. "I really have no idea. All I know is that I got a call from the prosecutor, Ellie McCoy, and she told me the arresting officer called her to let her know they would no longer cooperate with the prosecutor on my case. Ellie said she had no choice but to dismiss the charges."

I bit my lower lip. "Do you have any idea why the arresting officer would ask that of Ellie?"

"No, but what a relief. As a nurse, I can't have something like that on my record. Literally. I'd have lost my job if I was convicted of that drug charge. I had to pay $10,000 for an attorney to fight it. I got none of that money back, but I guess it was money well-spent, even though my attorney literally did nothing to bring about this dismissal. That's a lesson well learned – never get involved with a no-good guy."

"That's a lesson well learned for sure," I said. I didn't know that much about bad boyfriends, considering Axel was really my first boyfriend. Considering I didn't meet him until last year, at the age of 35, it was embarrassing to admit to myself that Axel was my first boyfriend. That was because of my rape, of course. In that way, sympathized with Ariel, because I knew about bad men like Michael.

"So you really don't know who the arresting officer was?"

"No." She shook her head. "It was the same guy who came to the house all three times, though. The same guy. He was with different partners each time, but it was one guy who came all three times."

"What did he look like?"

"Pretty generic, really. Average height, average weight. Just kinda average. I guess I'd describe him as being kind of shlubby. Do you know what I mean by that? Just a guy you wouldn't look at twice on the street. Invisible, really. That would be the best way to describe this guy – invisible. Like a ghost."

"Do you have a copy of your paperwork that you were given when you were arrested?"

"I do. But I keep it in my office at work. I have a filing cabinet there. I don't have one here. I don't think it's safe to have personal papers in this house – there have been a rash of burglaries around the neighborhood. I'm always afraid somebody will burglarize me and take a personal paper and find out my information. They can steal my identity. Believe me, I have an excellent financial record. Somebody can screw that up in a heartbeat. So I keep all my personal papers in my office. Under lock and key."

"Can you-" I wanted to ask her if she could get a copy of the paperwork, but I thought better of it. I thought the better way to go would be to contact Ellie and find out more about why the charges were dropped.

"Can I what?"

"Nothing," I said. "Ariel, thanks for meeting with me. You've really been a big help."

"I have?" She looked surprised. "I didn't really tell you anything useful."

"Oh, but you did. You did."

Twenty

"What did you want to talk to me about?" Ellie asked when I showed up at her office the next day. After I spoke with Ariel, I knew Ellie would hold the key for me. I somehow knew that speaking with her would enable me to figure out exactly why Stephen was killed.

"I need to speak with you about a case you have. A case you were prosecuting. Ariel Tucker."

She looked perplexed, as if she was trying to remember what case that was. "Ariel Tucker." She shook her head. "I don't think-" Then her face lit up. "Oh, right, right. Ariel Tucker. The name didn't immediately ring a bell because I didn't do much on that case. It was assigned to me then sat on my desk for a week or so. Then I get a call from the cops on this case telling me they wouldn't cooperate with us anymore, so we needed to dismiss the charges. Which I did."

"When did this call come through about dropping the charges?"

"Last week. Last Thursday, as a matter of fact."

Last Thursday. Stephen was killed last Wednesday. "Last Thursday, huh? Can I ask who is the officer on that case?"

She sighed. "Oh, Harper, I wish I could. But you know how it is in this office – we get hundreds of cases in here a week. I never got a good look at the file. I hadn't had the chance to start working it up yet."

"Can I see the file?"

"Well, it's in the closed file room," she said. "I can send one of our runners to get it, but it'll stake a minute."

"When can you get that for me?"

"Could be a day. Could be a week. I doubt it'll be longer than that, though."

"Thanks," I said. "I appreciate you helping me out with this."

"Sure. I'm curious, though, why do you want to see this file?"

"I got a hunch," I said. "And I need to build on it."

When I got back to my office, Pearl informed me I had a visitor. "Her name is Ginger," she said. "She's in your office. I'm sorry, I tried to tell her not to go in there, but she didn't listen to me."

"That's okay, Pearl," I said. "I asked her to look me up when she got out of jail. I guess she did."

I went into my office, and there she was. Ginger. She was dressed down some, compared to the last time I saw her – she was wearing jeans, a red t-shirt and a jean jacket with boots. Her hair wasn't blonde anymore but was more auburn. She wore it in a ponytail and didn't seem to have a bit of makeup on. She looked very different. It occurred to me that she looked much younger than she looked when I saw her in the jail. She could've passed for a college student.

"Hiya," she said, her face lighting up when I walked through the door. "I hope I'm not just barging in here. I mean, I know I'm barging in here, but I hope you don't mind."

"Not at all, actually. You're lucky – you've caught me at a good time. I don't have potential clients coming in and don't have court for a couple of hours. What can I do for you?"

"I wanted to see about maybe getting you on retainer. I got money. I just need someone who can bail me out when I need it. Do you do any cases like mine? Is that something you do?"

"Sure, sure," I said. "I've done prostitution cases before. I've even done some felony prostitution cases."

Her eyes got wide. "Felony prostitution. I didn't even know there was such a thing."

"Oh, yeah. You'd be surprised. I've never actually pled anybody to that, though. I've pretty much gotten my clients off either completely or get probation for them. How many priors do you have?"

"20," she said. "I know, I'm probably going to have to think about another line of work soon. But I gotta eat and right now I don't have no skills. But I got money. How much you want to a retainer?"

I raised my eyebrow. "Actually, let's talk about that later. Right now, I want to know more about your encounters with Officer Cooper."

"What do you want to know? Other than what I already told you about him being a perv. A sick perv."

"Well, here's what I'd like for you to do. Keep your ears open. Your eyes open. Report to me anything you hear anybody saying about Officer Cooper. Can you do that for me? You do that for me, and we'll call it good. No retainer – I'll just go ahead and represent you whenever you need me. I just need you to keep your ears to the ground about him. Can you do that?"

"Sure, sure. Anything special you want me to bring you?"

"No. Just bring me anything you hear. He's the arresting Officer for one of my clients and I'm trying to run down an alternative theory of the case. I need all hands on deck for this one."

"You got it," she said.

"Thanks. Now, what do you have? You have any new cases?"

"No, just the one you know about. I'll try to keep my nose clean, though. No promises."

"Well, give me the court date for that offense and I'll show up."

"It's December 11," she said. "In the municipal court."

"I'll be there."

Twenty-One

I got home, and Axel was waiting for me. He was sitting in the living room with the girls, watching some kind of tween-friendly movie. I nodded as I laid my purse on the dining room table.

"Hey," I said. "I'm sorry I haven't been returning your calls." I looked down at the ground. Axel had been calling, but I hadn't been picking up. I hadn't felt like talking to him. I just got the feeling he thought Stephen was guilty of that awful crime, and I didn't want to be around anybody who could think that for even a hot second.

"Why haven't you been returning my calls?" Axel asked.

"Yeah, Mom," Rina said. "What's up with that?"

"Let's go into the sun room." I motioned to the room.

We went in there and shut the French Doors.

"So, what's going on? I've been worried about you, lass. I know Stephen's death hit you hard."

"It did. But what's hit me even harder is that you think he was guilty of murdering a 13-year-old girl. You saw how he was around Rina and Abby. He never looked at either of them inappropriately. Ever. You heard all those people at his memorial. They loved him."

Axel looked exasperated. "Harper, Ted Bundy was beloved in his early years. Remember? Remember me telling you about how he worked at the suicide hotline and was great mates with that Ann Rule woman who went on to write a best-selling novel about him? You read that book, *The Stranger Beside Me.* She had great affection for Ted Bundy. She really fancied him. She sounded just like you when you defend Stephen Heaney."

I turned to face the door. I didn't want to look at Axel anymore. I didn't want to see his judgmental face. Truth be told, this confrontation had been coming for awhile. I didn't like his attitude about my clients, in general. He was a cop. I was a defense attorney. We had very different ways of looking at the world. Of looking at the criminal justice system. Of looking at people who are accused of committing crimes. He had no sympathy for the accused. He saw things through a different lens – that of a cop who sees criminals as nothing but scum. I was very different – I saw all my clients as human beings first.

"Mate," he said, coming over and putting his hands on my shoulders. "Maybe he's innocent. Maybe he was. I'm just saying you shouldn't necessarily believe that about him. I know you like to see the best in everybody, but you can't be so naïve."

"Go," I said. "Please, just go. Stephen was my friend and now he's dead. And all you can do is try to convince me he was a murderer and pervert. And what does that make me? Huh? What does that make me? I'll tell you what it makes me. It makes me an accessory to murder. It makes me responsible for Alaina's death. If he really did it, then I should've just let well enough alone and left him in the woods. If I'd have left well enough alone, Alaina would be alive today. That's if he did it. So, yeah, maybe I'm selfish or maybe I just really cared about the guy. I think it's a little of both. But the fact that you can't even see that..." I shook my head. "Please go."

"Harper."

"Go." I didn't turn around. "Before you go, though, look through the bathroom that's attached to my living room. There's some stuff in there – your shaver, your electric toothbrush, your after-shave. Take those items and go."

I could feel his anger radiating towards me. I didn't even have to turn around to feel it on my neck. "You're bloody shitting me, mate," he said. "You're breaking up with me? Seriously? Because I'm not some kind of pie-in-the-sky Pollyanna who thinks the world is made up of unicorns and rainbows? There are some seriously bad blokes out in the world, Harper, but you don't see that. You see everyone as victims. You feel sorry for everyone. A guy can bloody cut you in your sleep and you'd excuse him because his mommy didn't love him enough."

I finally turned around. "This. This is the reason why I'm breaking up with you. You're sitting there fucking making fun of me for having compassion. You don't seem to realize that my clients really have had fucked-up lives. I know, I know, you had a fucked-up life too, and look how well you turned out. Well, bully for you." I started to clap my hands. "I guess you deserve a medal for coming out of your hard life unscathed. Well, guess what. Not everyone is as lucky as you."

I was yelling by then, my anger boiling over. Axel was no longer the man I fell in love with. He was just another black and white thinker. The world is good and bad and if you're a criminal, you deserve no sympathy. He was impugning everything I did with his attitude. My life's work amounted to less than nothing in his eyes. All he could see was that I was defending a bunch of punks who were lower than low. Punks who didn't deserve an advocate. Punks who deserved to die.

He bowed his head. "Mate, I'm sorry about what I said. I didn't mean to insult you."

"And yet you did." I just stared at him with my arms crossed. "And yet you did."

He leaned against the wall and I turned my back on him again. "I'll count to 20, and I want you gone by the time I get to 20. I hope I've made myself perfectly clear."

I counted out loud and, by the time I got to ten, I heard the

French Doors open and shut. I closed my eyes and bowed my head. I felt absolutely empty.

I leaned my head against my window pane and cried.s

Twenty-Two

I cried myself to sleep the night Axel left, but the next day I was over it. I was over him. I questioned why I was so quick to dismiss Axel, even though we'd been together for over a year, almost two.

I realized I still had a huge scar that covered my body and soul like a shroud. I might never become whole. I might always be a woman who can't get close to anyone.

I didn't like his conservative views about the justice system. In fact, I couldn't stand them. He was no better than those rabid about the death penalty. He was no better than those who scream about turning the Middle East into a parking lot and bombing them until the sand glows. I was always a firm believer in looking at people according to their experiences and what happened to them growing up and not judging them. Each of my clients was an individual with their own backgrounds and pain. I could never look at my clients as so much cattle that need to be locked away because they are less than human.

Not that Axel saw my clients that way. But he didn't have sympathy for them, let alone empathy, and that I couldn't abide. The final straw was his apparent refusal to believe Stephen was innocent. He couldn't entertain that thought.

I'd prove him wrong.

I'd prove Axel wrong, but I was also working Darnell's case. I needed to focus on that.

I called Anna to get her working on things. "Anna," I said when I called her. "I need you to run a few things on a case I'm working."

"Sure thing, Harper," she said. "What do you need from me?"

"I need you to track down a Leonard Jefferson," I said. "Find out if he has a criminal record. He owned the murder weapon in my case with Officer Parker. While you're at it, try to find out where he lives. Anything you can find about Leonard would be helpful."

"Will do."

Not twenty minutes later, Anna called back. "Okay, yes, it looks like Leonard Jefferson has a criminal record. What do you need to know about it?"

"The arresting officer?"

"Looks like Officer Morgan Cooper."

I raised my eyebrow. Officer Cooper was certainly popping up all over my case. Then again, it was probably a coincidence – Officer Cooper had that beat. If Leonard Jefferson lived near the Church's Chicken place, Officer Cooper would be the one to arrest Leonard.

"Address?"

"Yes," she said. "He lives on Gillham Road. 33rd and Gillham." She gave me the address and I wrote it down.

"Thanks. I'll probably go down there today."

"Good luck."

I nodded. "Hey, Anna, while you're at it, maybe you can tell me more about Officer Cooper. Find out his background. Find out if he has a criminal record himself. I've heard rumors about him, but I need something more concrete."

"Will do."

I got off the phone and decided to immediately see Leonard Jefferson.

Maybe he could give me some more information about his

arrest and when his gun went missing. I hoped Leonard Jefferson didn't know Darnell. That would complicate things considerably. If Darnell and Leonard knew one another, then maybe Darnell stole Leonard's gun.

I drove down to the address and found the house where Leonard lived. This house was more of a typical house for this area than was Ariel's – it was run-down, with peeling paint and tall weeds in the front yard. I was intimidated by a large pit bull dog that bounded to the front fence and started to bark loudly. I drew a breath and made sure not to make eye contact with the dog. I wasn't afraid of dogs, except for dogs like this one, because he was barking and going crazy. Nonetheless, I needed to talk to Leonard, so I opened up the front gate and walked on through.

The dog started to sniff me, his tail wagging warily. I put out my hand for him to smell, and he did. I tried to stay calm, because they always said dogs smell your fear. It seemed to work and I proceeded on to the front door of the house and knocked.

A tall black man answered the door. He had an Afro cut into a flat-top and was wearing brown pants and a red t-shirt. His feet were bare. He looked at me curiously. "I'm sorry," he said. "Whatever you're selling, I'm not buying."

He attempted to close the door, but I put my foot in between the door and the doorway. "Mr. Jefferson," I said. "I'm not here to sell you anything."

He furrowed his brow. "You the police?"

"No. In fact, that's what I want to talk to you about. My name is Harper Ross. I need to speak with you about my client. His name is Darnell Williams. He's been accused of murdering an undercover policeman with your gun."

"You an attorney?"

I nodded. "Yes. I'm an attorney. I'm Darnell's defense attorney."

He opened up the door. "Come on in," he said.

I walked in and smelled an old house. It reminded me of when I'd visit my great aunt at her old house. Her house always smelled like Filipino food, because she was married to a Filipino man, but it also smelled musty. That's what this house smelled like – mustiness. The house needed a lot of work, that was for sure – the hardwood floors were worn, as was the furniture, and I could see on the ceiling where the roof leaked. There was a bucket underneath the leak filled with dirty water.

Leonard had apparently been busy rolling some joints right before I came to the door. There were rolling papers and pot on his coffee table. "I guess if you a defense attorney you won't say nothing about this," he said, motioning to the stuff on the table. "You want some? My prices are real cheap. A C-Note for an ounce."

I shook my head. "No, thank you." Marijuana was never my thing, and it was legal now anyhow. I tried it in college, as did most everybody I knew. The only thing pot did was make me lay on the couch and feel paranoid. Whenever I smoked pot, I always imagined horrible things happening around me – like when I got high when my mother was in the hospital and all I could think about was that she would die that night. Suffice to say that me and pot didn't get along well.

"Cool," he said. He motioned to a chair. "Sit down, sit down. Make yourself at home."

I sat down and watched him roll his pot.

"So, what did you want to ask me about?"

"Do you know Darnell Williams?"

He looked at the ceiling, with a look on his face that told me he was thinking. His eyes were squinting and his mouth was turned down. "Darnell Williams, Darnell Williams..." He finally shook his head. "Name doesn't ring a bell."

"Tell me about a your stolen gun."

"Yeah, man," he said. "That was some trifling bullshit right there, man." He shook his head. "I came home one day from work and found it gone. Just gone, man."

"Did you report it stolen?"

"Nah. No point. I've been jacked so many times it's not even funny. I ain't never got my shit back. I don't even bother with police reports anymore when shit gets stolen."

"Did anything happen before you got the gun stolen? Anything unusual."

He shrugged. "Not really, man. Nothing I can think of. Why you ask?"

"The cops didn't come to your house at any point before the gun was stolen?"

"The police are always coming to this neighborhood," he said. "They're always in the neighborhood harassing us. But they ain't coming in here. Not without a warrant."

"Have you ever had an encounter with an Officer Cooper?"

When I asked him that he rolled his eyes and made a snorting sound. "Man, I hate that mother-fucker," he said. "That mother-fucking Officer Cooper is the worst mother-fucker around, man." He shook his head. "That dude shot my friend Ron Hicks. Cooper's one of the ones who roll into the neighborhood and harass the shit out of us."

My ears perked up when Leonard was talking about Officer Cooper. "Tell me more. Why did he shoot your friend?"

"Shit, I don't know. Ron's okay now. He was lucky. Cooper just shot him in the shoulder." He looked at the wall again, his eyes narrowed. "No, wait, I do know. I do remember why he shot him. Ron was walking while black one day. Minding his own goddamned business. Then this pig Cooper rolls up on him, gets out of his car and slams Ron against it. Ron don't know what he did wrong, and Cooper kept hollering and screaming at Ron to keep his hands in the air."

"He did that and Ron had no idea why?"

"Yeah. Turns out there was a robbery in the area. Some cat jacked a liquor store and Cooper was looking through the neighborhood for a black dude about Ron's height." He started to laugh. "They actually caught the cat who robbed the liquor store, and he ain't looking nothing like Ron. Guess pigs like Cooper think we all look alike."

I nodded my head. "So, Cooper comes into the neighborhood

and he harasses Ron and slams him up against the car. What happened then?"

"Ron's got warrants. He ain't paying his child support. He's got no driver's license 'cause he's ain't paying his child support. He's not so bright so he decides he's gonna try to run. He knocked Cooper in the face and ran off. Cooper shot him in the shoulder."

"Did he get arrested?"

"Of course he got arrested. Cooper arrested him for assault. Served 6 months for that in the pen."

"Have you ever had a personal encounter with Cooper?"

"What you mean?"

"Has he ever harassed or arrested you or anything like that?"

"Oh, yeah. He harasses me all the time. All the fucking time."

"Tell me about his harassment."

"When hasn't he harassed me, man? I mean, seriously." He shook his head. "But, yeah, he was around the neighborhood when my gun got stolen, for sure." He paused. "In fact, yeah. Yeah. Yeah." He pointed wildly at the ceiling and then at me. "My roommate told me he was in the house the day the gun went missing. I remember now. He told my roommate he got a tip we be selling drugs up in here. We ain't selling no drugs. We ain't even doing drugs, man."

I looked meaningfully at the pot on the coffee table.

"Well, except weed man, and that don't even count, man. Shit's legal, man. Thank God."

"Go on," I said. "Officer Cooper came into the house and said he had a tip about you and your roommate selling drugs. By the way, what is your roommate's name?"

"Antoine Harrington. Anyhow, yeah, that cat Cooper came in here and had a look around. He ain't finding nothing illegal."

I wrote all this down. "And then the gun went missing..."

"It was missing that night, man. That very night. I get home from my job at the Taco Bell, man, I'm a night shift manager, you know, and it was like 2 in the morning. Antoine wasn't home. He was with his baby momma. I get home and check on where my gun was stashed. I always do that whenever I get home from work, 'cause I need to know it's there in case some cats break into this place and try to jack some shit."

He shook his head. "Trifling niggas always be jacking shit, you know. I get home that night and that piece ain't in the night stand where it's supposed to be. I call Antoine and chew his ass out, but Antoine says he don't know what happened to it. I'm pissed but I got another piece at the pawn shop the next day. I ain't gonna live in this neighborhood without a piece."

"And when did this happen?"

"I don't know. September something."

I was seeing a pattern. Cooper comes into Ariel's house and drugs show up out of nowhere. Cooper comes into Leonard's house and a gun disappears.

Cooper seemed to be the link through all these incidents.

Leonard continued to roll his joints while I stood up. "Thank you, Mr. Jefferson," I said to him. "I appreciate your help."

"Not a prob, Miss. I don't know what else I can tell you. I hope I don't catch no case from you being here."

"What does that mean?"

"That means Cooper is weird, man. Really fucking weird. That's what I mean, man. And, yeah, he arrested me one time. He did. That was about six months ago. Drug possession. Wasn't a big deal, I got probation and walked it down. I just hope that cat ain't casing this place and seeing you snooping around, that's all."

I wrote this down. The pieces were starting to fit. "Thanks again, Mr. Jefferson."

"Whatever I can do to help you in pinning something on that bastard Cooper, I'll do. Just ask me anything. Here's my cell phone."

I wrote it down, smiled and shook his hand.

He ran his hand through his Afro and looked around. "Talk soon, huh, Miss?"

"Yes. Talk soon."

Twenty-Three

"What you got for me?" I asked Anna when I got back to my office later on that day. I knew she'd already gotten her research done on Cooper. Anna was the fastest and most thorough researcher I'd ever known. If something could be found, Anna could find it.

"Can I come in?"

"Sure, sure. I'd like you to."

"Be there in a half hour."

About a half hour later, Anna showed up. "Man," she said, when she came into my office and sat down. "That Cooper is weird one. A really weird one."

"In what way?"

"He's worked at like ten different police departments."

"Ten different ones?" I pictured Cooper in my mind. "I wonder how old he is?"

"I found his birth certificate," she said. "He's 50."

I got out my slinky and played with it while I thought about what Anna was saying. "50 years old and has been shuffled around

10 times over the course of his career. That's weird. Different cities, I'd imagine?"

"Yeah. Let's see..." She looked down at her notes. "He lived in San Francisco, Las Vegas, Orlando, Tulsa, Boston, Dallas, Nashville, and in Butte, Montana." She shook her head. "Sorry, that's only 8."

"Still, 8 different places. Do you know why he's moved around so much?"

She shook her head. "No, there's nothing in his personnel records that stands out. Nothing that says he shuffles around for this reason or that. I guess he just goes from one force to another because he gets bored."

"Bored," I said. "Bored." I looked up at the ceiling. "Does that sound weird to you? What's strange to me is that Cooper keeps moving around but keeps going from one big city to the next. Aside from Butte, Montana, I mean. That's not the biggest city in the world, but the others are pretty major places." I raised an eyebrow. "But maybe it's not strange. Sometimes people get bored. Others decide just to move from one city to the next because that's how they are – they want to experience living in a bunch of different cities before they die. Maybe he's just adventurous that way."

"Maybe. Anyhow, that's what I have for you. And, no, Cooper doesn't have a criminal record. Nothing I could pull up, anyhow, and if I can't find it, it doesn't exist. I can find anything, even records which have long since been expunged. Even juvenile records. So, he's clean."

I sighed. Anna gave me something to chew on. But what it was, I really didn't know.

I decided the best thing would be to talk to Olga Morosky. I'd seen her at Stephen's memorial service and was meaning to speak with her then, but I never got the chance to. She came in, paid her respects, and left.

I went to the Crossroads nursery where she worked after finding out her work schedule. She was at the cash register, ringing somebody up, when I walked through the door. "Don't forget to water this tree at least once a week, about five gallons. You need to saturate the ground, but use this water gauge to make sure the water is penetrating to the root system. Good luck growing this beauty in your greenhouse. When you plant her in the ground in the spring, make sure you give her nourishment and water and always monitor to make sure the ground is moist. She should bloom for you beautifully."

The lady nodded her head, shook Olga's hand and left.

Olga was around 50 years old with salt and pepper hair, smiling green eyes and about 20 extra pounds. Nothing about her really stood out but she was still an attractive woman. Her smile made her more attractive, of course, because a smile always makes everybody more attractive, but she would be cute even without a smile.

Olga saw me and grinned. "You're Harper," she said, holding out her hand. "I remember you from Stephen's service. That was a lovely service, really." She looked around the nursery. "You put that together, didn't you?"

"I did."

"Stephen would've been tickled about that service. Just tickled. He really liked his whiskey. He made some amazing whiskey in his bathtub." She looked sad. "I was trying to encourage him to sell his recipe to a place that bottles whiskey. It was quite different, quite smooth. He was very proud of it."

"I wish I could've tasted it," I said. "When I met him in the woods, he wanted me to taste his whiskey. He was desperate for approval, really. That was what I thought about him – he'd been in the woods for so long, just all by himself, cut off from the outside world, and he was desperate for feedback. Feedback on his rabbit stew, feedback on his whiskey. He really wanted to talk, too. He needed company."

"Yes," Olga said. "I know. I realized that when I met him. Being in isolation, even self-imposed isolation, does something to your soul. We're human beings. We're social creatures. You look at our evolutionary profile, and you realize that early humans needed each other to survive. They needed their tribe to defend them, to procreate and do the things humans do with one another. It's the height of cruelty to be alone like that."

I nodded and looked around the nursery. It was a cute place, with little butterflies you can put into the ground, birdhouses, plants, statues, bird baths and flowers. Since it was the wintertime, or almost would be wintertime, the place didn't have much outdoors, but, indoors, it had plants that anybody can grow in their home, along with tiny trees meant to either grow indoors or in a greenhouse. "Yes," I finally said. "And it's the saddest thing what happened to him. I'm having a tough time coming to terms with it."

Olga took the next customer, giving advice and a friendly smile, and then turned back to me. "We aren't crowded right now, of course. This isn't exactly our busy season. Would you like to talk to me about Stephen? I can take my break right now and Amy can take my place."

"Yes. I'd like that."

"Good." She nodded and went back to speak with Amy who was a young girl, probably in her early twenties, with blonde hair. She was thin and wiry and her hair was retro, in that it was cut in a semi-mullet and seemed to have been subjected to a perm within the last month or so.

"Would you like to go to Jack's Stack?" she asked. "My son, Peter, is working there as a bus-boy. I like to go there at least once a week. Not just because Peter can use his employee discount for me, but also because I happen to really love the food there."

"Sounds yummy." I loved Jack's Stack. It was a Kansas City tradition. It was a barbecue place but wasn't like an ordinary barbecue place. Kansas City was known for its barbecue, but most of the barbecue joints in Kansas City were just that – joints. Arthur Bryant's was perhaps the most famous of all the barbecue places and was in the inner city. It was a no-frills place, where people lined up and ordered from the counter and ate their food in paper boats. Gates and Sons was probably the next most famous and popular place, with many locations throughout the area. It was also a place where you lined up and ordered and ate on paper plates and boats. And so it was for most places around the city that served up amazing barbecue.

But Jack's Stack was different. It had amazing barbecue in the Kansas City tradition, but, unlike most places, it was an actual restaurant. You sat down at a table and a waiter took your order. It was more expensive than most of the barbecue joints, but was worth it because of the atmosphere. There were different locations around the city but all were actual restaurants with hostesses, bartenders and waiters.

And the food was divine. I'd traveled to different places around the country and could never get barbecue as good as I got in my hometown. There were other places famous for barbecue, such as Memphis and Texas, but, for me, there was no place like home.

We went down to Jack's Stack, which was close to where she worked. "It's noon," she said. "So expect a rush."

Indeed, there was a rush, but we were seated soon enough.

"I'd like to treat you to lunch," I told her.

"I wouldn't hear of it. I'll treat."

I put my hand on hers. "Please. Let me do this. You're doing an enormous favor just sitting down and speaking with me. I need some information from you, so I'd never let you buy lunch."

She drew a breath. "Okay, but if we go out to lunch again, it'll be on me. I insist."

I nodded but knew I'd never let her pay for lunch. Whenever I went to lunch with a witness, I made it worth their time to speak with me. They didn't have to talk with me. I knew this. I was taking up their time. I never wanted to take a witness for granted, so I made sure I didn't.

We both ordered and I sipped my water. "Where is your son?"

"He's around here somewhere. He works in the back, usually, doing dishes, but he buses the tables, too. I think he's in the back today, though."

"How old is Peter?"

"Just turned 17. He turns 18 next May when he graduates high school. He goes to Lincoln Prep."

Lincoln Prep was one of the last magnet schools in the area. Back in the day, in the early 1990s, a judge decided the kids in the Kansas City school district would get a better education than what they were currently getting. Kansas City responded by making their high schools magnet schools and taking away the boundaries. For instance, one school was designated as a foreign language magnet school, where kids could enroll and learn different languages. Another was a Greek magnet school. All that I could remember about that particular place was its indoor swimming pool. Other schools might be a tech magnet school, where the kids would have all kinds of different media to play around with. The overall goal of the magnet school program was to make the schools so state-of-the-art that they would attract more white students to the district. The plan was noble and expensive – it cost the Kansas City taxpayers over $2 billion. It also ultimately failed in its stated purpose of desegregating the schools – the school district was currently only 9% white and I don't think it ever got above that.

But Lincoln Prep was something different. That was a school where you had to have certain test scores to get in and the curriculum was challenging and diverse. I substitute taught at Lincoln Prep and that school was more desegregated than any other in the district. The entire focus of Lincoln Prep was preparing children for college, so it featured AP classes as well as more challenging courses such as calculus, physics and advanced foreign languages.

Lincoln Prep was also the school where Darnell was attending. I wondered if he knew Peter.

Olga sipped her water and got quiet. "You probably wanted to talk about Alaina, huh?"

"Yes," I said. "I need to talk to you about her." I put my hand on hers and rubbed lightly. "When you're ready."

She shook her head. "I have to work myself up to talking about her," she said. "I can't just come out with it." She sighed and looked at the ceiling and then took a sip of her water. "Alaina was my baby. My beautiful, perfect baby. Her father died when she was just a small child. She and Peter had the same dad, Seth Morosky. My maiden name was Ivanov. I lived in the former Soviet Union and emigrated here when I was just a young girl after the wall went down. We experienced many hardships in my homeland and I got tough. Very tough. But I guess I wasn't tough enough, because when Alaina was found..." She shook her head. "When Alaina was found, I didn't want to live anymore. I just didn't want to live. I couldn't imagine who would do something like that to her."

"You don't think Stephen did this, though?"

"No. I don't. Not for a minute. Not for a split second. Stephen was good and kind. He'd give you the shirt off his back. I always thought he was grateful for every second on earth, moreso than anybody I'd ever known. You know, you work with people and you see them get cross and get in bad moods and all that. Not Stephen. Never a cross word from him. Never got snippy or snappy or anything like that. Always went out of his way to help our customers no matter what they asked for. My boss told me she wished for 100 Stephens because you could never catch him on a bad day."

I took a sip of my water and the bread came. I broke off a piece, put some butter on it and handed it to Olga before buttering my own piece of bread. "Is there anybody who you might suspect might've done this to her? Was she seeing anybody?"

"She was 13," she said. "I admit, I was a bit protective of her. I didn't want her to go out with anybody from school. I wanted her to concentrate on her schoolwork and not get so wrapped up in boys. I was always afraid she'd end up pregnant. That happened to me when I was her age. I put the child up for adoption but it was really a stressful experience. I didn't date anybody until I was in my early thirties, when I met Seth and fell in love. I was so focused on survival that I didn't have time to date. I put some of my neuroses on poor Alaina. I didn't let her have much of a social life."

She looked sad. I could imagine why. I'd probably regret stifling the social life of a young girl, if that young girl ended up being killed at such a young age. She meant well by making sure Alaina didn't date, but where did it get her?

"So Alaina didn't date," I said. "She didn't run away ever, did she?"

When I said that, Olga's eyes filled with tears. "She ran away one time. I was frantic when I went upstairs to her bedroom to find she wasn't in bed. I was beside myself. She was gone for two whole weeks before she was brought back to the house by a kind policeman. Officer Parker brought her back one day, said he found her eating out of a dumpster and he recognized her face from the missing posters plastered all around town."

My ears perked up with she mentioned the name of Officer Parker. My victim. "Officer Jake Parker?"

"That's the one. He wasn't dressed in a uniform but explained he was plain-clothes. Undercover." She clapped her hands in front of her and looked towards the heavens. "I was so relieved, so relieved. I go to church, Harper. I had the whole church praying on her safe return. When she showed up at my door, it was nothing short of a miracle. An absolute miracle."

She then got silent and more tears came to her eyes. "A miracle," she said quietly. "Little did I know how short-lived that..." She shook her head. "I'm so sorry. I'm really trying to talk about my little girl. I want to talk about her. My priest tells me I shouldn't push myself to talk about her if I just can't. But I have to talk about her. She exists now only in my memories and in my heart and in the hearts and memories of the other people who loved her. I have to keep her in my heart so I need to talk about her without falling apart."

Olga started to sob and I silently handed her a Kleenex from my purse.

"Thank you," she said. "You're an attorney, so you always have to have Kleenex on you, huh?"

"Yes," I said. "I've long since found that having Kleenex is a necessity, to say the very least."

"I guess so. When you talk to witnesses and the families of victims, I'd imagine there are a lot of tears involved."

"You might say that."

"So," she said, taking a deep breath. "Alaina was gone for a couple of weeks and didn't say how she survived. I found out, though, soon enough." She shook her head. "Best laid plans, I guess. I tried so hard to make sure she didn't go out with boys because I was afraid she might get pregnant and what happens? She runs away from home, stays away for two weeks, and ends up pregnant."

"Alaina was pregnant?" This was news to me. There wasn't anything about that in the paper. Yet, this was a significant piece of information. "How did you find out about that?"

"She didn't get her period so I took her into Planned Parenthood. She wasn't very far along when she..." Olga made a motion with her hands, and I got the drift – she still couldn'tverbalize that her daughter was murdered.

I wrote down that Alaina was pregnant. This was significant to me. That, to me, gave somebody motive to kill her. She was 13 years old. If the father was ever identified, that man would end up behind bars for statutory rape.

"What do you think about that?" Olga asked me. "My daughter falling pregnant?"

"I think that if we identified the person who got her pregnant we can find our killer. That's what I think."

"Why do you believe that? I mean, I thought the same thing when Alaina was found. I immediately thought the father of Alaina's baby was who did that to her. But I was wondering what your thoughts were."

"Well, statutory rape of a child as young as Alaina is a very serious offense. It could result in life in prison. The person who killed her probably did it because he wanted to cover up his crime of raping her. That's assuming Alaina willingly had sex with the man, whoever it was. If she didn't, and it was forcible rape, then the penalties would be even stiffer. That would give the man motive to kill Alaina."

Olga nodded. "You know, Alaina told me the man didn't force himself on her, whatever that's worth. She said he told her she could stay with him if she agreed to have sex with him. She told me she didn't know what else to do so she went along with it." She started to speak softly under her breath in a different language that sounded like Russian. Her hand flew up to her throat and then landed back down on the table. "She went along with it. She didn't want to come home. She didn't want to see me anymore. She ran away because she felt like I was stifling her, imprisoning her. Do you have children, Harper?"

"I do. Two young girls, age 13. They're identical twins."

"Well, don't do what I did. Don't try to put a short leash on them. They'll strain against that leash, Harper. They'll do anything to get away from that leash. Anything. Even stay with a man in exchange for sex, just because they're that desperate not to come home. I didn't think something like that would happen to me, but it did. It did."

"I'm very sorry," I said as sincerely as possible. "I know how this must feel."

"No. You don't. You couldn't possibly. And, for your sake, I hope you never know how this feels. I hope you never do. Because it's like having your heart ripped out every second of every day. It's like that Ancient Greek Titan who stole fire from the Gods and was sentenced to having his liver eaten out by a bird every single day for eternity. That's what this feels like, losing a child in this way. It's an intense pain that never goes away and never lessens. Never lessens but becomes more painful with every passing second."

Olga was a broken woman. Her ready smile for me and for everyone in that nursery covered up that she was broken. I thought about Rina and Abby and how I'd feel if either of them was murdered in such a way. I couldn't imagine the pain and the devastation I'd feel if something like that happened. I'd feel as if somebody had come along and severed one of my limbs without anesthesia. And that pain would just never go away.

"So..." Olga said and then shrugged. She started to cry again and dabbed her eyes with the Kleenex.

"Olga," I said. "Do you have any idea who Alaina stayed with when she ran away?"

"No. She didn't tell me anything about him. She was afraid to say anything, I think. She was afraid I'd come after him like a mama tiger and she was right. She was right. If she told me who he was, I probably would've come for him with a gun." She looked into the distance. "I'm handy with a gun, Harper. I am. I lived for the first 22 years of my life in the old Soviet Union and I was around when it was crumbling. It was chaotic and violent. My father gave me a gun to defend myself with and he taught me how to shoot to kill. I had to kill a man in Russia. He was attacking me, wanting to rape me, and I shot him and killed him. So I'm not afraid to kill somebody."

She revealed her heart and soul at that moment and knew she was a strong woman who would do anything to protect the people she loved. I had no doubt that Olga probably would've killed the man who impregnated young Alaina.

"I don't really understand, though. The papers never said Alaina was pregnant."

"The papers withheld that information at my request," she said. "And the police department thought it would cut down on the people claiming to have done this. Whenever there's a high-profile murder such as, such as..." She shook her head. "Whenever there's a high profile murder, there's always a danger of crazy people claiming they did it. The police department suppressed that information from the public to cut that down."

I understood that. That was a common thing in cases like this – suppress some piece of pertinent information, so that, when people try to claim responsibility, the cops would ask them information about the victim, and if they didn't know the important details, they were routinely ignored.

"That information wasn't in the police reports, either." I bit my lower lip. "That's so weird. I mean, that's the most important piece of information, yet it wasn't in the reports."

OIga cocked her head to the side. "It wasn't? That's odd."

"Yeah. Very odd." I bent down my head to suck on my straw as I thought. The good news was, this piece of information could very well clear Stephen. Assuming the police did their job and did a DNA analysis on the fetus, it might be easy to clear Stephen. All I'd need would be a hair from one of his hairbrushes or something that has his DNA on it and I could clear him.

The information about the pregnancy made me wonder why the police never made Stephen give DNA. Might it be because he'd have been ruled out as the father of the baby, which would make it more difficult to railroad him for Alaina's murder? If so, who were they protecting? It seemed obvious they were protecting somebody, because, well, that would be the only reason why the detail about Alaina's pregnancy was missing from the police report.

"Olga," I began. "Since Alaina was found, have you experienced anything out of the ordinary? Anybody following you, or maybe you've seen the same person coming into your shop time and again without buying anything? Maybe you might've been getting odd hang-up phone calls at all times of the day or night? Anything happening like that?"

Olga looked at me for a few seconds and then shook her head. "No, nothing weird like that. But maybe I just haven't noticed it. I've not been noticing much around me these days. I've been lost in a fog, Harper. The early morning is the absolute worst time of the day, because I remember each morning what my life has become. I remember each morning that I no longer have a daughter. Night-time is the only time I can survive because I have dreams all night that Alaina is still alive. Then I wake up and go to her room and remember. I have to remember each morning and then I just want to die. That's my life, Harper, that's my life. It won't get better, either."

"Could you do me a favor? Could you make note if there's anybody who seems suspicious to you? Maybe you see a car following you, or maybe, as I said, you see somebody coming into the nursery a few times without buying anything. Not that this means the person is suspicious or anything, but you never know."

"Sure. I'll try. What are you thinking about?"

"I don't really know. I just think you might be targeted by Alaina's killer since you know she was pregnant and nobody else really did. You have a piece of information that somebody will try to keep silent. I don't want to see you get hurt, that's all."

"You really think somebody will come after me?"

"I don't know. I'll ask around the police department about why Alaina's pregnancy was kept silent. I hope somebody did a DNA analysis on the fetus because that would be the most important clue on who killed your daughter."

I was happy I saw Olga. I didn't like seeing her pain, of course. I couldn't imagine the depths of her agony. I was an empathetic person, so her pain became my pain.

Yet she gave me perhaps the best piece of information I could have possibly had.

Twenty-Four

"Anna," I said when I got back to the office. I'd called her from my car after I spoke with Olga and asked her to meet me in my office. She was waiting for me when I got there, talking to Tammy, back in town after an extended vacation to Europe. "Come in my office. I need to ask a few things of you."

"Sure, sure."

"Hey, Harper, don't you want to see my pictures?" Tammy asked me.

"Of course, of course. Let me talk to Anna and I'll come in your office and check them out. How does that sound?"

"I'll see you in a few."

A part of me wanted to see Tammy's pictures because she'd spent three months in Europe and I was sure she had amazing photos. A part of me, however, didn't want to see the pictures. I was jealous that Tammy had the kind of life where she could chuck work aside for months and go on a sight-seeing trip to Spain, Italy, Germany, France, Romania and The Czech Republic. I'd always wanted to see Prague, myself, as I'd always heard it was the most beautiful city in the world. Yet I knew I couldn't enjoy myself for that length of time. I always had so much on my plate that I couldn't relax for very long. I had to really plan ahead for any kind of a trip - I'd have to cease taking cases for months, otherwise I'd inevitably have court appearances that would crop up while out of the country. I was too much of a control freak to let other attorneys handle my court appearances, however minor, so I was stuck.

I could maybe handle a vacation of a week or two, but I could never get away for three months at a time. I was jealous of Tammy because she could. She didn't have court appearances the way I did so she was much more flexible.

"Okay, Anna, here's a few things I want you to do for me. First of all, I need for you to do some digging on Alaina Morosky. She was pregnant. That was apparently covered up because it never appeared in any police reports. I need you to figure out why and find out if there is any information on the fetus' DNA. Secondly, find out the active cases Officer Parker was working. I need a list so I can figure out if anybody had cause to ice him besides my client, Darnell. This will be phase two of my investigations of both cases. I have a few hunches, so I need as much information about these hunches as I can get."

She wrote down the requests and then looked up. "Alaina was pregnant?" she asked. "But she was only 13. How is that even possible?"

I cocked my head, looking into her quizzical brown eyes.

"I mean, of course it's possible," she said. "I just think that's horrible, though. To be that age and pregnant..."

"I know." I nodded. "I know. Believe me, I'm thinking the exact same thing. It's weird, to say the very least, and creepy. But more than that, it gives somebody motive to murder her. I just need to know who that might be."

"I'll do my best to find out," she said. "But I don't think this stuff would be on-line anywhere. After all, it was buried by the police department, right? The most important piece of information about your victim was buried. They'll keep it buried. It won't be easily accessible even by somebody like me. But I'll try. As for the Officer Parker case, I can find that information out pretty easily. Just give me a few hours on that."

"Thanks."

"You're welcome. Is there anything else you need?"

"No, nothing else right now. I just wonder..."

"What?"

"Oh, nothing." I drew a breath. "Just thinking out loud."

"What are you thinking?"

"I'm thinking about Alaina and her plight. I need to clear Stephen's name so I need to find out who did this. I'm getting close to that information, Anna, but, for some odd reason, the closer I get, the more scared I get. I'm opening a can of worms that can't be put back. And that thought terrifies me."

"You, scared?" Anna smiled. "I never thought of you being scared about anything. You're a badass, Harper."

"Boy do I have you fooled."

Anna left and I went to Tammy's office. She was rifling through the pictures she took on her trip and she looked up and smiled.

"Well," I said to her. "Let's see these pics."

For the next few hours, I saw pictures of castles and beaches and landmarks while trying hard to tamp down my jealousy. *Someday, Harper, you will get to Europe.*

Someday...

Twenty-Five

That night, I got an urgent phone call from Katy, Stephen's girlfriend. "Harper," she said. "I need to speak with you." She was crying. "My landlady found I have Stella and told me I need to get rid of her. I was hoping you might know somebody who can take her."

I thought about Stella, the beautiful golden retriever who Stephen said changed his entire life. No, actually, he said Stella *saved* his life. As I recall, Stephen said he was on the verge of suicide when sweet Stella showed up at his door. Stella then gave Stephen the will to live.

"Uh," I said, looking at Rina and Abby, who were staring at me as I spoke with Katy. I sometimes thought Rina and Abby had a sixth-sense. They just knew I was talking about getting a dog.

That was something the girls had been asking me for some time. They wanted a dog so desperately. "We've never had a dog," Abby informed me. "Our other mother was allergic. But we're not allergic, Mom. We've both been to many houses that had a dog. Rina and I have never sneezed around these other dogs."

"Hang on, Katy," I said. "Can I call you right back? I need to discuss this with my twins."

"Oh, yes, yes," she said. "Does this mean you might take her?"

"Might is the operative word," I said. "I work a lot of hours, so..." I looked at Rina and Abby who were still staring at me, and, for some odd reason, Rina was nudging Abby excitedly. How did they know I was talking about getting a dog? "I'll call you back."

I hung up and looked at my two girls. "That was Katy, Stephen's girlfriend," I began.

"Yes?" Rina asked while she watched me. Her eyes were lit up and she looked like she was about to burst out dancing around the room. "What did she want?"

"She wanted to let me know that Stella the dog is about to become Stella the homeless dog and did I know anybody who can take her."

At that, Rina let out a shriek and I suddenly realized that Rina probably already knew about this situation. "Rina, did you know about this?"

Abby, just as happy as Rina, but was, as always, more subdued about it, ratted her out. "You had your computer up again and Rina's always sneaking around and reading your emails. You should probably make sure you log out from your emails next time, Mom, just a heads-up."

I groaned. "Rina, I asked you not to read my emails. But you're right, Abby, it's my fault for being careless." I didn't mind Rina reading the emails because I had nothing to hide. Axel, for his part, disappeared just like I asked him to. He hadn't begged me to reconsider, and I wouldn't, so I was happy he didn't beg. But his emails would be the only ones I'd be worried about, as far as Rina reading them. Everything else in my personal email was spam that I hadn't yet bothered to get rid of – mainly because I was lazy and just hadn't gotten around to deleting everything. I didn't care if Rina read my endless emails from Travelocity, the Democratic Party or any of the companies who sent me daily pleas for one thing or another.

"So, Mom, you got an email from Katy and she said she'd call you about it right about now," Rina said. "So I knew why she was calling you. And Stella is beautiful and sweet and well-behaved and please take her in. Please, Mom. Pllllleeeeeaaassseeee....."

"I agree. Stella is all those things. But she's used to having somebody around who has time for her. When she lived out in the woods with Stephen, she was around him literally 24/7. Even here in Kansas City, Stella was around Stephen a lot, because he only worked part-time. I, on the other hand, don't work part-time. Nowhere near. That means you girls will have to care for Stella when I'm not here. That means picking up dog poop in the backyard, brushing her, feeding her and giving her water when she needs it. That means walking her several times a week. That means talking to her, petting her and loving her. She's probably in mourning for her Stephen right now, so she'll need extra attention. Can you girls handle this?"

Rina was rapidly nodding, and Abby was now jumping around excitedly. "Oh, yes, Mom, yes, yes, yes."

"Now, are you sure? I won't be happy if I come home late one night and hear from Sophia that she fed and walked Stella and picked up Stella's poop in the backyard. If that happens, I'll be extremely angry. When I get home early, before 6, I'll feed and walk her, but if I'm not home early, it'll be up to you two. I'll make sure Stella has what she needs, but I'll need help. You two girls can't just get the dog and decide after a week or two that she's too much trouble – when Stella gets here, she's here for good. This will be her forever home. That means you girls will have to stick with it as far as caring for her."

"Mom, we won't let you down," Abby said. "We promise. We swear. We'll do everything for Stella that you ask of us. Promise."

I finally sighed. "Okay. I'll call Katy back and tell her I'll take Stella." I shook my head. I hoped and prayed I wasn't doing the wrong thing. I never wanted a dog before because of my work hours. I didn't think it was fair to any dog to be away from his or her pet parent for such long periods of time.

But Stella was special. She'd maybe end up in the dog pound if I didn't take her and I couldn't face that. Seeing animals in the pound always made me sad, anyhow, but it really made me sad when the animals lost their lifelong companion. It was bad enough not being around their person, but to end up in the pound - lost, lonely and abandoned after losing their person...that was the saddest situation I could possibly consider.

I called Katy. “I’ll take her,” I said, hoping I wouldn’t regret it. “When can I come and get her?”

“Anytime,” she said. “You can come and get her tonight if you like. I’ll be up until 11. Or anytime tomorrow.”

“No time like the present,” I said. “Give me your address and I’ll be there within the hour.”

I hung up and the two girls screeched and gave me giant hugs. “Thank you, Mom, thank you, thank you, thank you,” Rina said over and over again.

Abby was crying too hard to thank me, but I knew they were happy tears.

“Well, come on, girls,” I said. “Let’s get Stella before Petco closes and then go to Petco and get everything she needs.”

The girls and I went to my SUV, with the two girls literally dancing their way to the car.

As I drove, Rina and Abby were singing along in the back to some Drake tune streaming on their Apple Music app, one earbud in each girls’ ear. They were rapping and singing along at the top of their lungs.

By the time I arrived at Katy’s apartment, which wasn’t all that far, I was ready to brain both my girls. I liked pop music as much as the next mom, but my taste leaned more towards Adele and Ed Sheeran. I even liked Harry Styles. Hip hop of any kind was not my thing, even though I knew most tweens were listening to Drake, The Weeknd, Lizzo and people like that. I felt hopelessly old-fashioned but that was just how it was.

“Okay, girls,” I said. “I’ll get the dog and come back out with her. Then we’ll go to the pet store.”

“Okay, Mom,” Rina said enthusiastically. “Oh, goody, goody, goody....”

I knocked on Katy’s door and she opened it. Stella was on a harness and leash, ready to go. “Thank you so much for taking her,”

Katy said. "I wish I could keep her but I'm glad she'll have a better home. She needs a backyard and kids to love her. I can't give her either of those things."

"Well, she'll certainly have both of those things with me. A backyard and two very excited little girls who will smother her the second I get her to my SUV."

I took Stella, who looked up at me with her big brown eyes, and I melted just a little. There was something about looking into the eyes of a dog that always got me. They were so innocent, so trusting, so eager to please. I often hoped I could find a man with those qualities, but, alas, that didn't seem possible. Then again, I didn't know if I really wanted a man like a dog. I wouldn't respect him if he were.

"By the way, how are things going with Stephen's case?" she asked.

"I think I might've gotten a break in the case," I said. "Alaina was pregnant. If I could figure out who impregnated her, I could figure out who did it."

Katy shook her head. "That's tragic that Stephen should have to die for somebody else. That really makes me angry, every time I think about it. Somebody killed that girl and Stephen paid for it. I hope you find out who did that, Ms. Ross, I really do."

"Oh, I'll figure it out. I always do. And that person will fry if I have any say about it."

At that, Katy kneeled down and put her nose on Stella's. Stella licked her face. "Now, Stella, I'll miss you. I'm very sorry I couldn't keep you. I wish I could because you're such a beautiful girl. Such a beautiful girl." Katy smiled at me. "You'll have a great girl there, Ms. Ross. You can't find a dog with a sweeter disposition."

"I'm sure you're right about that," I said as I looked down at Stella. "Thank you for caring for her so well."

"I was happy to do it."

I took Stella out to the car, and Rina and Abby both leaped out at once. They hugged Stella, who wagged her tail and licked both of their faces. I shook my head. I had no idea where that tongue had been, but I wouldn't be my mother. I would let the dog lick my girls and not say anything about it.

An hour later, with leashes, harnesses, collars, food, toys and a dog bed in hand, we arrived home. I felt like I bought that pet store out, but Stella wouldn't want for anything. She didn't know it was her lucky day when I went to that apartment and got her.

But she soon would.

Twenty-Six

The next day, I went to my office with Stella. I was officially a crazy dog lady. I'd die one day in a house full of dogs, both large and small, because I fell madly in love with Stella overnight. Once I let down my guard and realized what a snuggle-bunny I had in her, I knew it would be difficult to separate us. She had her own bed but slept in mine, her tiny snore charming me and keeping me awake at the same time.

I also brought her into the office because I had to inquire about doggie daycare places. I wasn't ready to leave Stella at home alone because I didn't want her to get lonely, yet I didn't have a doggie daycare place set up. So I brought her into the office with the intention of getting a daycare facility lined up by the end of the day.

"Who is this?" Tammy asked as I walked through the door with Stella. She bent down and pet her and Stella eagerly wagged her tail and gave Tammy kisses on her cheek.

"This is Stella. She's my dog. She belonged to Stephen."

Tammy cocked her head. "Stephen. Why would he give her up? I know how much he loves this dog."

"Stephen is dead," I said. "He was arrested for the murder of a young girl and was murdered in jail. I'm still getting to the bottom of his murder while trying to figure out who killed Alaina, all while getting evidence together for a capital murder case. It's been rough."

Tammy's face got pale and her mouth flew open. "Stephen's dead?" she asked. "That poor man. Who killed him and why was he arrested?"

"A guy in jail named Jock Tucker killed him," I said. "And I don't know who killed Alaina, the young girl who Stephen is accused of killing. I haven't a clue on that one, although I'm getting closer to finding out. Jock is an Aryan Brotherhood member who-"

"Is dead himself," Tammy said. "I was reading the paper today and there was an item about Jock killing himself in jail." She went into her office and brought out the newspaper. "Here," she said, pointing. "In the Metro section."

I sat down to read the newspaper. It was a small piece on the inside of the paper that talked about how Jock was found hanging in his jail cell. It mentioned that he'd recently been accused of murdering Stephen, forever going to be known to the general public as Alaina Morosky's killer. At least he'd be known as her killer until I found and exposed her real killer.

I'd do that if it was the last thing I did.

"Well," I said. "I'd say I was sad, but I'm not really all that sad. Jock Tucker had a short and ignoble life and now he's dead." I should've felt worse about it after speaking with Ariel Tucker, his sister. After all, she told me Jock was a child pornography victim until the age of 8, when Ariel's family adopted him. Ordinarily, a sad story like that would be enough that I'd absolutely have sympathy for Jock or a person like him.

Ordinarily that would be true, but, in the case of Jock, I couldn't bring myself to feel sorry for him. He killed my friend and that's all I knew.

Tammy sat down across from me and looked at me sympathetically. "How are you feeling about all that? About Stephen being killed?"

"Horrible. Absolutely horrible. I really cared about that guy and losing him was devastating. And it led to my breaking up with Axel, too." I looked down at the desk, suddenly feeling a pang about Axel. I didn't know where the pang came from or what caused it, but it was there. Right in my heart.

"What do you mean, you broke up with Axel because of it?"

"Well, Axel thinks Stephen killed Alaina Morosky and I couldn't be around him or anybody else who would think that about such a gentle man as Stephen."

Tammy said nothing, but just stared at me.

"What?" I demanded.

"Nothing."

"I know that look. You're thinking something. Out with it."

She finally sighed. "Harper, it's just that not everybody is always as sure as you are, that's all."

I knew she was right. That was probably one of my biggest weaknesses – I was certain about my certitude. But in this case, I was certain Stephen didn't kill Alaina. There wasn't a shred of doubt in my mind. The father of Alaina's child, whoever that was, killed her. I wouldn't entertain anything different. "So, you're saying..."

"I'm saying that maybe Axel simply said he wasn't sure. There's the possibility Stephen killed that girl. After all, Stephen's fingerprints were all over that house where all those children were killed. You just bought his story on faith. I'm not saying the man is guilty of anything but there's always a possibility he is, however slight. I can see Axel's point. After all, the guy is a cop."

I crossed my arms in front of me and looked away. "Okay, maybe. Maybe there's a 1% chance that Stephen was a crazy serial killer who went away into the woods to overcome his murderous urges and then was brought back into society and resumed what he was doing before. Maybe." I blinked back tears and Stella whined softly. "Maybe I owe Axel an apology."

Tammy clapped her hands and smiled. "You're making progress, Harper. Now if you want to know the truth, I'm with you. I never got bad vibes from Stephen, not in the least. But Axel doesn't have the same sensitivities you and I might have. Perhaps Axel isn't as intuitive as we are. He just goes by clues and facts and things like that. And-"

"The biggest clue, besides the fact that Alaina was pregnant, was that Stephen apparently wrote out a confession on his computer. He said he knew nothing about it. I believed him when he said that. I-"

"You what?"

"I…" I shook my head. "Well, I think somebody must've gone into Stephen's apartment and wrote that confession out. I don't know who would have had access to his apartment except his landlord, though." I looked up at the ceiling. "Which means I'll have to pay a visit to his landlord. I'll have do that today."

"You have any court appearances today?"

"Of course. But I'll go over there around 4 or so after my court appearances are done. I'm also waiting on the Grand Jury verdict for my death case, Darnell Williams. I assume he'll be indicted, then I'll get going on this case with Aisha. I can't get a deal for him, though, mainly because I don't think he did it. I mean, he was caught at the scene with drugs in his pocket and his hand on the gun, but I'm thinking it's a perfect frame for the person who did it."

"And you're sure that-"

"Yes. I'm sure Darnell is innocent. I'm also sure Stephen was innocent. I have a bunch of moving parts on this whole thing, and I'll make sure these moving parts fit together in the end. In the meantime, I need to make an appointment with the landlord. After I find Stella the right day care place."

I did both of those things, and Stephen's landlord, Jared Ford, was waiting for me when I got there at 4. I'd gone through my court appearances for the day and had a list of questions I needed to ask him.

I met him in his apartment. He was the same guy with the man-bun when Stephen moved into the place. He had since grown the Civil War beard that had grown in popularity, much to my dismay.

This guy was currently sporting two of the worst trends of the current day, yet I could tell that, underneath all that hair, he was an attractive guy. He was wearing a t-shirt and jeans. On his forearm was an enormous tattoo that looked like a bunch of circles radiating out. "Hey," he said when I got to his place. "What's up?"

His eyes were narrowed like slits and I realized he was stoned. He was a peculiar choice for a landlord and I wondered if he was related somehow to the owner of the building. I didn't imagine that *he* owned the building. I assumed the building's owner appointed this hipster to collect rent money and call maintenance people.

"I wanted to ask you some questions about Stephen Heaney," I said. "You knew him, didn't you?"

"Yeah," he said. "I try to know everyone in the building." He sniffed. "Which isn't hard, as there's only the four units. But, yeah. I knew him. Good dude."

"He was a very good dude," I said. "But what did you know about him? Did you ever see him with anybody quite a bit younger than him?" I had to ask that because I had to clear up a nagging thought that perhaps Stephen took Alaina in in exchange for sex. Tammy was right – when I was sure about something, I was really sure. I needed to not be so sure and be open to things I didn't want to be open to. And, really, it made sense that Stephen might've been the one who took Alaina in. After all, he knew her mother. That might give him access to Alaina herself.

He shook his head. "No, I never noticed him with a young girl. He had that one chick, that Katy chick, but she's at least 50. I guess she was younger than him, but you're talking about-"

"A 13-year-old."

"Then no. I never saw any 13-year old."

I breathed a sigh of relief. "Did you happen to let somebody into Stephen's apartment when he wasn't there?"

His face got red. "That would be bad, huh?"

"Well, yes."

"Man, I need this job. I can't get fired. I work this job part-time for my dad. He owns this building and he's threatening to fire me.

I'm out of work right now, looking for work, and this is my only income besides my unemployment check, which will run out soon."

"Okay," I said. "I won't tell anybody what you did. I just need to know if you let somebody into Stephen's apartment at any time for any reason."

He sighed. "The dude had a search warrant," he said. "He had a search warrant for Stephen's premises. This was before Stephen got arrested. I let him in. I didn't know. That search warrant looked legit."

I raised my eyebrows. "Of course there was a search warrant. Did you ever let anybody into Stephen's apartment besides that time with the search warrant?"

He hung his head. "Yeah. There was one other time about a month or so before Stephen was arrested. I let this dude into the apartment. It was the same dude who came back later with the search warrant. He was a cop, and, I don't know, I panicked." He made a face and looked up at me. "He told me he'd arrest me if I didn't let him into Stephen's place. He could've arrested me, too, because I got some weed growing on my balcony that's more than the 18 plants you're allowed under law. He saw it when he knocked on my door to ask me about Stephen."

"Really? Did you get this person's name?"

"Yeah. It was Officer Morgan Cooper."

I nodded. "I see. So, he threatened you with arrest if you didn't let him into Stephen's apartment?"

"Yeah. I can't get arrested, ma'am. My dad is a pretty tough guy. He let me have this job managing this property in exchange for free rent and a small salary. Not that this place is Gracie's Mansion or anything like that, but it's a roof over my head which is better than what I had before I moved in here. I gotta keep my nose clean until I can figure out a better job and can get out from under my father's thumb."

"And you just let him in?"

"Yeah."

"When you let him in, did you go in with him?"

"I stepped into the apartment with him, yeah, but he gave me a look like he wanted me to scram, so I did."

"Did you happen to notice if Stephen's computer was turned on at the time? If he was already on the Internet?"

"Yeah, it was. It was on the Internet. He doesn't use a screen-saver and it was up and running. I said something to Stephen about not doing that, ever, but I didn't want him to know that I let somebody into his apartment. I figured I could collect his rent and pretend like I noticed his computer on and say something to him about it. You know, so he didn't know I was snooping."

Okay, then. That would explain the note. Cooper got in there and wrote it.

Then something occurred to me. "You said this happened about a month before the search warrant?"

"Yeah, about a month before. Why?"

I suddenly got excited. If Cooper wrote out that note, he did it *before* Alaina was killed.

I'd have to prove that with a forensic analysis of that note. The computer indicated the note was written after Alaina was killed, but a good forensic analysis could tell if the note's time stamp was altered in some way.

"Thank you," I said. "If I have any other questions, I'll call you. But you really helped."

"Sure," he said. "Just call if you have anything."

Twenty-Seven

I went right to the prosecutor's office after I spoke with Jared. I'd see Bill and find out if I could get that computer analyzed. I assumed he hadn't yet closed Stephen's case, and, even if he did, he probably had the computer stashed around as evidence somewhere.

"Hey, Harper," Bill said when I went to see him. "You wanted to speak with me some more about Stephen's case?"

"Yeah. It's not closed yet, is it? I need to find out if I can get a forensic analysis on his computer."

"Well that computer has been released as evidence," he said. "But we have it on our premises. I'll get somebody to retrieve it for you. I'll call my runner and she can probably have it to you today. You want to come and pick it up?"

"Yes. I'd like that."

"By the way, you were asking Ellie about Ariel Tucker, right? You wanted to know her arresting officer?"

"Yes. I needed to know who arrested Ariel."

"She's down the hall if you want to talk with her."

"Thanks."

I went down the hall to see Ellie. She was on the phone, but her door was open, so I stood outside the door and waited patiently. I heard her click off her phone and I rapped lightly on her open door.

"Come in," she said. "Oh, hey, Harper. I have Ariel's file. I don't know why I couldn't remember her arresting officer. I read through my notes and remembered this was an odd case. The arresting officer called my office and told me he wouldn't cooperate with her prosecution so I needed to dismiss the case. But it was Officer Cooper. He arrested her and he was the one who told me he wouldn't cooperate with her prosecution anymore. I had no choice but to dismiss the case against her."

Officer Cooper. His fingerprints were everywhere. Literally everywhere. He arrested Ariel, he was in Leonard's home before his gun went missing and he was in Stephen's apartment before Alaina was murdered. I wondered if he planted the drugs in my car. Maybe he did and called in a tip to Officer Campbell that I was harboring drugs, which was why Campbell pulled me over and searched my car. The smoking gun would be if the forensic analysis came back that Stephen's "confession letter" was composed before Alaina died.

I wondered if Alaina stayed with Officer Cooper while she ran away. At any rate, I was getting the puzzle pieces together that Officer Cooper might've killed Alaina. I'd have to figure out two more things before I put it all together – one, if anybody in Officer Cooper's neighborhood noticed him having a 13-year-old girl around his apartment at any time, and two, when that confession letter was actually composed. I was anxious to get that computer in my hot little hands so I could have it analyzed.

My working theory was that Officer Cooper had Stephen killed in jail because Stephen was being railroaded for Cooper's crime. Then he had Jock killed in jail, too, and made it look like a suicide. Jock did the crime because he was already serving several life sentences for different murders, so he had nothing to lose, and Officer Cooper offered Jock the chance to see his sister, Ariel, have her drug charges dismissed. Her drug charges were probably resulting from Officer Cooper going into her house and planting the drugs in the first place.

"Thanks," I said to Ellie. "I appreciate the information."

"Did that help?"

"More than you know."

The next day two things happened that made me sure Officer Cooper killed Alaina. One was that the computer came into my possession. I took it to my professionals for forensic analysis and they confirmed the confession note was composed on October 3, a week and a half before Alaina was killed. That coincided with the date Cooper went into Stephen's apartment after threatening poor Jared with arrest for drug possession if Jared didn't let him in.

The other thing that happened was I spoke with Cooper's neighbors. He lived in Armour Hills, an area of Kansas City where most of the houses were built in the Tudor style. It wasn't exactly a wealthy enclave, but it was probably upper-middle-class and a very desirable neighborhood.

I spoke with Cooper's next-door neighbor. Her name was Lily Fuller. She was a heavy-set woman with short curly hair, glasses and a poodle named Sasha. She was still dressed in her pajamas when I arrived and knocked on her door.

"Hello," she asked in an inquiring tone. "I ask that you please respect the sign on my door that clearly says 'No Soliciting.'"

"My name is Harper Ross," I said. "I'm an attorney." I showed her my Bar card and she lifted her glasses and inspected it. "I need to ask you some questions about your next-door neighbor, Officer Morgan Cooper."

She shook her head. "Name's Lily Fuller. Cooper's a weirdo. Come on in, I'll make you some coffee. You drink coffee, don't you?"

"No," I said. "But I'll take a glass of water."

"You don't drink coffee? I don't know if I can trust a person who doesn't drink coffee."

She didn't smile when she said that, so I didn't know if she was joking or not. I decided to chuckle politely. When I did, she smiled, but just barely, so I knew she wasn't serious about not trusting me just because I didn't like coffee.

We sat down at her kitchen table. She squinted behind her eyeglasses and looked out the sliding glass door, which was right by her kitchen table. "It'll be snowing soon. I hate the snow. I always have to dig my car out, every winter. I don't have a garage I can put a car into. My garage is full of crap. I'm always meaning to clean the crap out of my garage but never get around to it. My grandson tells me I have procrastinitis, whatever that means."

I smiled. "How old is your grandson?"

"18. He's in his first year of college down at Mizzou."

"Ah. My alma mater. What's he studying?"

"He's a physics major. Wants to go to med school. He's a bright boy. Claims he doesn't suffer from procrastinitis."

I found that word particularly humorous. I was once a sufferer from procastinitis myself. The motto of procrastinators everywhere is "Why put off until tomorrow what you can put off until the day after tomorrow?" I had to will myself out of that bad habit when I became a lawyer because I simply had to. I couldn't put things off because then they would pile up and stress me out.

"Now, what did you want to talk to me about?"

"Officer Cooper. You said he's a weirdo. What do you mean by that?"

"He's a weirdo. He always has young girls at his house. They swim in his pool and stay with him. There's not anybody staying over there right now, for whatever reason, but he usually has one or two girls staying with him."

"Does he explain to you who these young girls are?"

"No. I don't mess with him. I don't talk to him. He used to try to be friendly with me, years ago, but I didn't like the way he has loud parties over there and I don't like what he does." Her voice got low. "I was looking down at them one time from my window upstairs." She pointed at the ceiling. "And I could've sworn he had two young girls together by the pool. They were topless and kissing on each other and Morgan Cooper had a video camera out on them." She shook her head. "I wanted to call the police on them but then I remembered Morgan *was* the police. There wasn't much I could do about it so I just pay them no mind anymore."

Child porn. Officer Cooper was making child porn.

Was it a coincidence that Jock Tucker was a victim of child porn too?

"How young were these two girls you saw kissing each other by the pool?"

She shrugged. "Those girls I saw over there were never much older than 13. Some of them looked quite a bit younger even than that. Some of the girls didn't yet have their breasts. But those two girls did. The two girls I saw kissing on each other had their breasts. They were quite developed. I doubt they were much older than 13, though."

I got out a picture of Alaina, which was stored on my phone. "You ever see this girl at that house?"

Lily lifted up her glasses and looked at Alaina for a split second, and then looked away in disgust. "Yes. I saw her over there, all right. She was one of the ones kissing in front of the camera. I saw her a lot over there, then nothing. I didn't see her no more. Then I saw she went missing and was found floating in the Missouri River. What a waste. A beautiful girl, too. Just beautiful."

I suddenly realized something. Doing a DNA analysis on Alaina's unborn fetus wouldn't necessarily show Officer Cooper was the father of the child. If she was making child porn with Officer Cooper, it was entirely possible somebody else impregnated her. That was no guarantee, of course – Officer Cooper might've impregnated her, too. But there was not a guarantee.

He was connected to everyone, somehow, someway. Everyone I spoke with in this investigation turned up his name.

Was I getting closer to proving that Officer Cooper was somehow involved in Officer Parker's murder? That seemed unrelated to any of this, but where there's smoke, there's fire.

Who would know the identity of the person who made child

porn featuring a young Jock Tucker? Ariel Tucker might know who that was, or her parents.

But Jock was put into foster care once it was found he was victimized in child porn. There was a connection I didn't think I'd see, but it was apparent this connection might exist. I assumed Jock was some random guy put up to killing Stephen. I didn't think maybe Officer Cooper and Jock had a prior connection, which would be why Cooper chose Jock.

"Thank you," I said to Lily. "You've been a huge help."

She shrugged. "Good luck to you, whatever you're doing with that sleazebag Cooper. I wish he'd move away. I'd move away, but, golddurnit, I've been here for 40 years. He's only been in this neighborhood for less than 10. If I had an HOA, I'd bring up the possibility of buying him out to get him to leave, but no HOA, either. I don't know what to do, but I know I can't sell this house without telling the new people there's a child porn ring going on next door, and that a cop is the ring-leader." She shook her head. "Who would ever believe that?"

Who indeed?

I left the house, knowing where my next stop would be.

Ariel Tucker.

I hoped she wasn't working.

I got to her house and happened to see her walking from her car in her scrubs. I smiled, hoping she was getting home after a nursing shift as opposed to coming home for lunch or something like that. If she was coming home for lunch, she might not be able to talk very long.

She saw me and smiled. "Harper, hello," she said. She had a bag of groceries she just got of the car. "How are you?"

"Great," I said. "I have some information for you about who arrested you, but I also wanted to ask you a few questions. I hope you have a minute or two."

"I do," she said. "I worked the graveyard shift last night and I'm getting home to get some rest." She went to her door and opened it. "What do you need to know?"

"Officer Morgan Cooper arrested you. He probably was the same cop who came to your house prior to that arrest. I was hoping you might have some more information for me about Jock's situation when he came out of foster care. You said he was sold into the porn industry when he was five. And your parents adopted him when he was 8. Right?"

"Right. That's right." She nodded. "Why do you ask?"

"Do you know where I can find those adoption papers? Actually, I'm interested in the file for Jock's foster care. There's a piece of paper lawyers get when dealing with foster care situations. It details why the kid was taken out of the home. Do you know who might have that file?" This was a long-shot. I could get it from the adoption lawyer, but it was a closed file and I didn't think the county would allow me to see that file. I could get Anna on the case, if that file made it onto the computer, but I had a feeling it was so long ago that the file was probably only in paper form.

I hoped Ariel knew where that file was.

She bit her lower lip. "It's in a safety-deposit box," she said. "My parents put those papers in that box. I have access to it. Would you like me to get it for you?"

"Yes, please," I said.

"When do you need it?"

Today. Right now. "Whenever you can get to it."

"Well, treat me to lunch, and I'll go right now."

"You got a deal."

Twenty-Eight

We got to the bank that had the safety deposit box and Ariel got the file out of it. "Here," she said. "What are you looking for?"

I took the file eagerly and looked at it. There were handwritten notes on Jock's situation, but there wasn't an identification of the person caring for him at the time. There wasn't an identification of the person filming him, in other words. I assumed his caretaker was the same person who filmed him.

I shook my head. Of course this would be a dead-end. The person making the child porn would've been arrested if there was a correct identification. It stood to reason that Officer Cooper hadn't yet been caught in doing what he was doing. Otherwise, he'd never would've been allowed to become a police officer.

Still, perhaps there were some clues in the file somewhere. "Do you mind if I keep this file and look it over?" I asked Ariel.

"No, of course not."

"Now, where do you want to go to lunch?"

"You call it."

I nodded. "Grand Street Café."

. . .

We ended up at the Grand Street Café right around noon so it was packed. This was a restaurant right off The Plaza and was always extremely popular. It served basics such as burgers and salads, along with some limited pasta selections and a few things that were Asian-inspired, such as spring rolls, but these spring rolls had mushrooms and cheddar in them.

I ordered the seared tuna superfood salad, while Ariel got the southern-fried chicken sandwich. "I'm starved," she said. "It was a long shift on my feet."

"Thanks for seeing me again," I said. "And for getting that file out for me."

"Sure," she said. "Anything I can do to help out a criminal investigation, I'll do. Especially since it involves my brother."

"I'm very sorry to hear about your brother."

"Yeah. He's always in so much trouble. I know he'll be in prison for life. I wish I could help him, but there's only so much you can do. Jock was damaged way before he came to our family."

I took a sip of water, wondering what was going on. "Oh, I'm sorry. I read in the paper-"

"That Jock killed himself. I read that too. I called the jail and they said that it was a mistake. The newspaper made a mistake. As it happens, there was another inmate named Jack Tucker. He killed himself in prison. Somehow, the reporter messed that up. But, no, my brother is unfortunately very much alive. And I mean it when I say unfortunately, because I know he stirs up a lot of trouble in prison. Nobody is safe from him."

Hmmm...Jock was still alive. He could help me himself. He apparently killed Stephen in exchange for letting his sister go free. I wondered if he was a mercenary and might help me, too. He might give me necessary information.

"Ariel," I said. "I think I'll have to talk to Jock again. How close are you with him?"

She shrugged. "Close enough, I guess. I've always done what I can to protect him. I guess I didn't do a very good job, after all." She looked sad. "But we're not estranged. Not at all. He always tells me he loves me whenever I see him and I tell him the same. That makes this whole thing that much more difficult." She took a bite of her salad, which had just arrived. "Why do you ask?"

"I'm thinking Jock and Officer Cooper might've had an arrangement from way back. I just wonder if Officer Cooper might've been the one making movies with Jock. That might explain a few things on why Jock killed my friend, Stephen."

Ariel looked perplexed. "Come again? I don't quite understand what you're getting at. If Officer Cooper was making those movies, why would Jock do a single thing for him? And why wasn't he caught?"

"I don't know. I'd really like to find out if there was a connection between Jock and Officer Cooper. That would fill in the final piece of the puzzle for me to prove Officer Cooper murdered Alaina Morosky."

"My head is swimming," she said. "How do you get from A to B to C here?"

"Well, Stephen was accused of killing Alaina. Officer Cooper wanted Stephen dead because he didn't want Stephen to go to trial on this case. He knew that if Stephen went to trial, I'd keep on the evidence trail until I proved Stephen was innocent. He figured that if Stephen was dead, I would quit. Especially since I have a capital murder case I'm working. If Stephen is dead, the case is dead too. But I'm getting more and more evidence that Officer Cooper killed Alaina and framed Stephen. The biggest thing is that he went into Stephen's apartment and apparently wrote out a confession to Alaina's murder before Alaina was killed. He somehow made it look, on the computer, that it was written just after the murder, because the time-stamp said that, but I had a forensic team examine the note. They confirmed the confession was written before the murder, not after."

Ariel followed along, nodding her head. "Go on."

"Well, here's what else I found out. I found out from Alaina's mother that Alaina ran away for a couple of weeks and came back pregnant. I went to Officer Cooper's next-door neighbor and she told me that not only did she recognize Alaina as being a young girl who stayed with Officer Cooper, but she saw Officer Cooper making porn films in his backyard. She saw them from the upstairs window, which looks down into the pool in his yard."

By this time, Ariel's mouth was open, and she didn't say a word. "Oh, my God," she said. "Why doesn't she call-"

"The police? She told me that since Officer Cooper *is* the police she didn't think it would do any good to call the cops. She figures he'd get out of it. But this investigation brings me to Jock. Jock killed Stephen. Jock was a victim of child porn. If Officer Cooper and Jock have some kind of agreement, I don't know what that would be, but if they did, that's the final piece of the puzzle. It's all circumstantial evidence, but it's enough for me."

Ariel shook her head. "Wow. That's quite a story. But, yeah, I'll talk to Jock about it. I'll ask him point blank about Officer Cooper and if Jock has some kind of agreement with him. I know it's strange that Officer Cooper arrested me and then told the prosecutor's office that he wouldn't cooperate on my case so they had to drop it."

"That's the other thing. I figured that was Jock's motivation for killing Stephen – he did it in exchange for prosecution on your case being dropped. That was the original arrangement I figured those two men had. I still think that. I figured Cooper and Jock agreed to that. I think Jock did it because he has nothing to lose. But what if he killed Stephen for another reason? Maybe Cooper has something over him. Maybe you can find that out."

"Maybe. I don't know if Jock will talk to me about all that, but I can try."

"That's all I can ask."

Little did I know that I'd soon get my answer.

I got home and Officer Cooper was waiting for me on my porch.

Twenty-Nine

"Hello," I said to him. He was sitting on my porch swing, swinging back and forth, back and forth.

"Harper Ross," he said to me. "How are you doing?"

"I'm doing just fine. How are you?" It was weird sharing pleasantries with this man. This weird man who was quite possibly a murderer.

"Good, good. Your girls are inside." He nodded meaningfully. "Two beautiful young girls, they are. Gosh, I'd hate for something to happen to them."

My heart started to pound and I opened the door. "Abby, Rina," I shouted.

"What, Mom?" Rina asked me. She and Abby were in the living room playing a video game. "Some guy is here to see you. Did you see him on the porch?"

"I did." I turned back to Stephen. "Okay, what do you want?"

"You're getting too close, Harper. Too damned close. Whatever I'll say right now will between you and me, and if you tell anybody, I'll just deny it. After all, I'm the law enforcement officer and you're the common criminal." He smiled. "I know about that drug possession thing. I know all. In fact, I tipped Officer Campbell off about you. Told him you had drugs on you. Gave him your license plate number and told him where you lived."

"Oh, I see. I get it now. You planted those drugs on me."

"Sure as shit did. But what you gonna do about it, Harper? What you gonna do about it? You can't prove nothing. What is clear, though, is that you have a drug possession charge and you're in danger of losing your license to practice law. I know all about that probation you got yourself on. Guess you screwed the pooch with some client of yours and pissed him off enough that he hauled you before the Missouri Bar to answer for your treatment of him. Guess that court didn't find quite enough cause to revoke your license in full, but guess they went ahead and put you on probation. I know what pleading guilty to possession of more than 3 ounces of marijuana would do to you. Yeah, the prosecutors will give you drug court and all that, but your pleading guilty to that charge will make your license to practice law go bye-bye. Won't it?"

I sat down. "What do you want?"

"I want you to back the fuck off. Stephen is dead. The whole world thinks Stephen killed that young girl, Alaina. Let the whole world continue to think that. That's what I want."

I shook my head but then looked to the house. "Alaina didn't run away, did she? You kidnapped her, didn't you?" My heart started to pound. Would Rina and Abby be safe if I didn't do what Officer Cooper asked me to do? If Cooper kidnapped Alaina, could he do the same with my girls? Would their bodies be the next to wash up on the shore of the Missouri River?

He shrugged. "Maybe I did, and maybe I didn't. But, yes, Alaina stayed with me. I made some movies of her. Yes I did."

"But she made it back home."

"She did." He nodded. "And Jock, yes, I was involved in his movies back in the day. It was always easy to manipulate Jock to do what I wanted. He was involved in several different murders that I had nothing to do with. He was serving multiple life sentences. So I asked him to do certain things for me in exchange for doing things for him, like getting Ariel's drug charges dropped and..."

"And what? What else did you hold over Jock's head? What else did you threaten or promise to get him to shut Stephen up for good?"

"I have his videos stored in my home. Every once in awhile, I'll threaten to put them on-line and that keeps Jock on his toes. That keeps him doing what I want him to do. He knows that if those videos made it on-line, his life in prison won't be worth a damn. His Aryan Brotherhood would disown him if they knew all the nasty things he did as a kid with other boys. He knows his beloved sister, Ariel, would access those videos. I would send them to her directly. I never did because Jock has been a good boy. He's done what I've wanted him to do."

Officer Cooper was evil. Looking at him, I saw the face of pure, unadulterated evil. He made a porn video of a young boy and then used that video to threaten him into doing his bidding. He killed Alaina, framed Stephen, and then had Stephen killed to shut him up. He set me up to be arrested for drug possession, knowing that if I pled guilty to the charge that I'd be suspended from practicing law for at least six months.

I felt rage at his smug face. I wanted to take a knife and smash him with it. I wanted to get some lighter fluid, light a match, and roast marshmallows on his burning flesh.

I bit my lower lip. I'd have to control myself. One thing about psychopaths – you need to outsmart them. You need to beat them at their own game. If I didn't, then not only would Rina and Abby be in danger, but I probably would as well. This man would stop at nothing to cover up what he did to Alaina. He proved he'd do anything at all.

"My drug possession charge?"

He shrugged. "I needed some insurance in case you started to snoop around too much. Which you are. I knew you would. I thought once Stephen was dead that you'd stop snooping. You have that other case to work, after all. I figured you would just work that other case and let Stephen's death be the end of the investigation into Alaina's death."

He narrowed his eyes. "But just in case you wanted to keep on the investigation, I wanted some kind of insurance. Now, I have some sway with Officer Campbell. I can either ask him to back off your drug possession charge, and work with the prosecutors to drop the charges, like they dropped Ariel's charges or..." He shrugged. "You'll have to plead guilty. You know how these drug cases go, Harper. You know how they go. You won't beat that charge. Never in a million years."

I turned my back and opened the door. "You better leave," I said.

"Or what? You gonna call the police?" He grinned and started to laugh. "I *am* the police. Or did you forget that?"

I said nothing, but opened the door, walked in my house and locked it behind me.

And called Axel.

Thirty

"What is Officer Cooper doing on your front porch, mate?" Axel asked when he came over.

"Oh, God, it's a long story. Such a long story. But thank you for coming over." I started to cry. "Oh, Axel, I'm sorry, so, so sorry for being such a bitch."

He smiled. "I figured you'd come around after our row. I didn't think it would take this long, though. I'm glad you finally came to your senses."

"I did. I mean, I need you, too. I do. But I was stubborn and pig-headed and judgmental."

"And silly. Don't forget silly." He wrapped me up in his arms. "Lass, I never believed Stephen was guilty of killing Alaina. But I wasn't as sure as you. I was only 98% sure Stephen didn't do it. You were 100% sure, and you had me tarred, feathered and run out on a rail because I had a tiny bit of doubt."

"I know, I know," I said, my tears starting to flow. "It's just that Stephen meant something to me. He did. I can't even explain it because I didn't know him all that long. But he was just such a lost soul and showed such kindness to everyone he met. I loved the guy. I really did. I never wanted to even entertain the thought that he'd do something like kill Alaina. And he didn't. He didn't."

"And you can prove this?"

I shook my head. "Not right now, I can't. I mean, I just got a confession out of the guy who killed Alaina. It's the guy on that porch. Why he's still on the porch, I don't know. I guess he wants to intimidate me. He already threatened the two girls. He admitted he set me up for my drug charge. He planted drugs in my car the night before I got pulled over and then called in a tip to another officer, Officer Campbell, that I had drugs. It looks like I'll have to plead guilty to drug possession unless I can figure something out beforehand but that means I'll have my license suspended for six months."

Axel and I sat down. I got out a handkerchief and blew my nose and wiped my eyes. I then took it and wrung it into knots and unwound the knots again. "I just don't know how to handle this. I've never gone against a dirty cop before. He's right, too. He confessed everything to me but it'll be my word against his, and I'll be the criminal before all this is said and done. I'll be the dirty druggie and he's a cop. Who'll believe me?"

"I believe you," Axel said, and he kissed my forehead. "I believe you."

"I know you do, but Axel, I need more than that. I need some way to bring him down. And he's-"

"He's what?"

"He's the witness on my death penalty case. My Darnell Williams case." I sighed. "He's the witness on that case. He's the arresting officer. I have to concentrate on working that case, Axel. That's the case I need to concentrate on. I've spent all this time and effort proving my friend Stephen wasn't guilty of killing Alaina and I've ignored Darnell."

I couldn't go on ignoring Darnell. But would I be an attorney by the time Darnell's case went to trial? My drug possession trial, such as it was, was scheduled for December 11. That was in a few weeks. Darnell's case hadn't even gone through the Grand Jury. That meant his trial would be scheduled in the new year. Assuming I had to plead guilty to drug possession, because I was assigned a bench trial, and the judge probably would find me guilty if I didn't plead, would the Missouri Bar just swoop in and take my license before I even had the chance to try Darnell's case?

I couldn't see Darnell's case passed on to another attorney. I hadn't done much work on the case, and I knew I'd have to step it up, but I intended to do a thorough job in proving Darnell didn't do it.

"Mate, is there anything I can do for you? I am a detective, you know. I work for the Kansas City Police Department. My ear is to the ground." He nodded. "Things are pretty entrenched in there, and Officer Cooper is a decorated officer who actually commands a lot of respect. Bringing him down won't be as easy as you think, but bringing him down, without somebody on the inside, will be impossible."

"How can a psychopath who killed a young girl and has been running a child porn ring for years command respect?"

"I don't know, except nobody knows all this about him. And if anybody does, I'd imagine he does whatever he can to silence them. He's well connected and probably knows where all the bodies are buried. He probably knows all the dirt on everyone else, so everyone is afraid to cross him. He doesn't know dirt on me, though. I don't have any dirt for him to trifle with. He can be brought down, Harper. We just have to figure out how to do that."

"What's going on?" Rina asked and then looked at Axel. "Hey, I'm glad you're back. I was wondering what happened to you."

"Yes, I'm back," Axel said. "And hopefully your mom won't kick me out again."

"I'm not planning on it," I said with a smile. "I really missed you, Axel. I didn't know how much I missed you until right this moment."

"I missed you too, lass."

"Aw, isn't that sweet?" Rina said sarcastically.

Abby came out of her room, where she'd been this whole time, saw Axel, ran to him and threw her arms around him. "Axel, it's so good to see you!" she exclaimed.

"You too, sweet Abby."

“We have a dog,” Abby said. “Stella. She’s in my room right now. She studies with me.” Abby called for Stella, who came bounding down the stairs, wagging her tail. She went right up to Axel and Axel kneeled down and put his face to hers.

“She’s beautiful,” he said. “Just beautiful.”

“That she is,” I said. “This is another reason why I have to bring this bastard down. He killed Stephen. He was responsible for Stephen’s death. He framed Stephen and then blackmailed Jock Tucker into killing Stephen. That whole thing makes me sick. Stephen was such a good person. He didn’t deserve what happened to him. He didn’t deserve to die like that. That bastard, that evil man, did this to Stephen. I have his dog, Stella, and she seems happy to be here, but I’m sure she misses her daddy.”

“We’ll get him, lass. We will.”

I hoped and prayed that Axel was right about that. I feared for Abby and Rina. If Cooper could get to Alaina and kidnap her, couldn’t he do the same with Abby and Rina?

Thirty-One

Darnell sat in his jail cell, counting the minutes until he could see his attorney again. She promised to see him once a week. A whole week went by, and he hadn't seen her yet. He didn't know what to think. He only knew his auntie Violetta told him about his mother and his brother and sisters, and it seemed things were under control out there. A mysterious benefactor made sure the rent was paid for the next six months and made sure the utilities were also paid. That same benefactor paid for a sitter to watch the kids full-time. It was almost a nanny, but he didn't like to use such fancy terms. All he knew was that somebody was at the house watching his brothers and sisters, and that person had moved into his mama's bedroom for the time being. Violetta was back home with her own kids, and, for now, nobody was going into foster care.

He knew the mysterious benefactor was Harper Ross, because she told him that she'd do that. Harper Ross was good people.

So, that, at least, was off his mind. He could think a bit clearer knowing the crisis brewing at home wouldn't become full-blown. Aunt Violetta also told him his mother would soon be out of the hospital. He hoped to see her. He hoped she could get down to see him. He didn't know if she could make the trip, though. She was still not 100%, but she could watch his brothers and sisters, and, since the rent was paid for the next six months, that hopefully meant she could keep the apartment, keep food on the table and the utilities paid without working her second job. She'd have to work one of the jobs, though, that much he knew. Could she?

Now, if he could just see his attorney and tell her everything he knew. Everything he was finding out behind bars. He was talking to some guys he met and was finding out some information about Officer Cooper, the guy who arrested him.

He also found out about Officer Parker the guy he was accused of icing. Officer Parker was a good guy, the other inmates told him. Officer Cooper was not such a good guy. Most of the inmates had heard of Cooper, and none of them had good things to say about him.

What he found out, that maybe his attorney didn't know, was that Officer Parker wasn't just a plain-clothes policeman investigating drug charges. He was a plain-clothes policeman also investigating sex crimes. He was getting close to breaking up a pornography ring based in Armour Hills, and the target of his investigation was Officer Cooper.

At first, Darnell didn't believe the talk. He didn't know what to think when he first got to jail. He'd never been around people like the ones he met behind bars. He'd always steered clear of drug dealers and gang-bangers and people like that. His mama taught him to steer clear of such people. But he had to survive and make friends and he did. He made friends with a guy whose name was Marcelo White. This was his third time down, he said, and could give Darnell the lay of the land.

One of the things he told Darnell was that he had to watch out for Jock Tucker. Jock was one of the fiercest members of the Aryan Brotherhood, which targeted minorities in jail and prison. Marcelo was a member of the Black Knights, which was a gang in prison who protected people like Darnell from the Aryans. And what

Marcelo told Darnell about Jock was something that made Darnell sick. Jock was apparently an assassin for Cooper, a guy who would do anything Cooper asked him to, and that meant killing people Cooper wanted dead.

"And you, my friend, are somebody on top of that list, for obvious reasons," Marcelo told him. "You gotta watch your ass, but don't worry, your ass is covered and will be covered by the Black Knights. We ain't gonna let anything happen to you while you're in here."

Nobody quite knew why Jock Tucker was Officer Cooper's assassin. There were rumors going around about Jock being Cooper's son, and other rumors that went that Cooper knew things about Jock that Jock didn't want getting around. Darnell didn't know the real story, but he knew he was in danger from Jock.

Darnell felt protected by the Black Knights. They had the upper hand on the Aryan Brotherhood, just because the AB didn't have too many members in that Jackson County Jail and the BK did. He knew that if the worst happened, and he went to prison, he'd have to become a full-fledged member of the BK and would have to kill a member of the AB as an initiation. He hoped and prayed it didn't come to that. He wasn't cut out for prison. Not that anybody was exactly cut out for prison, but he knew a lot of guys in his high school who could survive in prison without somebody protecting them.

Darnell wasn't one of those guys. He was terrified. Every night, in his cell, after his cell mate, Montel Jacobs, started to snore, Darnell let loose with the tears. He never cried in front of Montel and always had to wait until Montel was asleep before he felt brave enough to show his emotions. He wasn't raised on the streets like some guys he knew. He was never tempted to join a gang, because he knew what gang members had to do to become initiated, and he would never court trouble like that.

More than being terrified, though, Darnell was heart-broken. He had big dreams that were becoming out of reach. With every passing day, he was falling further behind in school. With every passing day, he knew his dream of going to MIT was slipping out of his grasp. His going to jail resulted in a cascade of dominoes that were falling, one by one, starting with his mama having a stroke and being unable to work. The latest domino was that he probably couldn't complete his senior year like he'd hoped. He was already a year behind because of his earlier learning disabilities that weren't diagnosed properly, so he didn't get an IEP, which is the specialized plan to help him overcome his learning disabilities, until he was in the second grade. He was helped immensely by his special education teacher in grade school, so he caught up soon enough, but he was still a year behind.

Now he'd be two years behind.

That was if he didn't go to prison. That was a real possibility. The situation didn't look good. He told Marcelo about what he was charged with, and how he was arrested, and Marcelo told him he probably wouldn't be acquitted.

"Those juries don't like those cop-killers," he said. "And you were caught with a quarter kilo of dope on you too?" He shook his head and patted Darnell on the shoulder. "Better you than me. Sorry, bro, but unless your lawyer is some kind of Houdini, it looks like you're going down. Let's just hope the jury takes pity on you and doesn't decide to needle you over this."

Marcelo's words haunted Darnell. Was that possible? Would he end up strapped to a gurney with a needle in his arm? He always heard innocent people have died on the gurney before. He couldn't imagine that could happen to him but was he being a naïve kid when he assumed things would work out for him? If there was any kind of justice in the world, he'd be acquitted. But Marcelo was right – he realized there was a good chance he'd be convicted of this murder, and he'd end up, at the very least, in prison for life.

He didn't know what else he could do about his situation except pray on it. Which is what he did – pray on it, night after night. His mama took him to church every Sunday - the chicken place let him off every Sunday so he could go – and he really believed in Jesus. Jesus was always with him, no matter what. It was just like that footsteps poem to him – Jesus carried him during times of trouble. This was definitely a time of trouble, so he took comfort in knowing that Jesus was with him, and that He had a plan for him.

He couldn't see what that plan was at that moment, but there was a plan, and he was part of it.

Thirty-Two

Four Weeks Earlier

Officer Parker couldn't believe the evidence mounting up about the porn ring in Armour Hills. He was doing double duty with the drug crimes division and the sex crimes division of the KCPD. His superior informed him that he'd transition out of drugs and into sex, which was fine with him. He was getting tired of the drug beat, to tell the truth. He was busting the same perps over and over again. And he was becoming known in the drug community for being a cop, so it was more difficult to make an arrest. Everybody was wary of him so people would no longer sell to him. He'd outlived his usefulness in the drug division so was happy to transition out.

For the time being, he was still working the drug beat, but was getting into sex crimes. At first, he was just busting some prostitutes. That wasn't a big deal. But now he was assigned some cases that involved child pornography. It wasn't just doing a sting on individuals possessing child pornography or stinging people selling it. He was also hot on some tips about an individual filming child porn out of his home. Parker was gathering evidence on this ring and was getting close to busting it.

And then he was assigned the case of finding out who raped and murdered Alaina Morosky. He couldn't believe he was assigned that case because this was one of the most high-profile murders in the city. He figured it would be a 30-year veteran who would get that case. But it wouldn't be a 30-year veteran on this case. It would be him.

"Are you sure you want me to investigate that murder?" he asked his superior, Officer Lee Philips.

"I'm sure. Officer Parker, you've been doing double duty as an undercover drug officer and as a sex crimes officer, and you've been doing commendable work in both those divisions. You're ready for the big leagues so I'll put you on this case. I want you to find the perp who killed Alaina and hopefully you can do it soon. *The Kansas City Star* has been all over this crime, and we haven't gotten close to making an arrest yet. Can you can handle it?"

"Of course. Who will be my partner on handling this case?"

"I'll partner you with Officer Cooper. I know Officer Cooper is in uniform and you're plain-clothes, but I think you and Cooper will make a good team on this. He's been in the sex crimes division for quite awhile, but I still want you to take the lead on this one."

Officer Parker didn't get along well with Officer Cooper, but he felt Officer Cooper was an upstanding guy. He heard word on the street that Cooper harassed prostitutes, but nobody had ever made a formal complaint against him, so Officer Parker figured these were just words.

Officer Cooper had a hard-on for Stephen Heaney right away. He thought Stephen Heaney was good for this crime. He told Officer Parker that, but Officer Parker wanted to wait to make an arrest. He wanted to get some evidence that Stephen Heaney did this crime, and, thus far, he hadn't seen anything that would point to Stephen killing Alaina. There was a connection between Stephen and Alaina's mother, Olga, but that meant exactly nothing, in Officer Parker's book. There was some scant evidence that Stephen Heaney was a serial killer back in the early 1970s, but, to Officer Parker's knowledge, the actual serial killer had long since been buried, and, for his money, he thought Stephen Heaney wasn't good for those crimes in the 1970s, either.

Cooper insisted and persisted, however, and wouldn't let up on Parker making an arrest of Stephen Heaney.

"Goddammit," Cooper said to Parker. "When will you arrest that bastard? Seriously. He's a pervert, he knew her mother, he murdered boys and girls, a lot of boys and girls, back in the early 1970s. He mysteriously went missing for all these years, and then he shows up, and a body is found. What more do you want? What other evidence are you looking for?"

The evidence that Parker was looking for was simple – something that demonstrated probable cause to arrest Stephen for Alaina's murder. The fact that Stephen worked with Alaina's mother and Stephen's identical twin brother was a serial killer weren't evidence. He simply wouldn't make an arrest on such flimsy evidence. It wasn't just that he was afraid of a lawsuit for false arrest or for a violation of civil rights. It was that he wasn't that guy. He wasn't that cop that made arrests based on nothing. He wouldn't be pressured to make premature arrests in response to that pressure.

He was a thorough officer, and the investigation of Alaina's murder was just beginning.

Then, one day, he ended up at the Church's chicken restaurant in Mid-Town. He'd pick up some chicken and head on home. He ordered a breast and wing combo with cole slaw and mac and cheese, with a large lemonade. For his money, Church's chicken was the best chicken in town. Sure, Stroud's really had the best chicken in town – maybe the best chicken in the world. But for fast-food, Church's couldn't be beat.

He took the food home and ate it slowly, watching a little television, intending to turn in somewhat early – midnight was an early night for him anymore.

He watched his show and stretched and yawned, wanting to hit the sack. It would be a full day the next day. He went to look for his phone to plug it in when he realized he couldn't find it. He looked everywhere around the house and simply couldn't find it. He couldn't remember where he last saw that phone, either. Was it at the chicken place?

He went back to Church's, hoping to find somebody working there. He hoped it was still open. Some restaurants stayed open late on a Friday night. But when he got to the restaurant he realized the doors were locked. He'd have to wait until morning.

After trying the door to Church's, he went back to the parking lot and saw Officer Cooper. "Hey, Morgan," he said. "What's going on?"

Officer Cooper looked around the parking lot. There weren't many cars in the parking lot because of the late hour. "I followed you," Officer Cooper said. "I've been thinking a lot about this case we're working on together. The Alaina Morosky case. I don't know why you just can't make that arrest of Stephen Heaney."

"Why do you want me to arrest Stephen so badly?" Parker asked Cooper.

Cooper looked around some more. It was almost as if he was afraid somebody was around who might hear him.

Then he brought out a gun. It had a silencer on it.

Parker didn't quite know what was going on.

"Make that arrest," he said. "And nobody will get hurt. You agree to do that or don't you?"

Parker shook his head. "No," he said. "I won't arrest somebody on no evidence. I'm confused on why you want me to so badly."

"I'll tell you something, and if I hear a breath about this, a word about this, anywhere in the police force, I will kill you. But I did it. I killed that girl. Alaina. She was pregnant with my child, man. I won't go to prison for having sex with a 13-year-old girl and she told me she'd name me as the father. She was talking to some of the working girls she got to know on the street and those working girls told her she needed to see a lawyer about my doing a DNA test so she could get child support. She's 13, man. 13. You know the law. I'd go to prison and you know how cops are treated in prison. You know how child rapists are treated in prison. I'm a cop and a kiddy-diddler. No way could I let her do that to me, name me the father like that. No way."

Officer Parker couldn't believe the words coming out of this man's mouth. Apparently, Officer Cooper was okay with letting an innocent man go to prison for his crime. He was apparently fine with ruining the life of another human being to cover up what he did.

He was apparently fine with murdering a young girl just because that girl was pregnant with his child. It was true that Officer Cooper would go to prison for statutory rape because he had sex with a 13-year-old girl. But killing that girl and pressuring him to arrest somebody completely innocent for that crime? Officer Parker concluded that Officer Cooper was a psychopath.

Officer Cooper still had that gun in his hand and was still pointing it at Officer Parker. Officer Parker looked towards the restaurant, hoping somebody would come out, but knew that wouldn't happen. There was only one blonde lady in the chicken restaurant earlier, working behind the counter, and he saw an African-American boy working in the back. There were two exits to the restaurant and he figured the other exit was the one the blonde lady used to leave the building.

"And what will you do if I don't do what you want?"

"Listen, if something happens to you, I take over Alain's investigation. One way or another, Stephen Heaney will be arrested for this crime. Either you arrest him or I will after you're dead."

"Morgan, even if Stephen Heaney is arrested, a good lawyer could get him acquitted in record time. A good lawyer could get him out of jail and sue this department for false arrest. You can't just arrest somebody with no evidence they did anything wrong. This is America. That simply isn't done, and when it is done, there's usually hell to pay."

Officer Cooper shook his head. "You have to agree to do this or I'll do something I don't want to. I like you, Jake. I really do. We could work well together. But if you don't do this one little thing for me, this one thing that'll take the heat off me, then I don't know what else I can do. I'm sorry."

Officer Parker put his hands up and backed away. "I won't do what you want," he said. "I won't arrest an innocent man, especially since I know he's innocent. I won't ruin somebody's life for your crime."

Officer Cooper bowed his head. "I was afraid you'd say that."

He then pointed the gun at Officer Cooper and pulled the trigger.

Thirty-Three

The next day, I was still absolutely freaking out about what happened with Officer Cooper. He threatened me and my girls. Axel was on the case, and he'd ask around the police department about Cooper, but that didn't make me feel safe.

It didn't make me feel safe in the least.

But I would put it behind me to focus on Darnell's case. I felt bad I hadn't visited him for a few weeks. I felt really awful I hadn't yet focused on his case. I was so consumed with trying to prove Stephen innocent that I neglected Darnell's case. Darnell's case was still early - it hadn't yet been through the Grand Jury, so he hadn't been arraigned and assigned a trial judge - but I was still feeling guilty about the neglect. I hadn't started interviewing witnesses, much less do the necessary background investigation of the victim, Officer Parker.

The victim background investigation was usually my first step when trying a SODDI (Some Other Dude Did It) defense. I always needed to determine if somebody else had cause to kill him, so that was why the victim background investigation was so pertinent. That usually led me to an alternative explanation of how the victim met his or her untimely end.

In this case, though, I was spinning my wheels. I resolved to stop spinning my wheels and start doing my shoe-leather investigation.

I'd start with talking to Sally at Church's and then do my intensive background work on Officer Parker. As he was a cop, there could've been any number of individuals who had it in for him. Any number of individuals who might've just iced him and left his body at the chicken place.

There was the issue of the drugs found on Darnell, though. He claimed they weren't his, but I wasn't entirely sure. The drugs could very well have been in the pocket of that coat, because that coat belonged to Antwan Jordan, Darnell's co-worker.

I got to Church's, where Sally was working. "Hello," I said to her. "My name is Harper Ross. I'm Darnell's defense attorney, and I'd like to ask you a few questions."

Sally smiled brightly. "Sure, sure." She turned to the tall and skinny African-American boy dumping french fries into the deep fryer. The fries sizzled below the surface of the oil and the boy got out a pair of tongs and made up a box of chicken. "Antwan," Sally said. "I need to speak with this lady for a few minutes. Can you take over the cash register for a bit?"

"Sure, Sally," Antwan said.

"I need to speak with Antwan next," I said. "Would that be possible?"

"Of course. I'll give him his break when we're done and you can talk to him."

We went and sat down at one of the booths. "I need to ask you some questions," I said.

"Ask away."

"Does this restaurant employ any kind of surveillance?"

"No," she said, shaking her head. "No, it doesn't."

"On the night of the murder, by any chance, did the drive-thru recordings pick anything up?"

"Not that late, no. We turn that equipment off when the restaurant closes."

"What about dumpster divers? Do you have anybody who regularly goes through the trash, looking for food? I'm just trying to figure out if there was a witness we didn't know about."

"We get dumpster divers all the time, of course, but I don't see any regulars, no."

"Now, the night in question, the night Darnell was arrested, what time did you leave?"

"I left the restaurant right at 11 PM. I left Darnell behind to clean up. I usually leave him behind to clean up. He does an excellent job."

"Did you see anybody in the parking lot at that time?"

"No." She shook her head.

"Now, he clocked out at midnight. Is that right?"

"Yes, that's correct," she said. "Would you like to see his time card?"

"Yes, I'd like to see his time card for the night."

She left for a brief time and then came back, the time card in her hand. "Here it is," she said. "As you can see, the time stamp shows he clocked out at midnight."

"Is there any reason why Darnell would still be on the premises at 1 AM?"

"No," she said. "No, I don't see any reason why Darnell would still be on the premises at 1 AM. I heard he was using the restaurant for drug deals." She shook her head. "I certainly hope that isn't the case. Darnell always seemed like such a good boy, but, then again, you just never know about these kids."

"What about Antwan? Do you think he'd be the kind to do drug deals?"

"Antwan? Why do you ask about him?"

"Darnell said Antwan left his jacket in the restaurant. Darnell was cold, so he borrowed it. He didn't wear his own jacket. The drugs were found in Antwan's jacket. Is is possible that Antwan deals drugs?"

"No," she said. "I know Antwan and he doesn't do things like that. No." She shook her head. "If Darnell was found with cocaine in his pocket, it must've belonged to Darnell himself, not Antwan. I'd like to think Darnell wasn't making a drug deal with that cop, but, as I said, you just never know."

"So, you're positive the drugs didn't belong to Antwan, but you're not positive they didn't belong to Darnell?" I found Sally's behavior and words peculiar. I expected her to be emphatic that Darnell must've been framed and he'd never ice a cop. That he didn't do something like deal drugs. Yet she was willing to throw Darnell under the bus.

"That's right. After all, Darnell was caught with drugs, not Antwan. Darnell was caught in the parking lot with a gun and a body of a cop, not Antwan. I don't know why Darnell wants to bring Antwan into this mess." She shook her head. "If Darnell did something like this, he shouldn't try to blame other people. That's just not right."

"With all due respect, Darnell wasn't blaming it on Antwan. He simply said the jacket he wore that night belonged to Antwan and he wondered if Antwan had the drugs in his pocket. He told me that was the only explanation for how the drugs got there, because he doesn't do drugs himself, let alone deal them. That's what he told me."

"And you believe everything your clients tell you?" Her face looked skeptical. "If you believe everything your clients tell you, then I'm sorry to say this, but you must not be a very good attorney. You have to know when somebody is lying, and Darnell was most likely lying when he said he doesn't know where those drugs came from. I feel sorry for Darnell now that I've talked to you because I don't think you'll do a very good job for him."

I stood up, feeling absolutely humiliated and chastised. This woman, who didn't know me from Eve, was accusing me of being incompetent. I shouldn't have let her words hurt me, but they did. They stung. I knew why, too – I was feeling incompetent. I felt I was letting Darnell down because I was so slow in gathering evidence. Sally's words would've rolled right off of my back if I felt I was doing a good job. But I felt incompetent so her telling me I *was* incompetent rankled. Hard.

"Could I still speak with Antwan?" I asked Sally. "I need to hear from him that he didn't put those drugs in his pocket." I wanted to speak with him and see if I could tell he was lying.

"Sure," she said. "But he'll tell you he doesn't do that type of thing. Antwan is a good boy."

She got up and left, and Antwan came and sat down across from me. "Hello, Ms. Ross," he said. "My supervisor told me you needed to speak with me about something."

"Yes," I said, extending my hand for him to shake. He shook it while looking at me warily. "I need to speak with you about Darnell Williams."

"Oh, yeah, yeah," he said. "That's too bad about him. He was my homey, you know?"

"He was?"

"Yeah. We was tight. He's been to my crib and I've been to his." He shook his head. "You gonna get him off?"

"I don't know. But Darnell told me he was wearing your jacket the night he was arrested. The cops found a quarter kilo of cocaine in that pocket. Do you know anything about that?"

"No, man. No." He leaned down. "That's a lot of drugs, man. A quarter kilo? You don't have a quarter kilo on you unless you're dealing, and I'm not dealing. I don't deal."

"Do you use?"

He shrugged. "No I don't use. Not coke, anyhow. I smoke weed and I've tried crack, but I don't like it much. Other than that, no, I don't use."

"So, you've never had cocaine on your person?"

"No and I've never tried coke, so I wouldn't have it on me. And I don't get into dealing. I try to be straight, Ms. Ross. I'm not trying to get in trouble or catch a case. I already got a brother in the joint because of drug dealing and gang-banging, and I ain't going down that path."

I bit my lip, thinking somebody was lying.

Unless Officer Cooper planted those drugs.

Was it all a coincidence that Officer Cooper was involved in the murder of Alaina, and then was the arresting officer for Darnell? Was it possible that Officer Cooper was covering for the person who killed Officer Parker? That would make the most sense, at this point – Officer Cooper planted the drugs on Darnell to give the cover story that Darnell killed Officer Parker because Officer Parker was trying to arrest him.

Or was it possible that Officer Cooper killed Officer Parker himself?

If so, why?

Why would he do something like that?

Thirty-Four

"What did you come up with?" I asked Anna when she came to my office. She was presenting me with a list of cases Officer Parker was working on before he died.

"Well, you'll never believe the case he was working on," she said. "He was working on the Alaina Morosky case."

The Alaina Morosky case.

The final piece of the puzzle was finally fitting in.

"Harper?" Anna said to me. "What's going on? You suddenly got a weird look on your face."

"Hmmmm," I said. "I think I know who killed him. Now, how do I prove it?"

That was always the rub. Always. I had my target - Officer Cooper. He was good for the Alaina Morosky murder and I now had no doubt he was also good for Officer Parker's murder. There were just too many coincidences to come to any conclusion but that.

Darnell was found with the body and his fingerprints were on the gun. But, but, but...that gun was stolen, and Leonard Jefferson, the rightful owner of that gun, told me Officer Cooper had been in his house right before the gun went missing.

Darnell was found with drugs. He insisted the drugs weren't his, and Antwan, the owner of the coat, insisted the same. So, the only other explanation was the drugs were planted by Officer Cooper.

The gun was stolen by Cooper. The drugs on Darnell were planted by Cooper. Cooper killed Officer Parker, and then found a convenient patsy in Darnell, an innocent kid just finishing up his shift at Church's who happened upon the body of Parker.

With the knowledge that Officer Parker was investigating the murder of Alaina, the entire thing fit. The puzzle fit together beautifully. Officer Parker investigating Alaina's murder gave Officer Cooper motive to kill him. Cooper obviously didn't want Parker anywhere near that murder. Perhaps Cooper wanted to ensure somebody else was implicated in the murder. Parker refused to try to implicate somebody else so Cooper killed him.

He killed him and then took over the Alaina murder investigation. It was so convenient for him to do so, too – he could arrest an innocent man, Stephen, and then have Stephen killed. He'd see the file on Alaina closed because the suspect died in prison, and nobody would suspect him of killing Officer Parker, because they had a convenient patsy in Darnell.

The more I thought about the whole situation, the angrier I got. Darnell, as a young, poor, African-American boy, was just so disposable. In Officer Cooper's world, people like Darnell and Stephen could be sacrificed to cover for his evil deeds. They were both poor. Both of them were insignificant. Nobody would miss either of them, at least that was what Officer Cooper obviously thought.

Would he get away with murder? I'd make sure he didn't. I'd prove Officer Cooper killed Officer Parker if it was the last thing I did. And, while I was at it, I would also prove Officer Cooper killed Alaina. He couldn't just use people like this. He was destroying lives. He destroyed Stephen and was trying to destroy Darnell. He killed Alaina, which destroyed Alaina's mother Olga. I didn't get the chance to meet Peter, but I'd imagine that he, too, was probably destroyed by Alaina's death.

So many lives ruined by the caprices of one man. By the whim of one evil man.

An evil and, unfortunately, a powerful man. He had the power to still put me behind bars. Officer Campbell might've arrested me, but Officer Cooper planted the drugs on me. Officer Cooper said he'd have those charges against me dropped if I played ball.

I wondered if he'd try to force me to plead out Darnell.

I'd have to play this entire case under the radar. I was afraid for Rina and Abby. Cooper was dangerous - he kidnapped and killed Alaina, and he could do the same to my girls.

Somehow, someway, I'd have to prove Cooper killed Parker, killed Alaina, and framed me for drug possession. How I'd do all that, I didn't know.

What I knew was that Darnell was wasting away in jail because of Officer Cooper. He'd be there at least until his trial, and at his trial, I'd have to do all I could to convince the jury that Darnell was innocent. I'd have to show the jury that the person who had the motive, means and opportunity to kill Officer Parker was none other than the arresting officer, Officer Cooper.

How in the hell would I to pull that off?

Thirty-Five

December 11

"I have to get to my court date," I told Tammy. "For my drug possession charge."

"You're representing yourself?"

"Yes, of course. Who else would I get for this?"

"You know what they say. A person who represents himself has a fool for a client."

"Ha ha. I'm pretty sure that saying applies to lay people who represent themselves, not attorneys. Besides, I haven't had the time to try to hire somebody. I've been so waist-deep in this Darnell Williams case, I haven't had the time to breathe."

Truth be told, I wasn't quite sure how to pull this whole thing off. I'd challenge the stop – Officer Campbell had to have reasonable suspicion to pull me over in the first place. Unfortunately, I found out, after the fact, that Office Campbell had reasonable suspicion to pull me over, even if I wasn't hugging the shoulder, which was the official reason for the stop – Officer Cooper told him I had drugs in my car. He used the dreaded "anonymous tip," which pretty much meant he made it up out of whole cloth, but that would be enough for the judge to find enough reasonable suspicion to declare me guilty as charged.

This entire thing was bogus. Absolutely bogus. Yet, the stakes couldn't be higher for me – if I was found guilty of this drug possession charge, the State of Missouri could swoop down the next day and suspend my license. Then where would Darnell be? Where would his case end up? Who would take it?

Of course, this was Officer Cooper's plan all along. That was why he made sure I was pulled over and why he planted drugs in my car. He wanted to hobble me because he knew it was a matter of time before I was onto him about Officer Parker's murder, and he knew I'd tie him both to Parker's and Alaina's murders. The best way to neutralize me would be to get me out of the way. The best way to get me out of the way would be to pull a stunt like he pulled.

The only good thing was this was a bench trial, not a jury trial. It was a misdemeanor drug possession, so I wasn't entitled to a jury trial, which was fine with me. No way did I want to go through the hassle of picking a jury. It would take a few hours, tops, and that was what I wanted.

I got to the court and went in and sat down at the defense table. The prosecutor, Tom Houston, was at the other table, and he came up to me.

"It's not too late for a plea bargain," he said. "I can give you an SIS on this, since I know you don't want to hassle with Drug Court."

An SIS was shorthand for "Suspended Imposition of Sentence," which meant the imposition of the sentence was suspended and the person was put on probation. Since the imposition of the sentence was suspended, if the person completed the probation without incident, the sentence is never imposed, and the charge does not go on the person's permanent record.

An SIS was contrasted with what was called an SES, which was known as "Suspended Execution of Sentence." Unlike with an SIS, an SES involved an actual criminal conviction which went on the person's record. In an SES, the sentence is imposed, but suspended, which meant the person would still be on probation. If the probation is completed, the sentence isn't executed, but the conviction remained.

An SIS was therefore the best thing in this case, because it wouldn't ever be a criminal conviction, as long as I stayed clean for the length of the probation. Which wasn't a guarantee, considering Officer Cooper was out there, just waiting to frame me for something else.

"For the last time, if I pled guilty to this charge, even if the imposition of the sentence is suspended, I probably will lose my Bar License. I'm in the middle of a capital case and I can't lose my license right now."

"Harper, the only reason why I'm encouraging you to take this plea is that I don't want to see the judge throw the book at you. I'm looking out for you."

"Thanks," I said to him. "But I'll take my chances."

"Your call," he said. "But what would you advise a client in this situation?"

"In my exact situation? Where the client was framed and had drugs planted in her car, then was pulled over for a bullshit reason, and my client's Bar License was on the line? I'd tell her to try the damn thing. I'm not guilty. I'm a victim of a conspiracy and I'll be damned if I let the person pulling the strings on this get away with it."

"A conspiracy." Tom shook his head. "You're sounding like a crazy person."

"Be that as it may," I said. "But I'm not a crazy person. I'm absolutely sane. I'm the victim of a conspiracy and I won't let the person trying to bring me down succeed."

"All rise," the bailiff hollered. "The case of the State of Missouri v. Ross has now come to order, the Honorable Richard Jackson presiding. You may be seated."

Judge Jackson looked at me. "Ms. Ross, you're representing yourself, is that correct?"

"It is," I said.

He nodded. "Is the prosecution ready on this case?"

"I am, your honor."

"Please call your first witness."

"The state calls Officer John Campbell."

At that, Officer Campbell came through the double doors and walked to the stand.

"Please raise your right hand and repeat after me. I swear to tell the truth, the whole truth, and nothing but the truth, so help me God," the bailiff intoned.

"I swear to tell the truth, the whole truth, and nothing but the truth, so help me God."

Tom approached.

"Could you please state your name for the record?"

"John Campbell."

"Mr. Campbell, could you please tell the court what your position is?"

"I am a police officer with the Kansas City Police Department."

"Let me take you back to the evening of October 20 of this year. When did you first encounter the defendant, Harper Ross?"

He cleared his throat. "I encountered her on Main Street as she was driving between the cross streets of 30th and 35th. I noticed she was weaving slightly within the lanes and driving too close to the shoulder of the road. As I observed her driving, I called in her license plate and was informed there was an anonymous tip that she was in possession of more than 3 ounces of marijuana. This gave me reasonable suspicion to stop her."

"What happened when you stopped her?"

"I went to her front window to ask for her identification and the registration for her vehicle, and I noticed she was acting nervous."

"What do you mean by acting nervous?"

"She spoke rapidly, her eyes didn't meet mine, and her hand was shaking when she gave me her identification. Because I was suspicious about her actions, I asked her to get out of the car so she could perform the field sobriety test."

"Did she pass?"

"No, she did not. When she was asked to walk in a straight line, she stumbled. Then, when she was asked to recite the alphabet backwards, she had problems doing so."

I rolled my eyes. Most people would have problems with reciting the alphabet backwards.

"Did you ask her to blow into a breathalyze?"

"I did."

"What was the result?"

"She was not under the influence. The breathalyzer read 0.00."

"What happened next?"

"I was suspicious because she had problems passing the field sobriety test, even though she wasn't under the influence of any drugs or alcohol, so I had suspicions that she was hiding a controlled substance in her car. When I combined the anonymous tip about Ms. Ross possessing marijuana with her nervous manner, this gave me probable cause to search her car."

"And you asked her if you could search her car."

"Yes."

"And did she give you permission?"

"Yes."

Probably the stupidest thing I ever did. I should've known somebody planted drugs in my car. Then again, how was I to know? I didn't know I was dealing with a psychopath.

"What was the result of your search?"

"I started the search from the back of her car. I lifted up the panel that held her spare tire, and I saw a small bag of marijuana right next to her car jack. I thoroughly searched the rest of her car, and I did not find anything more."

"How did you know this bag held marijuana?"

"I was suspicious that it was a controlled substance, just because the contents of this bag appeared to be marijuana. The quantity was more than 3 ounces. I could tell that by sight. I arrested Ms. Ross, and I presented this bag for analysis. The analysis showed this bag contained marijuana."

"And how much marijuana was in this bag?"

"It was twelve ounces."

"I have nothing further for this witness."

"Ms. Ross, your witness."

"Thank you, your honor." I stood up. I knew I'd lose this case, but I hoped the judge would go easy on me. It was possession of more than 3 ounces of marijuana, big deal, and I was an esteemed member of the Bar. Of course, my kidnapping charge a few years back would work against me, as would my Bar complaint against me. Unfortunately, almost everyone in the criminal defense bar knew about my probationary status.

Perhaps my probationary status with the Bar would help me. The judge had to know I'd have my license suspended if I was convicted. I'd always gotten along with Judge Jackson. I hoped he'd take pity on me.

I walked over to Officer Campbell. "You stated you received notice of an anonymous tip that I was in possession of marijuana, is that correct?"

"Yes, ma'am."

"And you don't know who called that tip in, is that correct?"

"Yes. That is correct."

"Is it possible that nobody actually called this tip in?"

"I don't know what you're getting at."

"Is it possible that a member of the police force, specifically Officer Cooper, created this tip out of thin air?"

He shifted uncomfortably in his chair. "No."

"No? How would you know if this tip was legitimate if it was anonymous?"

"I don't know the tip is legitimate."

"That's right, because many of these anonymous tips are not legitimate. Is that correct?"

"Well, yes. Not every tip ends up being correct."

"In fact, anonymous tips are often called in by people who have agendas, isn't that correct?"

"What do you mean?"

"People who have agendas. Such as an estranged wife calling in an anonymous tip on her husband, so the police will harass him, for instance."

"Yes. That is not unheard of."

"And isn't it possible that this anonymous tip was created by an Officer whose intent is to hobble an investigation that concerns him?"

He got closer to the microphone. "That is a possibility. There's always the possibility of something like what you're describing happened. I never rule anything out."

"And isn't it also true that I was not weaving within my lane or getting to close to the shoulder?"

He looked uncomfortable. "No, that is not true. I saw you weaving within your lane."

"Isn't it true that what actually happened was that you got notice from Officer Cooper to watch out for me because I was in possession of marijuana, and Officer Cooper knew my route home from work, so he knew you would encounter me on the road?"

"I'm sorry?"

I realized that was not the most clearly worded question in the world, so I tried again. "Isn't it true that Officer Cooper contacted you while you were patrolling, gave you the description of my car, and my license, and asked you to pull me over because he had evidence I had marijuana in my car?"

He cleared his throat and looked embarrassed. "Yes, that is true."

"Then you didn't actually see me weaving and hugging the shoulder, then?"

He looked embarrassed again. "No. I didn't notice you weaving and hugging the shoulder."

I was getting somewhere. "Then you actually only pulled me over because Officer Cooper asked you to, isn't that right?"

"Yes," he said. "That is correct."

"And isn't it correct that Officer Cooper didn't tell you he was acting on an anonymous tip?"

"No, he told me he was acting on an anonymous tip."

I had him nailed, so I decided to rest. I'd form my closing argument based on this testimony, and I hoped the judge would decide there really wasn't reasonable suspicion for the stop, which would mean he'd throw the whole case out.

"Mr. Houston, do you have any rebuttal questions?"

"No, your honor."

"Officer Campbell, you may step down."

"Counselor, do you have any other witnesses?"

"No, your honor," Tom said.

I stood up. "Your honor, I'd like to ask for a directed verdict of not guilty at this time."

Judge Jackson took off his glasses and stared at me. "Counselor, let's hear your arguments for a directed verdict, and I will consider it."

I smiled. "You heard the testimony of Officer Campbell, the arresting officer and the only witness that Mr. Houston is planning to call. He clearly stated he didn't see me weaving within my lane or driving too close to the shoulder. He stated the only reason why he pulled me over was because Officer Morgan Cooper gave him a tip about my having drugs in my car. Officer Cooper is not here to testify about the anonymous tip, so I have no way of knowing how reliable this anonymous tip actually was. I cannot cross examine Officer Cooper on this tip. Because there is no way to cross-examine Officer Cooper about this tip, and this tip appears to be the only reason why I was pulled over, I have no way of ascertaining if Officer Campbell actually had reasonable suspicion for stopping me. If there was not reasonable suspicion to stop me, then anything that happened after the stop must be discarded."

Judge Jackson looked over at Tom. "Mr. Houston, Ms. Ross makes a good point. Why isn't Officer Cooper here to testify about the tip he received about Ms. Ross?"

Tom stood up. "I couldn't secure him, your honor, as a witness."

I knew better. Tom had the reputation for sloppy work. I assumed he thought he only needed the arresting officer there. He didn't imagine the officer was lying about the real reason he pulled me over.

Judge Jackson grimaced. "Well, it looks like you messed up, counselor, when you chose not to bring Officer Cooper in here. Here's what I'll do. Ms. Ross, I agree that the stop seems suspicious at best. However, I cannot ignore the fact that you actually were in possession of marijuana. I'd like to remind you, Ms. Ross, that possession of more than 3 ounces of marijuana is still illegal in this state."

Judge Jackson paused and bit the end of his eyeglasses. He took a sip of water. "I also cannot put aside that you are an esteemed member of the Missouri Bar. I understand that the Missouri Bar does not take kindly to members who have drug convictions, and it's my understanding that you are currently on probation with the Bar for another offense. As such, a conviction in this court might be enough to have your license suspended, so I am mindful of that factor as well."

He finally sighed. "Taking everything into account, here's what I'll do. I will reduce your marijuana possession charge to a moving violation, which is an infraction, and won't affect your status with the Missouri Bar. You are to pay a fine of $500. It is so ordered."

I smiled. It was bogus that I had to pay any fine at all, but I'd take this penalty without complaint.

As long as I wasn't stripped of my license, and I could try Darnell's case, I was good to go.

Axel and I were working on a way to bring down Officer Cooper. It was a risky plan, one that probably wouldn't work, but if it did, it would be the answer to my prayers.

And Darnell's prosecutor knew nothing about it.

Thirty-Six

January 15 - The day of Darnell's trial

"Okay, counselors," Judge Wright addressed Aisha and me. "It's time for voir dire."

It was the day of Darnell's trial, and I was as ready as I'd ever be to try this case. Not that I wasn't nervous. I was. Very nervous. Yet, I knew I'd done all I could to unearth as much evidence as possible to show that Darnell didn't do it.

I didn't yet have the goods on Officer Cooper, though. Axel was working on that. He was diligently working on getting the Internal Affairs investigator for the KCPD to look at Officer Cooper's background. He was getting close to convincing the Internal Affairs investigator that Cooper was dirty.

I had some other ideas on how to bring down Cooper and make sure he served the rest of his life in prison for the things he did. I just couldn't believe how arrogant he was and how willing he was for innocent people to be punished for the things he did. Stephen was dead because of him. Darnell's life was thrown off-track because of him, and, quite possibly, Darnell would go to prison because of him. I'd do my level best to make sure Darnell didn't serve a single day in prison, but nothing was ever a guarantee. And because of the Rules of Evidence constrained me from going all-out in showing that Cooper killed Officer Parker, not Darnell, my trial strategy would be constrained.

The worst part was that the Death Penalty was still on the table for my client. The prosecutor wasn't willing to take the Death Penalty off the table because the victim was a decorated police officer and the community was thirsty for blood. The politics of this whole situation dictated the prosecutor's decisions and there was little I could do about that.

My client could end up on Death Row with the most hardened of criminals. He was 18 years old, and, before October 13 of last year, he was full of big dreams. I'd visited Darnell in jail as often as I could, because I knew his mother couldn't get down to the jail to see him – she was still recovering from her stroke, and her doctor told her that visiting Darnell would be too stressful. His brother Jamal came to see him on occasion, but his little brother Cyrus and two younger sisters Alisha and Nicole never came to see him – they were 10, 7 and 8, so were too young to visit.

Because I knew Darnell was frustrated, lonely and scared, I went to see him at least once a week, for an hour at a time. I got to know him, and he told me about how he wanted to go to MIT on a scholarship. He was carrying a 4.4 GPA at Lincoln Prep and had a combined SAT score of 1550, in the 99th percentile. That was an impressive GPA and SAT score combination for any kid, and I knew that, with Darnell's underprivileged background, combined with his stellar GPA and SAT score, MIT wasn't out of reach.

I learned Darnell's main focus was to make enough money to take care of his mother, brothers and sisters. "I don't really know what I want for myself, Ms. Ross," he told me. "I only want to make sure my mama doesn't always have to work so hard."

The kid had dreams. He was interested in nuclear energy and he wanted to go into that field as an engineer.

But those dreams were replaced with the dream that he could walk as a free man into his tiny apartment that he shared with his mother and siblings. That was the most tragic thing to me – he went from having lofty dreams to just hoping he didn't end up on Death Row.

All because that bastard Officer Cooper.

The weirdest thing was that Darnell didn't even seem bitter about his situation. He seemed resigned to what happened to him.

"The Lord never gives you more burdens than you can handle, Ms. Ross," he said. "That was what I always learned in Bible Study. I've known plenty of people who have had things much worse than me. All of my brothers and sisters are still alive and they're all walking the straight and narrow. That's more than most of my friends at school can say, because many of them have had at least one brother or sister murdered. Many of them have a sister who got pregnant by the age of 14 or 15. I just hope my mama can handle my brothers and sisters if something happens to me and I serve time." He bowed his head. "That's really the only thing I worry about. I'm alright in here, Ms. Ross. I have people protecting me here, but I'm afraid of what will happen if I go to the penitentiary."

I wondered if Darnell could ever survive the pen. He was such a soft person. He could either be a target or, if he was lucky, he might attract a protector.

I hoped and prayed he never had to find out if he was a target or if he was protected, because I hoped and prayed I'd win his case.

Voir dire was the most important part of the trial process. I had to pick the right jury because the jury would decide Darnell's fate. The jury panel was composed of 50 men and women from all walks of life. I knew what I was looking for, although, because this was a death penalty case, I wasn't liable to find exactly what I needed.

Picking a jury in death penalty cases was trickier than picking a jury for a regular murder trial. The reason for this was that the jury had to be pre-screened to ensure they could impose the death penalty if the situation warranted it. This meant the people who didn't believe in the death penalty, such as myself, wouldn't be eligible to sit on this jury. That necessarily meant the death penalty jurors were, as a whole, more conservative than juries for non-death cases.

I did find that, when I picked jurors from the general population of people who might or might not believe in capital punishment, I could choose more than a few people sympathetic to the accused. With a death penalty panel, I was much less likely to find people like that.

I had to make do with the people I had, however. I knew that Darnell, once he told his story, would be sympathetic to many of the jurors. He was young, fresh-faced, and soft-spoken. His demeanor was that of a good kid who didn't make trouble. My hope was that I could get seat a few jurors who might have a kid like Darnell, therefore would empathize with him. It was my job to humanize Darnell, make the jury see who they're dealing with, make them understand that, if they put him in prison, they'd be putting away a terrified kid with big dreams squashed because he was in the wrong place at the wrong time.

The prosecutor, Aisha Moran, began her questioning of the jury, and, when she was done, I did my own questions. Aisha's questions were centered on finding evidence of bias – specifically, she was looking for people who stated they couldn't judge the case on its merits. I was looking for the same thing, but on the opposite side. If an individual stated he was biased against my client, because perhaps he or she had a close relative or friend in law enforcement, and that person was killed in the line of duty, then I'd strike that person for cause. If, on the other hand, there was an individual who stood up and stated that he or she could not set aside his or her personal feelings, which would make them *less* likely to convict, then Aisha would have reason to strike that person for cause.

I stood up and addressed the jury. "Ladies and gentlemen, thank you very much for coming. I understand this might be an inconvenience for many of you, and, believe me, I am sympathetic to your concerns. I just need to ask you all a few questions, and I'd like you to answer each of my questions truthfully, to the best of your ability."

I paced around the courtroom. Because there were so many people seated on this panel, it was difficult for me to address each person, but I always tried to do just that. "The facts of this case concern the murder of an undercover police officer. Raise your hand if one of your close friends or family is a member of the law enforcement community."

About twenty people raised their hands.

I asked each one about their law enforcement relatives or friends, and they each told me. After I heard their stories, I asked each person if they could judge the case on the merits, and would not hesitate to find my client not guilty if the facts warranted it. All but one said they could.

And so it went. I asked if anybody knew a victim of a crime and then asked each if they could judge the case on the merits. I asked them if they had heard of this case, or knew specifics about it. Unfortunately, most of the jurors had heard of this case, so I had to ascertain if they had an opinion about it.

This was actually where I got my most fruitful responses.

"I've heard of this case," one lady said, standing up. "And I don't look kindly on no cop-killers. Especially if they were caught with drugs." She shook her head and sat down, and I marked her down as struck for cause.

A man stood up and exclaimed that "I've seen stories about this in the papers, and that Officer Parker looked like a nice gentleman. He was risking his life every day and it wasn't fair that he'd be gunned down and found near a dumpster."

He went on to say he could judge the case on its merits, so I decided to try to use my peremptory challenge on him.

Then I went ahead and asked the jurors what they thought about the Black Lives Matter movement. "Most of you have heard of a movement known as Black Lives Matter," I said to my panel. "If you have any kind of opinions about this movement, I'd be interested in hearing them."

This was my way of uncovering racial bias, and I found it was generally an effective one. When I was a baby lawyer, I used to come right on out and ask the jury panel if anybody was racially biased, and nobody ever raised their hand. I soon learned that this was an ineffective way of rooting out people who would be prejudiced against my client because of his skin color. I learned how to develop other ways of finding this out. My next question would concern affirmative action, and I'd take special note of the individuals who would say things like "the only discrimination left is discrimination against white males."

Of course, I didn't necessarily think strong feelings against Black Lives Matter meant the person was racially biased. It didn't mean that at all. Many people legitimately were against that particular movement because they felt it constrained police. What I was looking for, however, were "dog whistles" - certain phrases that were commonly understood by a certain group of people to be racially charged. It could be something as simple as referring to "those people," and it could be something as blatant as saying the "n" word - I've heard that word come out of a juror's mouth more than once.

And, in this particular case, asking about Black Lives Matter accomplished something else - seeing how strongly the person felt about law enforcement. Since this case involved killing a policeman, it was important to find out how strongly the person felt about the boys in blue.

"I've heard of that movement," one juror said. "And I think it's bullshit, pardon my language. Of course black lives matter, nobody is saying they don't, but I think the black lives matter movement is just a way to make cops look bad. And they burned down cities across the country after George Floyd, and I don't look kindly on that, either."

I made a note to make a peremptory challenge of this juror.

"It's a terrorist movement," said another individual. "I heard from Sean Hannity that the leaders of this movement, the people who formed the movement, are in prison for terrorist acts," said another juror.

"I think it's making our streets less safe," said still another. "The cops are afraid to do anything now for fear of being victimized by organized protests against them. I guess the leaders of the Black

Lives Matter movement think cops should be handing out roses when they make an arrest."

I was feeling discouraged with the responses I was getting, but I plowed through. At the very least, I could find some people to strike for cause and others I'd get rid of through my peremptory challenges. So, there was that.

Somebody else raised her hand. A petite blonde woman. I pointed at her. "I think the movement is necessary," she said in a small voice. "There's been so much violence against unarmed black men that somebody needs to be their voice. Somebody needs to hold police officers accountable. Everybody thinks policemen are these saints who can do no wrong, and most of them are good people. But when you have poor training that results in unnecessary deaths, or, even worse, bad cops who have a sadistic or racist streak, they need to be reined in. The only way police departments will reform is if they have pressure on them, and I think that Black Lives Matter is a necessary tool for this reform to happen."

A woman after my own heart. As she was speaking, I looked around the room and made note of who nodded their heads along with what she was saying, and I also made a note of who gave her dirty looks. I'd fight for this juror to be on my panel, but I also would fight for the 6 or 7 other jurors nodding their heads while she spoke.

After she spoke, a few other people felt brave enough to speak up for the movement, as well, although none were quite as eloquent as she was. I'd try to get each and every one of these people on my jury. I wanted them, not just because they were less likely to show racial animus than the others who spoke out against the movement, but also because they were more likely to see all sides of an issue. They were more likely to believe there were dirty cops in the world, and this was crucial to my case, because I'd have to hammer away at Officer Cooper. I'd have to walk the fine line between implying he killed Officer Parker, and framed my client, and going over the line to where the judge would slap my hand or call a mistrial.

That was always a delicate balance in these SODDI trials – the real culprit wasn't on trial, and there was only so much questioning you could do to show they did it. Yet you had to subtly show the jury this person might've done it and the questioning to bring that fact out had to be spot-on. It took me years, and many trials, to figure out that balance, and I still didn't have it quite right.

My next question about affirmative action was also designed to ferret out possible racial animus. None of these issues were perfect in telling me somebody was likely a closet racist but it told me something about the jurors' mindsets.

After I finished my questions, the jury was dismissed, and Aisha and I went over the panel to see who to strike for cause, who we wanted peremptorily dismissed and who we wanted on the jury.

Of course, Aisha wouldn't let me have everybody I wanted. I didn't let her have everybody she wanted either. I got my blonde lady and two of the people who were nodding their heads when she talked about the importance of the BLM movement. I let her have some of the people talking about how cops should always be given deference over any criminal, because cops risk their lives every day. It was a delicate compromise, but, in the end, I felt confident I had a jury that would be as impartial as any other.

The judge ordered the panel back in, and she called the numbers of the jurors selected. They sat down in their seats, one by one. He congratulated them, told them what a solemn duty they would be performing, and then turned to Aisha and me. "Okay, counselors, please submit your opening statements."

The fun was about to begin.

Thirty-Seven

"Ladies and gentlemen of the jury," Aisha began. "I'd like to tell you a little about the victim in this case, Officer Jake Parker. Officer Parker was a 20-year veteran of the Kansas City Police Department and was working as an undercover policeman. Being an undercover policeman isn't an easy job – it's a grueling one and is probably the most stressful job one can ever imagine. He constantly lived in fear he'd blow his cover. He constantly knew there might be a time when he'd be looking down the barrel of a gun meant just for him. Yet Officer Parker bravely performed this duty, day in and day out, protecting our city and the people who live here. I'd love it if every officer on the force was an Officer Parker, because he was one of the best officers there was."

"On October 13 of last year, Officer Parker was working in his capacity as an undercover drug officer. He was also working in the sex crimes division of the KCPD, so he was working in two of the most grueling and taxing divisions in the force. He'd seen a lot in his years of working undercover, and he was responsible for many people going to prison – people who were hurting others and hurting our community. You have to understand, when you're working as an undercover drug officer, you come in contact with some of the most violent individuals in the city. Drug dealers will often kill to protect themselves and their trade, and they often do not have qualms in doing so. Officer Parker knew the risks, but he willingly took them."

"On October 13, Officer Parker was attempting to make an undercover drug sale between himself and the defendant, Darnell Williams." Aisha pointed at Darnell. "The evidence will show that the defendant, Darnell Williams, shot and killed Officer Parker when Officer Parker attempted to arrest the defendant. The evidence will show that when Darnell was arrested, he had on his person a quarter kilo of cocaine. This was found in his jacket pocket. The evidence will also show that Darnell's fingerprints were on the murder weapon and that Darnell was standing next to Officer Parker's lifeless body, which was found by the dumpster behind the restaurant where Darnell worked, Church's Chicken. The evidence will further show that Mr. Williams clocked out at his restaurant at 12 midnight, yet he was still on the premises at 1 AM, which was when Officer Cooper arrested Mr. Williams."

She paced around and looked the jury in the eye. "I intend to present to you the full case. The full monty, as it were, because I intend to show you that Mr. Williams had the motive, the means and the opportunity to kill the victim, Officer Jake Parker. Thank you, ladies and gentlemen of the jury."

She sat down and I stood up. I got right into my monologue. "Ladies and gentlemen of the jury, do you know how sometimes you see somebody accused of a crime, and the newspaper might say something like 'he was no choir boy?'" I looked at the jury and noticed that many of them had a smile on their face when I said that, and one lady suppressed a giggle. Two or three of them nodded their heads. "You know what I mean. In other words, the kid in question wasn't exactly living a clean life. I've heard that term, and, I'll admit, that term probably applies to most of my clients I have represented through the years. Most of my clients have been around the block a time or two. Most of them have picked up a couple of priors, maybe burglary, maybe stealing, maybe minor drug possession or drug distribution. Many of them are in gangs which means they were usually up to no good at some point in their lives."

I went over to Darnell, put my hands on his shoulders, and then walked back to the jury. "Well, what I have to tell you is that my client really is a choir boy. Not literally, but he has the character of somebody who could be. He's 18 years old and has never been in trouble with the law. Not even a parking ticket." I shrugged. "He's never been arrested for drug possession, never been arrested for burglary, never been caught shoplifting. He's been too busy working two jobs while going to school and maintaining a 4.4 GPA for any of that nonsense. He's never been in a gang, hasn't had a girlfriend and has had little time for a social life. His life has been filled with work, school and helping his mother put food on the table and keep a roof over his family's head. He hasn't had an easy life – he shared a single bedroom with four of his siblings, but he's not one to complain. His goal was to get into MIT on a scholarship and change the world as a nuclear engineer."

I walked back over to Darnell, and leaned down. "Look over at the jury," I whispered to him, and he turned around and looked at them. "Take a good look at my client. This is the face of a good kid. This is the face of a kid who would make any one of you proud. This isn't the face of a murderer. It's not the face of a drug dealer."

I strolled back to the jury box and put my fist in the air. "Now, the prosecutor has given you a big story about how she's going to show my client killed Officer Parker in cold blood. She said his fingerprints were on the gun. Of course they were – my client was in the wrong place at the wrong time, and he came across the lifeless body of Officer Parker, which was lying by the dumpster where he worked, and he did what any one of us would have reflexively done – he picked up that gun without even thinking about it."

"She said Darnell was still on the premises a whole hour after he clocked out. He was, ladies and gentlemen, on the premises of his restaurant a whole hour after he clocked out – he always stayed late at the restaurant because he wanted to do a really good job cleaning up and was only allowed on the clock for an extra hour. He couldn't get all the work done he wanted to do in an hour, so he clocked out and continued to work. Also, you have to understand that my client shares a two-bedroom apartment with five other people – he treasures his alone time, so he lingers in that restaurant as long as he can, just so he can have some peace and quiet. That's understandable in his situation, I think you would agree." I smiled and winked at the people on the jury, and they smiled back.

"The prosecutor said Darnell was caught with a quarter kilo of cocaine on his person. A quarter kilo of cocaine. That much cocaine has a street value of around $12,000. Now, ladies and gentlemen of the jury, I want to ask you one thing – if you worked at Church's Chicken on Gillham Road and you were closing that night, would you just show up with that much coke in your jacket pocket? There's not a good place to put coats in this restaurant – just a small closet accessible to anybody working there. There's not a safe in this restaurant accessible for employees. There's no secure spot, not even a locker. Maybe a less intelligent kid might put thousands of dollars worth of coke into a jacket pocket and just hang it up, but I already told you my client is carrying a 4.4 GPA at Lincoln College Prep, which has the most rigorous curriculum in the city, so it's safe to say my client is too intelligent to do something stupid like that."

I shook my head. "As for the murder weapon, let me tell you about that weapon. It was stolen from a gentleman named Leonard Jefferson. Mr. Jefferson is not acquainted with my client, but he is acquainted with the arresting officer, Officer Cooper. He's very acquainted with Officer Cooper, and, in fact, he will testify that Officer Cooper was in his house the day that gun was stolen."

"Now, what we have here are two things – one, drugs appear on my client, drugs he has no clue where they came from. I've already established it would make little sense for my client to be carrying that much cocaine on his person, and there's one other thing you need to know – Mr. Williams, my client, rode the bus to and from his place of business. He didn't have a car. That means the story about my client being caught with drugs makes even less sense, because could you imagine getting on a public bus with that much cocaine on your person?" I shook my head. "I can't imagine that either."

"The other thing is that the gun used in this murder was stolen from a house recently visited by Officer Cooper." I looked meaningfully at the jury, hoping they would put two and two together. I couldn't come right out and say Officer Cooper framed my client by planting the drugs, but I hoped I was making my point clear. That was how I carefully walked the line between presenting my evidence and inviting a mistrial.

"Now the prosecutor tells you my client was caught standing near the body, his fingerprints were on the murder weapon, and he had cocaine in his jacket pocket. What she never told you was that nobody saw my client do anything. She doesn't have a witness to the murder. But I do. And my witness will testify my client wasn't guilty at all. She heard who did it, and you'll find out who it was, but spoiler alert – it wasn't my client."

"One more thing, ladies and gentlemen of the jury. There was a peculiar thing about the murder weapon. A very peculiar thing. I'll leave you in suspense on what that peculiar thing is, but it's an exciting twist, and when you find out, you'll realize why the story that the prosecutor will tell you is a load of nonsense." I nodded my head. "Thank you very much."

I sat down and looked over at Aisha and raised my eyebrows. I had a trick or two up my sleeve and hoped to have her on the run soon enough.

I tried to act more confident in my case than I really felt, however. My witness was a good one, but not entirely credible. She could easily be picked apart once Aisha figured out who she was. My other piece of evidence was better, however, but even that wasn't the smoking gun, as it were. I was on firm footing, but not firm enough for me.

After all, my client's life was literally on the line.

Thirty-Eight

"Ms. Moran, call your first witness," Judge Wright intoned after all of us took a short break after our opening statements.

I expected Aisha would call Officer Cooper to the stand first. I was ready and waiting to nail that bastard to the wall. That arrogant bastard. He was going down. It might not be today, it might not be next week, but it would happen.

But she didn't call Officer Cooper first. She called, of all people, Sally Monroe, Darnell's supervisor.

I nodded. *So this is the game she's gonna play.* She was trying to psyche me out by calling a witness who should be friendly to Darnell because she was Darnell's supervisor. I wondered what lies she'd tell, and then wondered who put her up to the lies.

I thought Sally was up to no good when I saw her at Church's. She clearly wanted to throw Darnell under the bus. Now, here she was, the first witness the prosecutor was calling and I knew something was afoot. Something I wouldn't like. I would have to figure out how to impeach her.

Sally walked to the front of the courtroom and sat down in the witness stand. Darnell looked at me, and then looked at Sally, and he wrote on a piece of paper. *What's going on?*

I shook my head and wrote back. *I have no idea. Somebody has gotten to her, and I'll have to figure this out quickly.* I watched Sally take the oath, raising her right hand, and then I quickly wrote back to Darnell. *Does she have any kids at home? Any young kids?*

Yes, Darnell wrote back. *Three kids under the age of 15. Why?*

A hunch, I wrote back. I thought about how Officer Cooper threatened Rina and Abby. Because of that, I made sure Rina and Abby were never home alone. I even got another dog as companion to Stella. It was a Rottweiler I named Sue, and, while she was gentle as a kitten with the girls and Stella, she was extremely protective of all of us. I also hired a man to help Sophia care for the girls when I couldn't be at home, and this man, Juno Lee, just happened to be knowledgeable about weapons and had a black belt in Karate. I wasn't taking any chances with my girls.

I thought about Sally and how she didn't have the resources I did, so, if Officer Cooper threatened her children, she couldn't protect them. I wondered if he was blackmailing her, and, if so, how I'd bring it out on the stand.

"Could you please state your name for the record," Aisha said to Sally.

"Sally Monroe."

"Ms. Monroe, could you explain how you know the defendant, Darnell Williams?"

She cleared her throat and still refused to look Darnell in the eye. I saw shame in her eyes. Her voice was wavering and she kept running her fingers through her bleached-blonde hair nervously. This was not the body language of a confident woman. It was the body language of somebody scared to death. "I'm the shift supervisor at Church's Chicken," she said, her voice slightly twangy. "And I was the supervisor for Mr. Williams the night that poor man was killed."

"How well do you know the defendant, Mr. Williams?"

"I know him very well."

Aisha walked to the end of the witness stand and walked back. "In Ms. Ross' opening statement, she described Darnell to the jury.

She said he was a good kid, never in trouble, never into drugs, never ran with the wrong crowd. She said he was studious, hard-working and wanted to go to MIT, one of the most prestigious colleges in the country. Does that accurately describe the Darnell Williams you know?"

She took a deep breath, her eyes not meeting Darnell's. "No, ma'am."

I inwardly groaned and closed my eyes. The lying was about to begin. I tried to tamp down my rising anger that this woman would do this to Darnell, but, then again, maybe she felt she had no choice.

"Who is the Darnell that you know?"

"The Darnell I know is probably the laziest worker I have," she began.

I wanted to object, because whether or not Darnell was lazy wasn't relevant to the case, but I opened the door when I talked about how hard-working he was. There was nothing I could do at that point.

"You say he's lazy," Aisha said. "Tell the jury more about why you think that."

In the corner of my eye, I saw Darnell bow his head and put his hand to his eyes. I knew he was crying and my heart broke more than a little. He looked so nice in his suit, with a yellow tie and a handkerchief in his pocket – I gave him that handkerchief, telling him it was the little touches that made the suit, and he gratefully accepted my little gift. And, for some reason, the fact that he looked nice and spiffed up made me feel even more sorry for him. He looked like the person he should've been – the person who would fit in at MIT. Now, here he was, having to listen to the woman he trusted throw him under the bus.

It was heartbreaking.

She sat up a bit straighter in her chair and her hand flew up to the collar of her shirt. She bit her lower lip and then looked down at the table in front of her. "He's always goofing off instead of working. I can't ever get him to do a lick of work around the restaurant, and I was ready to fire him because I just can't have kids like Darnell getting paid for doing next to nothing."

I put my arm around Darnell and I listened to him quietly sob. He took the handkerchief out of his pocket and dabbed his eyes and I whispered to him. "Don't worry, I'll get her. Somebody is putting her up to this, I know it. Don't hate her, hate the person who put her up to it."

He nodded, his hand still pinching his eyes.

"Okay," Aisha said. "So, let me tell you another thing that defense counsel said about Mr. Williams. She stated the reason Mr. Williams was still on the restaurant premises a whole hour after he clocked out was because he wanted to do an extra good job cleaning and he was only allowed to be on the clock for one hour after closing, so he stayed an extra hour on his own time to make sure the restaurant was spotless. Does that sound right to you?"

"No, ma'am," Sally said. "I don't like having Darnell clean the restaurant, really, because he always does a terrible job. The next morning, after he cleans the store, there's always grease on the floor and the deep fryer still has grease in it from the night before. He doesn't bother to change it. It's always a mess when he closes, so, no, that doesn't sound right to me. If he was there at 1 AM, two hours after the restaurant closed, then he was there for reasons other than that he was still cleaning the restaurant."

"What do you know about Mr. Williams' family?"

"I know they're poor. Darnell tells me he sleeps in a bedroom with his two brothers and two sisters and his mother works two jobs."

"What do you know about how Mr. Williams planned to bring his family out of poverty?"

"He told me he had a plan for his family. He told me he'd quit his job with our restaurant, because he was making so much money dealing drugs that he didn't need to work for us anymore. He told me he had big plans for his family to move into a five-bedroom apartment on The Plaza, and that his mother wouldn't have to work anymore. That's how much money he said he made dealing drugs."

She was a lying sack of shit but I had to give her credit – once she got her sea legs, she could tell these wretched lies with a straight face.

Next to me, Darnell continued to bow his head, his fingers to his eyes, his head rapidly shaking from side to side. *Don't worry, Darnell, I'll get her.*

"He told you he was dealing drugs, then?"

"Yes, ma'am."

Aisha nodded. "What about what the defense counsel told the jury – that Darnell wouldn't be stupid enough to bring a quarter kilo of cocaine to his work. Is that what you know about Darnell? Would he do something like that?"

"Yes ma'am, he would." She nodded and I wondered if she'd be stupid enough to say she caught him bringing drugs into the restaurant before. If she said that, I'd make her pay. She'd 100% lose credibility with the jury. Of that, I was sure.

"Why do you believe that about him?"

"Because he's not very bright and he's not very careful. I suspected him of having drugs at the restaurant one time, so I went back to the back room and looked through his coat. I didn't find drugs, but I found ten one hundred dollar bills. He had a $1,000 right there in his coat pocket and I just couldn't believe it. I asked him about it. I said 'Darnell, you best be careful bringing that much money around and just leaving it where anybody can steal it.' He just told me to mind my own damned business and stop snooping around."

"Do you believe Mr. Williams is the kind of person, based on what you know, who would kill a plain-clothes police officer in a drug deal gone wrong?"

I stood up, finally getting something to object to. "Objection, calls for speculation and a conclusion."

"Sustained. Move along, counselor."

"I have nothing further."

"Ms. Ross, you may begin your cross-examination."

Okay, time to unravel this bitch's lies, piece by piece. "Ms.

Monroe, you stated you thought Darnell was the laziest worker you have, or something to that effect. Is that an accurate characterization of your testimony?"

"Yes," she said, looking at the table.

"Please look me in the eye, Ms. Monroe, when you are speaking with me." I stood there, staring at her, my hands on the rail. I leaned down, closer and closer and closer, until her face was inches from mine. She still refused to look at me.

I turned to the jury. "Let the record reflect that I asked the witness to look me in the eye when speaking and she refused." I didn't have to tell the jury why Sally wasn't looking at me. It was painfully obvious.

She continued to look down as I went on with my questioning. "The laziest worker you have. Yet Darnell has worked for your restaurant for what, three years? Is that right? He's worked for your restaurant for three years?"

"Yes," she said. "Maybe he used to be a harder worker, but lately he's just gotten so lazy."

"Please just answer the question I ask," I told her. "If my question is a yes or no question, I only want you to answer with a yes or a no. Do I make myself perfectly clear?" I leaned down again, my face a few inches from hers and she appeared to shrink away from me.

"Yes," she said softly.

"That's better. Now, Darnell has worked for your company for three years and he's gotten raises and evaluations on the regular. Is that correct?"

"Yes," she said, and then opened her mouth.

"A simple yes will suffice," I said. "I'll let you know when I want an answer other than yes or no, okay?"

"Yes."

"In fact, I plan on bringing in a witness to testify to Mr. Williams' employee record, complete with paperwork, since you were called and told a story completely at odds with reality, so I caution you to tell the truth when I ask you a question. But isn't it true that, with every employee evaluation, Mr. Williams was found to be a conscientious employee, hard-working, polite and thorough." I'd seen his employee evaluations, so I knew Darnell was said to be all those things and more.

"Yes," she said, nodding her head. "But-"

"And, Ms. Monroe," I said, cutting her off so she couldn't elaborate further. "Isn't it also true that you asked Mr. Williams to close the chicken shop at least three nights a week?"

"Yes."

"Yet you told the jury you didn't like him to close because he did a terrible job. You told the jury he left grease on the floor, left the old grease in the fryer and the restaurant was always a mess when you came in the next day. Now why would you continue to ask him to close the restaurant if he was such a negligent and careless employee?"

"I couldn't find nobody else to stay," she said weakly.

"Nobody else? I wasn't aware that closing the chicken place was optional. So, you're telling the jury that you have, what, 10 employees who regularly work the night shift and you try to schedule those other employees to close, and they all just tell you no, so you're stuck with Mr. Williams, who does a terrible job? Is that what you're telling the jury?"

Sally looked confused and looked at the jury pathetically. But she didn't answer the question, so I decided to move on. The point was made. Her credibility was shot, so I decided to go for the jugular.

"Now," I said. "You told the jury that Mr. Williams was planning on living in a big, fancy home with all the money he's bringing in with his drug dealing. Is that a fair characterization of your testimony?"

"Yes," she said.

"Now I'll bring in witnesses who will testify that not only was Darnell riding the bus to his job, but his mother continued to work two jobs, and he continued to live in a two-bedroom apartment with his sisters and brothers and his mother. Yet, you're telling me

Darnell was bragging about all the money he made with his drug-dealing side hustle. Doesn't that strike you as a bit off? I mean, if he was making all this money, he'd have a car at the very least, and his family sure as heck wouldn't still be living hand-to-mouth in a two-bedroom apartment, would they?"

"Objection," Aisha said, standing up. "Ms. Monroe doesn't have knowledge of how Mr. Williams would spend his extra money from drug dealing. This question calls for speculation."

"Your honor, Ms. Monroe clearly testified that Darnell was bragging about how he'd spend his money, so this question is appropriate."

"I'll allow it," he said. "Ms. Monroe, answer the question."

"No," she said. "I guess probably they should be living someplace else by now."

I nodded. "And let me get this straight. According to your testimony, Mr. Williams straight-up told you he was committing multiple felonies. I mean, if your testimony is to be believed, Mr. Williams told you he was making regular drug deals. Yet you not only didn't call the police but continued to employ him. Is that correct?"

"Yes," she said, looking down at the table.

"Is it your practice to employ individuals committing regular felonies?"

"No," she said.

"And you also testified that Mr. Williams showed up one day with a thousand dollars worth of hundred dollar bills. Is that correct?"

"Yes."

"Did you question Mr. Williams where he received this large amount of cash?"

"No."

"You didn't? He's telling you he's regularly dealing drugs and shows up with a large wad of cash, and you weren't even in the least bit curious about where this cash came from?"

"I was, but I didn't ask him, no."

I nodded and pivoted to the next question lightning-fast. I wanted to ask the question so she wasn't prepared for it and didn't have the chance to think about the answer. "Ms. Monroe do you know Officer Morgan Cooper?"

"Objection," Aisha said. "Relevance."

"Your honor, Officer Cooper is the star witness in this case. He was the arresting officer for my client. It's fair to ask if this witness has any knowledge of him, specifically if he was known to come into the restaurant from time to time."

"What does her knowledge of Officer Cooper go to show?" Judge Wright inquired. "Come up, counselor. You too, Ms. Moran."

That the bastard put her up to lying. "Your honor, my theory of the case is that Officer Cooper is ultimately responsible for the murder of Officer Parker," I whispered. "I'd like to inquire how Ms. Monroe knows Officer Cooper, because, quite frankly, I think Officer Cooper put her up to her lying."

"Ms. Moran?" Judge Wright addressed Aisha. "What say you?"

"Anything that Ms. Ross will ask Ms. Monroe about Officer Cooper will involve hearsay," she said.

"Actually, no it won't, because Officer Cooper will testify. You can just cross-examine him about what he told Sally," I said.

"Ms. Moran," Judge Wright said, "It's relevant to Ms. Ross' theory of the case," he said. "So I'll allow it within parameters. I won't tolerate a fishing expedition, Ms. Ross, so I'll rein you in if you get too far afield."

"Thank you, your honor," I said.

Aisha took her seat and I returned to questioning Sally. "Do you know Officer Morgan Cooper?" I asked her.

She shifted uncomfortably in her seat. "Yes," she said. "I do."

"How well do you know him?"

"Intimately," she said.

I wasn't expecting that answer, although I probably should've been. "Please explain."

She rolled her eyes. "Do you want me to spell it out for you?

We've had sex three times. But that's really all. We're not dating. We're not even friends."

I suddenly wondered if Sally had a side hustle of her own. "Ms. Morgan, are you a prostitute?"

"Objection," Aisha said. "This really isn't relevant."

"Ms. Ross?" Judge Wright said to me. "What is the relevance of that question?"

"The relevance is that if Ms. Monroe is a prostitute that would explain how she knows Officer Cooper," I said, and then I went to the bench with Aisha. "And it would explain why she'd lie for him," I said in a low voice.

"In what way would that explain why she'd lie for him?" Aisha asked me in a whisper. "This is getting ridiculous."

"Aisha, you put Sally on the stand and let her lie like that. Maybe you knew she'd lie, and maybe you didn't, but she *is* lying. I'd like to get to the bottom of why she's lying."

"Ms. Moran," Judge Wright said. "Ms. Ross makes a point. It's pretty clear this witness is not telling the truth. She probably has some kind of motivation to not tell the truth on the stand, considering the penalty for perjury. Considering Ms. Ross' theory of the case, I will allow this line of questioning."

Aisha rolled her eyes and I smiled. "Thank you, your honor."

She sat down and I approached Sally. "Ms. Monroe, are you a prostitute?"

Sally looked like she wanted to melt into the floor. "Yes," she said softly. "I am."

"Is that how you know Officer Cooper?"

"Yes," she said. "That's how I know him."

"Has he harassed you on the street?"

"No."

"He hasn't?"

"No." She looked at me with a look of panic and then looked over at the jury.

"Did he threaten you before you came here to testify?"

"No."

"Did he threaten your children before you came here to testify?"

She looked over at the jury then at me and nodded slightly.

"Please verbalize your answer to my question."

"Yes," she said softly and bit her lower lip. She lowered her head and it looked like tears were about to start. I decided just to rest at that point. I got what I needed out of her, and, hopefully, the damage was done.

"I have nothing further for this witness." I went over to her, took the box of Kleenex off the stand and handed it to her. She took a Kleenex and nodded at me as if to say *thank you.*

"Ms. Moran, do you have any follow-up questions for this witness?"

"No, your honor."

"Ms. Monroe, you may be excused."

She nodded, and she slowly left the witness stand and slowly walked out of the courtroom. I almost felt sorry for her. I broke her down, but she'd already been broken down long before I got to her.

I sat down next to Darnell and put my arm around him. He was smiling by then, so I felt better. "I guess Ms. Sally doesn't hate me after all," he whispered.

"I guess she doesn't," I agreed.

The medical examiner was next on the stand. He testified about the examination he did on Officer Parker and talked about how he determined how Officer Parker died. He talked about the trajectory of the bullet, that Officer Parker was shot at close range, and the results of his overall examination.

I didn't have any questions for him.

When the ballistics expert came on, however, I knew I'd have questions for him. There was one piece of information that I'd found, after sending the gun in for my own forensic analysis, that was absolutely fascinating for me.

After the ballistics expert testified about the caliber of the bullet that killed Officer Parker, and Aisha rested, I approached him.

"Officer Watters," I began. "You testified about the caliber of the bullet found in Officer Parker, but I'd like to ask you a few questions about the gun itself if I may."

"Okay," he said, a bit unsurely.

"Now, you testified the gun used in this murder was a Smith and Wesson .45 revolver, is that correct?"

"Yes," he said. "That's correct."

"And you testified the bullets found in Officer Parker matched the gun found at the scene, correct?"

"Yes."

"And you carefully examined the gun found at the scene, correct?"

He nodded. "Correct."

I cocked my head. "But you neglected to testify that this particular gun had been fitted with a silencer prior to the gun being fired. But it was, wasn't it?"

"Yes," he said. "That is correct."

"In fact, the gun had the silencer on it when it was used to murder Officer Parker, is that true?"

"Yes. That is correct."

"When you were presented with the recovered revolver from the murder scene, did it have a silencer on it at that time?"

"No, it didn't."

"So, it's fair to say that Officer Parker's murderer killed Officer Parker with a revolver fitted with a silencer and took that silencer off the gun sometime prior to the weapon being recovered on the pavement next to the dumpster at Church's Chicken. Correct?"

"Correct."

"Now I'm sure you've also read through the police report for this case. Is this assumption correct?"

"Yes, I read through the police report."

"And you've spoken with the officers who arrived at the scene and arrested my client, correct? I'm referring to Officer Cooper and Officer Facinelli, the first responders."

"Yes, I've spoken with both Officer Cooper and Officer Facinelli about the crime scene and the arrest of your client."

"And did you see anything on that police report that referenced a silencer or a suppressor found on my client's person?"

"No. I didn't see anything about that."

"When you spoke with Office Cooper and Officer Facinelli about the arrest of my client, did either of them say a word about finding a silencer or a suppressor on my client's person?"

"No, neither of them mentioned that."

"In fact, it would be unusual if either Officer Cooper or Officer Facinelli found a silencer or a suppressor on my client and not mentioned that fact in the police report, isn't that correct?"

"Yes, that's correct. The fact the gun had a silencer on it is an important one, and it certainly would've been in the police report if your client had the silencer on his person."

"And there was no indication that Officer Cooper or Officer Facinelli found a silencer anywhere on the premises of the restaurant, correct? Not in the restaurant, not in the parking lot, and not in the bushes, correct?"

"Yes, that's correct."

"Did any of the responders who came to the scene, and there were, as I understand it, 7 patrol cars plus an ambulance, did any of those responders find a silencer anywhere on the premises of the restaurant or in the surrounding areas?"

"No, nobody found a silencer on the premises of the restaurant or the surrounding areas."

"Yet the officers who responded to the scene did a thorough search of the restaurant and the surrounding areas, is that right?"

"Yes, that is correct."

"Now, you weren't here for the medical examiner's testimony, but his testimony was that the time of death for Officer Parker was between 12:30 and 1 AM on the morning of October 13 of last year. You wouldn't dispute that, would you?"

"No, I'd have no reason to dispute what the Medical Examiner would testify to, as that's not my area of expertise."

"Do you understand the first responders got to the scene at 1 AM on the dot?"

"Yes, I understand that."

"So there was, at most, thirty minutes between that gunshot and my client being arrested. In your experience, would that be enough time for a suspect to hide that silencer somewhere so far away from that restaurant that none of the responders found it, and then run back to the restaurant to be apprehended?"

"Objection," Aisha said. "Calls for speculation. This officer couldn't possibly know whether or not Mr. Williams ran away from the crime scene to hide that silencer."

"Sustained," Judge Wright said.

I wanted to ask if he thought it was peculiar that, if Darnell managed to run far enough away to hide the silencer that he'd return to the scene of the crime, but I decided that this, too, would call for speculation. I put that question in my quiver so I could hammer Cooper with it.

"I have nothing further for this witness."

"Officer Watters, you may step down. Ms. Moran, you may call your next witness."

She looked hesitantly over at me. I was schooling her witnesses and she knew it. "The State calls Officer Morgan Cooper."

This was when things would get really good.

Thirty-Nine

"Could you please state your name for the record?" Aisha asked Cooper when he took the stand.

"Morgan Cooper."

"You are Officer Morgan Cooper, is that correct?"

"Yes, that is correct."

"And you were the first responder to the crime scene involving the murder of Officer Parker, correct?"

"Yes, that's correct."

"Take me back to the early morning hours of October 13 of last year. Around 12:50 that morning, what you were doing?"

He cleared his throat. "I was patrolling the area around the Church's Chicken on Gillham Plaza. I was at the 7-11, right next to the Church's Chicken, right across Linwood Blvd., within 100 feet of the restaurant. I was getting a cup of coffee and was leaving the 7-11 when I heard a gunshot coming from the Church's Chicken parking lot. I immediately ran across Linwood Blvd. in the direction of the restaurant where I found the defendant, Darnell Williams, standing next to the body of Officer Parker. The murder weapon was lying next to the body, and I immediately pointed my gun at Mr. Williams and asked him to spread against the wall of the restaurant."

"You asked him to spread against the wall. Did he cooperate?"

"Yes, he did."

"And what did you do next?"

"I patted him down, reached into his coat pocket and found a quarter kilo of cocaine on him."

"And then what did you do?"

"I put my handcuffs on him, read him his rights and put him into the squad car to be processed."

"Did Mr. Williams say anything to either of you in the squad car on the way downtown?"

"No he didn't."

I knew he did. Darnell told me he pleaded with the officers in the squad car and repeatedly told both of them that he didn't do anything wrong. He repeatedly asked them why he was being arrested, and he repeatedly told both of them that those drugs didn't belong to him.

"He didn't say anything at all?"

"No. I told him he had the right to remain silent so he remained silent in the car on the way over."

"What happened when you got to the station?"

"I took him into the station to be processed and then I left him."

"I have nothing further for this witness."

"Ms. Ross," Judge Wright said. "Your witness."

I nodded. "Officer Cooper, you testified you were at the 7-11 right across the street from Church's Chicken around 12:50 AM, and you heard a gun shot, so you ran over to the restaurant to check things out. Is that correct?"

"Yes, that's correct."

"Isn't it correct that Officer Facinelli actually wasn't with you in the squad car parked in front of the 7-11 at that time?"

"No, that's not true. He was in the squad car waiting for me in the parking lot."

"Actually, that's not true and I have the surveillance video to prove it. Would you like to revise your answer?"

He looked uncomfortable. He looked at Aisha, and then I looked at her as well. Guess she not only didn't figure out the revolver had a silencer that was taken off before the suspect exited the crime scene, but she also didn't know about the surveillance video. I personally couldn't believe Officer Cooper was as sloppy as he was, but I thanked God for that.

"Officer Facinelli was actually inside the 7-11 as well," he said. "Come to think of it."

"And what time did you arrive at the 7-11?"

"Around 12:45 in the morning."

"Where were you and Officer Facinelli prior to arriving at the 7-11?"

I knew where Cooper was – he was busy killing Officer Parker. I wanted to see what he'd say about where Officer Facinelli was at this time, though.

"We were patrolling the neighborhood," he said. "We responded to a call at 3209 Gillham Road at 12:10 AM, which was a domestic disturbance, after which we drove to that 7-11 on the corner of Linwood and Gillham at 12:45 AM."

"I see," I said. "Now, isn't it true that Officer Facinelli was at the disturbance at 3209 Gillham Road at 12:10 AM and you were as well, but you actually disappeared at 12:15 AM, leaving Officer Facinelli to handle the disturbance on his own?"

He was caught and he knew it. If he'd try to lie, I'd call the people who lived at 3209 Gillham Road to the stand. I was planning on calling them anyhow. Plus, Facinelli would surely testify that Officer Cooper left him there for a good half hour talking to the two people, whose names were Mark and Catherine Wood. "Yes, that's true."

"And why did you leave the premises of 3209 Gillham Road right at that time?"

He obviously had his story worked out before he came to the stand. "I left because while I standing there speaking with Mr. and Mrs. Wood, who were the people involved in the domestic disturbance at 3209 Gillham Road, I got another call about another disturbance in the same neighborhood. By the time we got to 3209 Gillham, the situation between Mr. and Mrs. Wood was under control, but I recommended to Officer Facinelli that he remain with the Woods until he was positive there wasn't a need for further intervention. Since Officer Facinell assured me the situation in control, I investigated the other disturbance I heard about, which was at 3309 Gillham Road, about a five minute walk from 3209 Gillham Road."

"Do you know what is less than a five minute walk from 3209 Gillham Road? Church's Chicken. I could walk from 3209 Gillham Road to Church's Chicken in 3 minutes."

Officer Cooper just sat at the stand, glaring and crossing his arms in front of him. "I wouldn't know how far of a walk it is from 3209 Gillham Road to Church's Chicken, ma'am, because I didn't walk from 3209 Gillham Road to Church's Chicken. As I said, I walked from 3209 Gillham Road to 3309 Gillham Road, which are apartments that are a five or ten minute walk from 3209 Gillham Road."

"So, it's your testimony that you walked from 3209 Gillham Road to 3309 Gillham Road to check out another disturbance?"

"Yes, that is my testimony."

"Huh. And what happened when you went down to 3309 Gillham Road? Did you have a certain apartment number that you went to?"

"No, the disturbance was in the street in front of these apartments."

"And when you went down there to check out this other disturbance, did you make any arrest of anybody or even counsel anyone?"

"No, by the time I got there, the people involved in that disturbance had apparently left the scene."

"I see. And did you then return to 3209 Gillham Road to see how your partner was doing with Mr. and Mrs. Wood?"

Just try to lie, you bastard. I'll get them on the stand and they'll say you didn't come back and you didn't even call Facinelli to see how things were going.

"No," he said. "I didn't."

"You didn't." I nodded my head. "And why not?"

"I knew Officer Facinelli had the situation in hand so I didn't see a need to go back to 3209 Gillham right away. I wanted to walk around the neighborhood and see if I could find the people who had been in the street earlier."

"Why were you so anxious to find the people in the street earlier?"

"Because they were causing a disturbance."

"And what was the disturbance again? I'm sorry, I forgot to ask you that question earlier."

"There were apparently two men in the street, one of whom was pointing a gun at the other one. I wanted to walk around the neighborhood to try to find these two men."

"And did you find them?"

"No."

"And you finally went back to 3209 Gillham at what time?"

"12:40. We then immediately went to the 7-11 and got there at 12:45."

"I see. So, let's see now...you left the scene at 3209 Gillham Road at 12:15, you walked down to 3309 Gillham Road, which was a 5-10 minute walk, so let's just say that it took you 8 minutes. So, you arrived at 3309 Gillham Road at around 12:23-12:25, and then you looked around the neighborhood for what, less than ten minutes? Because you had to have time to walk back to 3209 Gillham Road, so that shaves off another 7 or 8 minutes. So, according to your timeline, you were casing the neighborhood around 3309 Gillham for less than ten minutes. Is that your testimony?"

"That is my testimony," he said confidently.

"So, you were looking for somebody who had a gun pointed at somebody else and decided to give up your search for these individuals in less than ten minutes. Is that what you expect me to believe?"

"That is what happened. I got to the neighborhood, found nobody there, I walked around for about ten minutes and decided the two men probably left in a car. I was wasting my time so I went back to rejoin my partner."

"And did you happen to knock on anybody's door to ask if they saw two men arguing in the street, one of whom had a gun?"

"No."

"And why not?"

"Because it was late, almost 1 AM, and I didn't feel the need to disturb anyone."

"Disturb anyone? You're a policeman. Disturbing people in the middle of the night is what you do, isn't it?"

"No, that's not what we do."

"Oh, it's not," I said. I had another piece of information that perhaps Officer Cooper didn't bother to find out before he concocted this story. "Would you be surprised to know there was a party on the 3300 Block of Gillham Road that morning?" I'd found out this piece of information once I ascertained that Cooper and Facinelli were at 3209 Gillham Road at 12:15 in the morning. I actually lucked into this information through my prostitute client, Ginger, who knew a girl at that party. She, too, was on my witness list, and she'd testify that she left that party at around 2 AM.

Ginger turned out to be a gold-mine because she had the best piece of information of all. She was an eyewitness to the murder. I only hoped her story was credible.

"I didn't hear any party on the 3300 Block of Gillham Road that morning."

"Oh, you didn't." I nodded. "There was actually a party going on in the apartment complex right across the street from where you were. This party was at 3314 Gillham Road. So, there were plenty of people at that party who you could've asked about the disturbance in the street between these two men."

"3314 Gillham Road was not in the line of sight of where these two men were. I knew about that party but I didn't see a point in going in there and asking anybody about these two men."

"And there wasn't another apartment around that had their lights on you could ask?"

"No, I didn't see any other apartment with their lights on."

"So, you just gave up," I said with a shrug.

"Yes, I just gave up."

"And why, exactly, did you not look harder for these two men?"

"I told you, I figured it was a waste of my time."

I nodded and then turned my back to him. "Officer Cooper, isn't true that you never went down the street to check on a disturbance between men in the street, but, actually, you went to Church's Chicken to confront Officer Parker?"

"No, that's not true."

"Isn't it true that you actually got a call on your receiver, but it was a call from your dispatcher informing you that Officer Parker was just around the corner at Church's, which was perfect timing for you to go over there, confront him, kill him and then come back to rejoin your partner at 3209 Gillham? After all, Church's is a three minute walk from 3209 Gillham."

"No, that's not true." His face started to get red and little beads of sweat started to form on his forehead.

"Isn't it true that Officer Parker was investigating another crime that you were involved in, that crime being the murder of 13-year-old Alaina Morosky?"

"Yes, that's true that he was investigating that case, but no, it's not true that I was involved in that case."

"But it's true that after Officer Parker was killed, you were put in charge of the Alaina Morosky case?"

"Yes, that's true."

"Isn't it true, Officer Cooper, that you actually killed Officer Parker at around 12:30 that morning, left his body at the dumpster, and then waited for my client, Darnell Williams, to come out of Church's Chicken so you had somebody to blame for the murder?"

"No, that's not true." He crossed his arms in front of him. "I told you, I was right across the street at the 7-11 when I heard the gun shot at 12:50 AM. I told you where I was right before I was observed at the 7-11 getting coffee, and I told you what I did when I heard the gun shot."

"Who else heard the gun shot?"

"I was the only one who heard the gun shot. Officer Facinelli was inside the 7-11 at the time I heard the gun shot."

I knew what was going on with Officer Cooper. He didn't think I could determine the gun had a silencer on it because the gun recovered didn't have one. It was only after I took the gun to an expert that I found the gun had a silencer which was removed right before the gun was recovered. He was on my witness list to call as an expert.

"And what did that gun shot sound like?" I was laying a trap for him to walk right into.

"It sounded like a normal gun." He crossed his arms in front of him and glared at me. "It sounded like what a normal .45 revolver would sound like when heard across the street, less than 50 yards away."

"Oh," I said, walking over to the jury. I looked at all of their faces, and they were listening in rapt attention. "It sounded that loud?"

"Yes, it sounded that loud."

"So, the sound was at 157 decibels, which is also approximately the level of decibels of a race car or the launch of the space shuttle, and you were the only person who heard this gun shot?"

"I guess so. As I said, my partner, Mr. Facinelli, was inside the 7-11 at the time I heard the gun shot and raced over to Church's to see what was happening."

"Would it surprise you to learn that the gun in question was fitted with a silencer at the time of the murder?"

Officer Cooper shifted uncomfortably in his seat. "Yes, that would surprise me."

"And when you got to Darnell, Mr. Williams, you searched him, and didn't find a silencer. Is that correct?"

"Yes, that's correct."

"But you found a cell phone on him, correct? In fact, he was carrying his cell phone when you first came upon him, correct?"

"Correct."

"And when you arrested Mr. Williams, was he out of breath, like he was running?"

"No."

"So, the weapon was fitted with a silencer for this murder, no silencer was found anywhere on the premises, and Mr. Williams wasn't out of breath, like he ran away from the scene, hid the silencer in a location far away from Church's, and ran back?"

"No, he wasn't."

"Now, the revolver used in this murder was stolen, isn't that correct?"

"Yes, that's correct."

"And did you find out who the revolver belonged to?"

"It was registered to a Leonard Jefferson."

"A Leonard Jefferson. Leonard Jefferson who lives at 33rd and Gillham, that Leonard Jefferson?"

"Yes. He lives at 3313 Gillham Road."

"And weren't you in Leonard Jefferson's house in September?"

"No."

"You weren't?"

"No."

"That's funny, because I spoke with Mr. Jefferson, and-"

"Objection, hearsay," Aisha said, standing up.

"Your honor, Mr. Jefferson is on my witness list, and he will testify about his stolen gun. Ms. Moran will have the opportunity to cross-examine him, so this is not hearsay."

"Overruled," Judge Wright said with a smile. "Proceed, counselor."

"As I was saying, I spoke to Mr. Jefferson, and he told me you were in his house in September. He said his roommate, Antoine Harrington, let you in and you were acting on a tip that Mr. Jefferson and Mr. Harrington were dealing drugs. Do you remember that?"

"No, I don't remember that," he said. "I go on hundreds of calls a week, and, almost every day, I'm responding to a call in the neighborhood about suspected drug dealing. I can't remember every call I get."

"Fair enough," I said. "It's just that Leonard Jefferson's gun disappeared on the same day you went inside his house to inquire about whether or not Mr. Jefferson and Mr. Harrington were drug-dealing. I just found that a coincidence, that's all."

"I guess that's it. It was just a coincidence."

"And when you apprehended my client, did you do any tests to find gun residue on his hands?"

"Yes, we did."

"And did you find any?"

"No, but residue is easy to wipe away. All you have to do is stick your hands in your pockets and the residue is gone."

I figured I did all I could. "I have nothing further for this witness, your honor."

"Ms. Moran, any follow-up for this witness?" Judge Wright asked Aisha.

"No, your honor," she said.

"Very well. You are excused, Officer Cooper." Judge Wright took a sip of water. "Looks like lunchtime," he said, looking at the clock. "Everybody, we will break for lunch, and we'll meet back here at 1:15. Thank you very much for your patience."

Forty

Darnell and I couldn't leave the courtroom. He was still being guarded. So, I'd brought in a lunch from home that I shared with him. It consisted of a juice box, a caprese salad made with cherry tomatoes and mozzarella cheese, and a peanut and jelly sandwich. We ate our food at our defense table.

Darnell was quietly eating his food, glancing at me from time to time. "You were really good," he said. "You were really good at cross-examining that cop and Sally. And that other cop, the ballistics guy." He stabbed a cherry tomato with his plastic fork. "This food is so much better than what I get in jail," he said, making a face. "That's one of the things I miss the most. My mama's cooking."

"Do you think she'll be able to watch this trial at all?"

He shook his head. "Jamal said that she wants to, but she thinks it will be too stressful."

"What about Jamal?"

"He should be here tomorrow, maybe. But he has school, so he probably can't, either." He hung his head and knew he wished for more support.

I knew Darnell would at least see his Aunt Violetta - she was on my witness list. She'd testify about Darnell's living situation with his family. Her testimony would dispute the theory that Darnell was drug-dealing, because she'd confirm that Darnell and his family were still very poor.

"Tell me about your mama's cooking," I said.

At that, his face lit up. "Oh, she's a good cook, a really good cook. One of the best thing she makes is breaded hamburger she fries up in a skillet, with a side of mashed potatoes and gravy, grits and corn."

"She breads the hamburger?"

"Yeah. She puts herbs and stuff in the meat, rolls it in flour and breading and then fries it. It tastes like chicken fried steak like you get at Stroud's," he said. He put his hand on his belly and stared at the peanut butter and jelly. "But this is good, too," he said. "I hope I can get some home cooking again. I really hope-" He bowed his head and squeezed his fingers on his eyes, like he was trying not to cry.

"I think things are going well," I said. "I'm breaking these people down on the stand. I only need to put reasonable doubt in the jury's mind. Reasonable doubt, Darnell. Those are the magic words here."

"I know," he said. "I just don't want to get my hopes up, that's all, Ms. Ross."

I smiled. "Eat your sandwich," I said lightly. "You leave everything up to me. You'll see. I'll nail everyone to the wall."

Darnell and I chatted for the rest of the lunch period. I tried my hardest to take his mind off what was going on, and I think he appreciated it. "Thanks," he said to me.

"For what?"

"For taking me on. For taking my case seriously. I was afraid when I had an attorney appointed that I'd get somebody who doesn't care and wouldn't do a good job. But you've done a good job, Ms. Ross. A really good job."

"Well, it's the least I can do," I said. "And, just for the record, in Kansas City, the court-appointed attorneys at the Public Defender's Office are some of the most dedicated I've ever seen. They're rock star caliber. You could do worse than to get one of them. But your case is a death penalty case, so you got stuck with me."

"I'm glad to be stuck with you, Ms. Ross," Darnell said with a smile. "Really glad."

At 1:15, the jury filed back in. Aisha was back in her position at the prosecutor's table and the judge was back on the bench. We all stood when he came in, and we all sat back down.

"Okay," Judge Wright said. "I hope the ladies and gentlemen of the jury had a nice break and you all got your fill of some decent food. I hope you all didn't eat too heavy for lunch, because I don't want anybody nodding off during testimony."

He smiled and the people in the jury laughed.

"We will resume with the prosecutor's case," Judge Wright said. "Ms. Moran, please call your next witness."

I didn't think that she'd call Facinelli because his testimony would essentially be duplicative, and it might be harmful to call him. I didn't dispute that Officer Cooper was in the 7-11 right at 12:50. I also didn't think it was a coincidence he was there – I knew he went there for an alibi since the time of death of Officer Parker was within the window of 12:30-1 AM. He wanted to be seen in the 7-11 during that window, plus it gave him a reason to be across the street from the scene of the crime when he allegedly heard the gunshots.

Of course the gun shots were not heard at 12:50, like he said. The gun actually went off around 12:30. It was loud, even though it was muffled by the silencer, but not loud enough that anybody in the surrounding residential neighborhoods would've heard the shots, and not loud enough for even somebody at the 7-11, right across the street, to hear if they were inside the store.

I was surprised when Aisha stood up. "The prosecution rests," she said.

"Very well." Judge Wright nodded. "Ms. Ross, call your first witness."

"The defense calls Leonard Jefferson," I said.

The bailiff went out and got Leonard Jefferson, who was out in the hallway.

He took his seat. He was dressed in a suit and his Afro was closer to his head. He was also wearing glasses. He looked at me expectantly as the bailiff sworn him in.

I approached.

"Please state your name for the record."

"Leonard James Jefferson III," he said.

"Mr. Jefferson," I said. "Do you understand why you are a witness in this case?"

"I do." He nodded his head. "I'm here because I'm the owner of the gun used in that Officer Parker murder case."

"Yes, that's right. Now, are you familiar with Officer Morgan Cooper?"

He chuckled. "You might say that."

"How do you know Officer Cooper?"

"He has my neighborhood beat."

"What does that mean?"

"It means he's always rolling up in our neighborhood," he said.

"And did he come to your house one day in September?"

"Yeah. That was some trifling nonsense, man. Some trifling nonsense."

"What happened on that day in September?"

"He come into my house and be looking for some drugs. I mean, he says that he got a tip that we be dealing drugs. I wasn't home, my roommate was, though, and-"

"Objection, hearsay."

"Your honor, his roommate, Antoine Harrington, is available to testify. He's on my witness list if Ms. Moran would like to cross-examine him."

"Objection sustained," he said. "Let Mr. Harrington tell his own story."

"Okay," I said. "Now, did you notice your gun was missing?"

"Yeah, that night, man."

"Objection," Aisha said. "Until I get the testimony of Mr. Harrington, this testimony shouldn't be allowed. I don't have any idea what the time period Mr. Jefferson is referring to, and I don't think he knows, either."

"Sustained."

"Your honor, I'd like to briefly excuse this witness so that Mr. Harrington can testify."

"That's a good idea," he said. Then he addressed Leonard. "Mr. Jefferson, you are excused, but you will be recalled, so don't go very far."

He looked confused, but stood up and left.

"The defense calls Antoine Harrington," I said after Leonard left.

Antoine was called into the courtroom. I hadn't met with him before. He was shorter and pudgier than Leonard. He didn't try to dress up for the occasion, for he was wearing jeans and a t-shirt. His head was shaved but he had a goatee. I hoped and prayed he wasn't stoned.

He sat down at the witness stand and was sworn in. When I looked at him up close, I knew that my prayers weren't answered. His eyes were little slits and he had a shit-eating grin on his face. *Just great.*

"Mr. Harrington," I said, after he was sworn in and I asked his name for the record. "How do you know Mr. Jefferson?"

"He's my homey," he said. "And my roommate."

"Do you know Officer Morgan Cooper?"

"Yeah."

"Did Officer Cooper come into your home in September of last year?"

"Yeah." He nodded. "He did."

"And why did he come into your home?"

"He thought I was a drug dealer. He said he got some tip about drug dealing in my house."

"Did he ask to search your house?"

"Yeah."

"Did you allow him to search your house?"

"Sure, man. I got nothing to hide. There weren't no drugs in the house at that time." Then he laughed. "I mean, not even weed. I told him to go on and search."

"And, to your knowledge, did he search the house?"

"Yeah. He was in the house about a half hour, searching, and he didn't find nothing, so he left."

"Did you tell Mr. Jefferson about this search?"

"Yeah," he said. "When Leonard got home from work, I did."

"Thank you. I have nothing further."

"Ms. Moran, your witness," Judge Wright said.

"Mr. Harrington," Aisha said. "You said that Officer Cooper came to your house to search for drugs and he didn't find anything, is that correct?"

"Yeah, that's right." He grinned and laughed a little.

"Mr. Harrington, are you high right now?"

"Yeah," he said with a little giggle. "I am."

"So you're high right now and have you been busted for drug possession in the past?"

"Yeah." He nodded. "I have, several times. Just for weed, though."

"And is weed something you do frequently?"

"I'm pretty much a wake and baker."

"You're a wake and baker. Yet you expect the jury to believe that Officer Cooper came to your house and didn't find drugs at all?"

"Yeah, that's right. That's right. He didn't find no drugs. Me and Leonard were dry that week. The longest week of my life." He continued to grin and I inwardly groaned.

"And you have no idea when this happened? You just said September."

"Nah. I don't remember what date. I don't have a calendar in my house."

"Then how did you know it was September?"

"Because it wasn't long after Labor Day. It was probably a couple of weeks after Labor Day."

"But you don't know the date?"

"Lady, if somebody asks you when something happened, could you recite the date?"

I smiled. Good point, and it was the point I'd make.

She finally sighed. "I have nothing further."

"I thought so," Antoine said.

"Ms. Ross, any rebuttal questions?"

"No, your honor."

"You may step down."

Antoine left, and then the bailiff brought Leonard back in.

"I'd like to remind Mr. Jefferson that he's still under oath," Judge Wright said. "You may proceed, counselor."

"Now," I said. "On the date Officer Cooper showed up and looked for drugs in your house, did you notice anything missing after he left?"

"Yes," Leonard said.

"And what was missing?"

"My piece was missing, man," he said. "That policeman took my piece."

"By piece, you mean?"

"My gun was missing."

"Did you report it stolen?"

"No."

"And why didn't you report it stolen?"

"Because it don't do no good to make a police report," he said. "Nobody cares and you never get your stuff back no-how so why bother?"

"I have nothing further for this witness."

"Ms. Moran, your witness," Judge Wright said.

Aisha got up and walked over to the witness stand. "Mr. Jefferson, you just told Ms. Ross that the policeman took your piece, is that right?"

"Yeah."

"You didn't actually see Officer Cooper take your gun, did you?"

"Well, no," he said. "But-"

"What made you think Officer Cooper took your gun?"

"He was in my house, looking for drugs, he found no drugs, but he found my piece and took it."

"Again, what proof do you have that Officer Cooper stole your gun?"

Leonard crossed his arms in front of him and looked away.

"I'd like to ask you one more time. What proof do you have that Officer Cooper stole your gun?"

"I guess I don't have no proof," he said.

"In fact, isn't it much more likely that your roommate, Antoine Harrington, stole the gun from you and took it to a pawn shop, where Darnell Williams bought it?"

"Objection," I said. "Calls for speculation."

"Sustained," Judge Wright said. "Ms. Moran, please rephrase the question."

"That's okay, judge," Leonard said. "I'll answer that question, and I'll tell you that Antoine is my homey. He ain't stealing from me. He steals from me and I pop a cap in his ass."

I heard the jury chuckle and I shook my head. Leonard actually wasn't a bad witness.

"I have nothing further for this witness," Aisha said, disgust dripping in her voice.

"Ms. Ross, any rebuttal questions?"

"No, your honor."

"Mr. Jefferson, you may step down."

For the next four hours, I called one witness after another. I called Mark and Cathy Wood, the people having the domestic disturbance that Officer Cooper claimed he was called away from. I called the expert who testified the murder weapon was fitted with a silencer, and that the silencer was used in the murder of Officer Parker. I called Skylar Jett, the working girl at the party on the Gillham Block where Officer Cooper claimed he was called to when he went to break up the fight between the two men in the street. I called Tyler Green, the clerk at the 7-11 that night who testified that he never heard a gunshot, which was important, because it went to show the gun had a silencer that made it hard to hear from across the street. I called Violetta, who testified about how poor Darnell and his family were. I even called the bus driver on Darnell's usual route to testify that Darnell rides the bus every single day.

By the time I was done with these witnesses, it was 5 PM and time to break for the day. I'd timed it all perfectly.

I wanted my star witnesses to testify the next day. I wanted them to be fresh.

I wanted their testimony to have the impact that it deserved.

Forty-One

"How did things go, mate?" Axel asked me that night when I got home. He was chopping vegetables for a salad we would have for dinner, and I was making rice for the stir-fry I was preparing. Rina had a little friend over and they were giggling in front of the television, mooning over Harry Styles.

I actually didn't blame them for mooning over Harry Styles. I seriously thought that kid had it going on and I loved his music. I didn't find his solo music to be very boy-bandish, but actually showed a great deal of maturity. Not that I'd ever admit my secret love of Harry Styles to the girls, but I'd agreed to take them to a Harry Styles concert. I pretended I only wanted to go as a chaperone, but I really wanted to go because I wanted to see him myself.

"It went well," I said. "As well as I could hope. I made mincemeat out of Aisha's first witness, Sally Monroe, who flat-out lied on the stand. And I think I did a pretty decent job of shooting holes in Officer Cooper's lies. Tomorrow will tell the tale, though. It really will."

"Good," he said, humming a tune. "I have some news from our Internal Affairs investigation of Officer Cooper, I guess."

"Oh? Does Cooper know he's under investigation yet?"

"Well, no, because Internal Affairs doesn't want to open up one just yet. They need more evidence. I'm trying, though, mate, to find hard evidence to bring to the investigators, but there seems to be nothing. I know Cooper is corrupt as the day is long, but I think he has too many people protecting him. If I can just get IA on the case, things will start moving, mate. They can subpoena his bank records and mortgage records and all the rest. But they need evidence to even begin."

"A Catch-22," I said. "They won't start an investigation until you have evidence, but you can't get evidence until they start an investigation." I shook my head. "There must be something that can bring this asshole down. He can't get away with all he's done. Can he?"

"As long as all we have on him is circumstantial evidence, he'll get away with it," he said.

I stirred the meat and the veggies for my stir-fry. "I wish Lily Fuller turn him in," I said, referring to the older lady who lived next door to Officer Cooper. She'd be able to tell the investigators that Officer Cooper, at the very least, hangs out with underaged girls. But she also could tell the investigators that Officer Cooper was making child porn at his home. I'd spoken with her twice more after I went to see her the first time, but she refused to speak with me anymore about Cooper. That was frustrating, but I knew why – she was scared.

That was always the issue in dealing with a psychopath – the psychopath will kill anyone in his way. He doesn't have any kind of a conscience, so he doesn't care who he ruins. Because of this, most people are afraid to turn on the psychopath - for good reason.

"But tomorrow will go okay, right, mate?" Axel asked me.

"I think so. I know Darnell will testify, and I'm looking forward to that. He's soft-spoken, intelligent and polite. He makes a very credible witness."

"And your other witness?"

"She still wants to testify," I said. "We'll have to see if she chickens out, though."

Axel hugged me and kissed me on the forehead. "I'll be thinking of you tomorrow, mate. I wish I could be there."

"Well, I know you have your own investigations to do," I said. "So I understand why you're not."

"True, but I want to give you moral support."

"I love that about you."

The next day, I got to the courthouse bright and early. I'd instructed the guards to bring Darnell in early, too, because I wanted to go over his testimony one more time. I knew that I had nothing to fear from Darnell slipping up – he wasn't lying, so it would be difficult for Aisha to try to trip him up. That's what they always say about telling the truth – it's just so much easier than lying, because when you tell the truth, you never have to think about the details. The story just comes flowing out.

I also wanted to speak with my other witness, Ginger the working girl. I had to admit, my heart was pounding as I sat in the courtroom, waiting for Darnell to show. I had no idea if my other witness would show and it made me nervous. She wasn't the most reliable person in the entire world, I had to admit. She tended to drink a bit too much and smoke a little too much dope, which meant that I had no idea if she'd show.

I knew enough people in my career, people who drank and smoked as much as Ginger did, and one thing about them – they weren't reliable at all. I'd ask them to show up in my office at 9 AM and they wouldn't show at all. Then, a week later, at a random time, they would appear at my office. I'd inevitably explain to them that they had to make another appointment if they wanted to speak with me, and they would, then not show for that appointment. And then show up randomly a week after that. And so it went.

I'd never forget one of my first child protection cases. It was a druggie mother who used cocaine while her baby was *in utero*, so the child came out addicted to drugs. The kid was taken away, and the mother showed up to the first hearing seemingly fine, but she failed the drug test. At some point, I got off the case, so I never found out what happened. I knew this was a common occurrence. Another DWI case involved a guy who showed up to his court date so drunk he knocked me over with his breath. Then there was the guy who showed up to his DWI hearing not drunk but only because he took a snort of cocaine to bring him to sobriety. He still had the powder under his nose.

That was the thing about addiction – it made you useless and unreliable. I was lucky when I was an alcoholic because I could function. I knew my limits and knew there was a time and place to get sloshed and a time and a place where I needed to have my wits about me, so I just drank a little to take the edge off.

I hoped and prayed Ginger knew her limits and that she knew just how important this court case was.

I'd actually found that Ginger, of all the people in the world, was valuable to me, because she was the *only* witness to the murder. She didn't see the murder, exactly, but she heard the gunshots and she knew just what time she heard them. She also heard the argument between the two men. She knew Cooper's voice. She heard it in her sleep, she said, and knew the argument involved Cooper and another man whose voice she didn't quite recognize.

"Why didn't you tell me this earlier?" I asked her when she came to my office one day to offer me assistance on my case. "Really?"

I'd been helping Ginger with her various court appearances for over a month when she admitted to me that she heard the gunshots at the Church's restaurant on the night of the murder. "I was afraid," she said. "I was afraid of what Cooper can do to my business. I need to eat, Harper, same as everyone else, and Cooper's been leaving me alone lately. My boss, Vinnie Scarpelli, he got Cooper to lay off me and all the girls. Guess Vinnie agreed to give Cooper a cut, so Cooper has been backing off. I didn't want him coming after me again so I didn't say nothing to you about what I heard."

"But why are you coming to me now with this?"

"Because I decided to get out of town, Harper. I got a job in Los Angeles working in the adult film business so I don't need to deal with Cooper for much longer. I found that out and decided it's time to tell you what I know and how I know it."

"Okay, then, Ginger, tell me how you heard those gunshots and how you knew the exact time you heard them."

"Well, see, I got this regular john. Name's James Whittier, I guess, I don't know. He tells me his name is James Whittier, but I don't really know his actual name. But he likes to break into buildings and go on the roof and get blown. It's his thing. He likes to stare at the moon, on the side of the building, and let me blow him."

"Go on,"I said.

"So, yeah, you've been to that Church's, so you know there's this building right behind the parking lot. It's pretty tall, about six stories tall, and it's just right there. And I was up there with James that night. We were doing our thing, and he had his cell phone out, and he was filming me blowing him. I was going to town, you know, when I heard this loud shouting. It was one guy shouting at another guy, but he was the only one shouting. The other guy, he was real quiet. But I recognized that voice. The shouting voice. I couldn't make out words or nothing, but I recognized that voice, and I knew it was Cooper."

"Okay, so you heard Cooper shouting at another man, but you couldn't hear the other man's voice?"

"Right. I didn't hear what the other man was saying at all. I didn't hear his voice at all. And then I heard a loud pop. It didn't sound quite like a gun shot but was more muffled. It was more like a firecracker. But I heard it. It was plain as day."

"And when did you hear the gunshot?"

"It was at 12:30," she said. "I know that, because, when I heard it, I took James' cell phone away to call the cops. I saw the time on the cell phone. James took it back from me, told me not to call, told me he don't want to get involved in no criminal case. Told me he wanted me to go back to what I was doing and to ignore what I just heard."

"And you ignored it?"

"Yeah. I knew Cooper was involved, so that really made me want to ignore it. Like I said, Cooper was harassing me for months, making it real hard to make money, but he stopped harassing me, so I-" She shrugged. "I didn't want to get involved."

A part of me was angry with her for being so selfish, but a part of me understood. She was right, she had to eat just like everyone else, and Cooper could interfere with her livelihood.

Now, I was waiting for her to show, and I prayed she would. I said a prayer, out loud, right there in the courtroom. Nobody was there yet, so I almost felt I was in a sanctuary.

Darnell came in, dressed in a brown suit and blue tie. I bought him several suits to wear to court, and I had to admit, he cleaned up well. He smiled shyly at me as the guard brought him in. "Guess today is the day, huh?" he asked. "We're going to finish today, right?"

"Right," I said. "At least, that's the plan."

He shook his head. "Didn't think my whole life would come down to one day. One day to make or break the rest of my life. My fate is in your hands, Ms. Ross. You did a good job yesterday. I hope you can do an even better job today."

"I will, Darnell. You're my first witness. You're the most important witness, really."

"Do you think Ms. Ginger will show up today?" he asked anxiously.

I told him Ginger was on the schedule but I didn't want him to hold out hope she'd show. Darnell actually understood that Ginger was an addict, therefore we had a 50/50 shot of her showing, even though she was subpoenaed and would be arrested if she didn't show. I had to hope I did a good enough job putting reasonable doubt in the jury's mind with just my cross-examination of Officer Cooper, along with Darnell himself telling his story, that I could get an acquittal without Ginger.

I didn't know, though. I never knew. The jury could go either way, and it really help that this was a cop-killing case. Juries tended to want to put *somebody* away for cop-killing cases, so they tended to side with the prosecution more often than not in these cases.

Forty-Two

At nine AM, the jury filed in for the second day of trial. The bailiff called everyone to order, and Judge Wright got on the bench. "You may be seated," he said.

I closed my eyes and counted to ten.

"Ms. Ross, are you ready to call your first witness?"

"I am your honor. The defense calls Darnell Williams."

Darnell walked to the witness stand and sat down. The bailiff swore him in, I asked him to recite his name and I started right in with the questions.

"Mr. Williams, you are the defendant in this case," I said. "Where do you work?"

He cleared his throat and, in his characteristically soft voice, said "I work two jobs," he said. "One is at Church's Chicken and one is at a printing shop. Both places are on Gillham Plaza, near where I live."

"You work two jobs," I said. "I'm most interested in your job at Church's Chicken on Gillham Plaza. Take me back to the night of October 13 of last year, please."

"Yes. I was working the closing shift that night, 4 to close. I left school that afternoon and came right to work."

"Four to close. What time would you typically get off work when you close?"

"The restaurant closes at 11 PM, and I can only work one extra hour when I close. I need to be off the clock by midnight."

"By off the clock you mean?"

"I have to punch my time clock at midnight and no later."

"But do you actually quit working at midnight?"

"No, ma'am."

"You stay after hours?"

"Yes, ma'am. I do. I like to take my time cleaning up, and there's a lot to do. It's a lot for one person, cleaning up the restaurant. I have to mop the floor of the restaurant, clean and stock both bathrooms, mop the floor behind the counter, change the grease in the fryers, restock the napkins and paper cups, clean out the pop machine, take out the trash, and clean all the counters and tables in the restaurant."

"That typically takes you more than one hour?"

"Yes, ma'am. I'm a very thorough person, and I like to make sure everything is done 100%. I don't like to do things less than 100%."

"So, after one hour cleaning up, what happens?"

"I clock out and keep on working until my work is done," he said. "I take pride in what I do. My job at Church's might just be a fast-food job, and it might be menial to most people, but my mama always taught me to treat every job as if it's important. That was how I was taught, and that's what I learned."

"On the night of October 13, you closed, right?"

"Yes, I did."

"And how do you make the time go faster?"

"I listen to music on my iPhone," he said. "I have earbuds and plug in my iPhone and listen to tunes while I work."

"And that's what you were doing the night of the murder?"

"Yes, that's what I was doing."

"What time did you leave the restaurant that night?"

"I didn't leave the restaurant," he said. "I never got the chance to leave. I intended to leave, because I have to make the late bus to get home, otherwise I have to walk five miles to my house. But I took out the trash and opened up the gate to the trash cubicle - our trash can is surrounded by four wooden walls – and I saw the body of a man laying there next to the trash can. I also saw the gun." He shook his head. "He was still warm. I knew he was dead, but I tried to revive him anyhow. I gave him mouth-to-mouth and CPR, but he was gone."

"What did you do after you found him?"

"I picked up the gun," he said. "I wasn't thinking. I touched the trigger, too." He shook his head. "I wasn't thinking."

"And then what happened?"

"I went back inside the restaurant to find my cell phone and put on a jacket left by another co-worker, Antwan Jordan. I knew I might have to stand in the parking lot and wait for the cops and it was getting cold. I should've brought a jacket of my own, but it was warm early in the day and I didn't think about it."

"When you went back outside to call the cops, what happened?"

"This policeman came out of nowhere. I showed him the body and told him what happened, but he made me spread on the wall and he patted me down."

"Did he find anything?"

"Yes, he found a bag of cocaine in my jacket pocket."

"Was that cocaine yours?"

"No, ma'am." He shook his head emphatically. "I've never done drugs and I've never possessed them. I've never touched them, not even marijuana. No, ma'am."

"What happened after he found the cocaine?"

"He slapped the cuffs on me and read me my rights. I knew I was being arrested for murdering that man but I didn't know why. When I got to the station, I was told I was arrested because I was in possession of cocaine and they thought I murdered that man because he was an undercover cop. They thought I was trying to deal to the undercover cop. When he tried to arrest me, I shot him dead. That's what they thought."

"Now, let me get this straight. You were standing near the body, your cell phone in your hand, when the policeman came out of nowhere to arrest you?"

"Yes, that is correct."

"Did you murder Officer Parker?"

"No, ma'am. I'd never do something like that, not in a million years."

"When you were brought into the station, did they question you?"

"Yes, ma'am."

"Did you confess to murdering Officer Parker?"

"No, ma'am."

"How long were you questioned?"

"For four hours."

"When did they stop questioning you?"

"After I told them I wanted an attorney. I was hoping I could convince them of my story which is why I didn't ask for an attorney earlier, but that didn't happen, so I had to ask for an attorney."

"I have nothing further."

I sat down and Aisha stood up.

"Ms. Moran, your witness," Judge Wright said.

"Thank you, your honor," Aisha said. "Now, Mr. Williams, you stated you stayed late after your shift at Church's because you want to get everything done right, is that correct?"

"Yes."

"And you listed out the different chores you have to do to close up, correct?"

"Yes."

"And how large is that Church's Chicken?"

"About..." Darnell squinted his left eye and looked to the ceiling. "Probably about 2,000 square feet. I don't know. There's about ten tables out in the lobby and then we have our kitchen, our counter and cash register. I'm really not that good at judging square footage of places."

"About 2,000 square feet. Is it fair to say, then, this restaurant is not particularly large?"

"No, ma'am. It's not large at all. It's a fast food place and not a large one at that."

"And it takes you two full hours to clean and close up?"

"Well, yes, ma'am, but I take my time," he said. "You have to understand, there are seven people living in my two-bedroom apartment with me. I share a bedroom with four of my siblings. Our apartment is probably less than 800 square feet and it's always a mess. I love my mama and my siblings but I need some quiet time to think. That's the main reason why I like to stay later than normal."

I smiled. In my view, Darnell was hitting it out of the park.

"And you testified you had no clue where those drugs came from, correct?"

"Correct."

"Yet they were in your pocket."

"Ma'am, Officer Cooper patted me down. He could've slipped those drugs into my pocket and I never would've known. I was wearing a bulky coat and was in shock when the Officer came up on me. I was in shock because I saw that body and then when that officer made me spread up against the wall, I was really stunned. If he'd have slipped something in my pocket, I wouldn't have felt it."

"And why would a decorated officer do something like that?"

"You'll have to ask him," he said. "I don't know why except he was eager to pin that murder on somebody and I happened to be in the wrong place at the wrong time."

I looked at Aisha and could almost see her wheels turning. She had no tricks to play with Darnell. No gotcha moments, where she could dramatically ask him about a prior statement he made that contradicted what he was saying now. No bringing up prior convictions for forgery or some other dishonest act to show he was a no-good liar. Darnell was clean and she knew it.

"I have nothing further," she said, and she sat down.

"Ms. Ross, do you have anything further for this witness?"

"No, your honor."

"Mr. Williams, you are excused. Ms. Ross, call your next witness."

I closed my eyes and prayed Ginger was in the hallway. I crossed my fingers on my left hand and counted to ten. My heart was thumping and my hands were shaking. "The defense calls Ginger Perry," I said.

The bailiff went out into the hallway and opened the door. I turned around and saw Ginger come through the door. She passed me and leaned down and whispered. "I'm sorry I was late," she said. "I had to get a ride from some loser who didn't show so I had to call one of my johns. Guess I owe him one, huh?"

I smiled. "Guess you do."

Ginger looked as presentable as she could possibly look. She was dressed in a too-tight sweater, jeans that were also too tight and red high heels. But at least she didn't choose a shirt with a plunging neckline paired with a micro-mini. Her wild blonde hair was tied back in a ponytail and she wore less makeup than usual. It was still a lot of makeup, but at least she didn't go with false eyelashes, red lipstick and blue eyeshadow.

She took the stand and the bailiff swore her in. I approached.

"Please state your name for the record."

"Ginger Michelle Perry," she said. "And that's my real name, too. My mama thought my hair would be red, because hers was, so she named me Ginger." She smiled and looked over at the jury. They seemed amused by Ginger.

I decided to lay it all out on the table. No use trying to hide what she was. "Ms. Perry, what is your profession?"

"I'm a working girl."

"By working girl, you mean?"

"I'm in the sex trade. But not for long. I'll be making movies in Los Angeles soon." She nodded. "I mean, I'll still be in the sex trade, but just not on the streets no more."

"Are you familiar with Officer Cooper?"

"Yes, I am," she said. "Too familiar with Officer Cooper, if you know what I mean."

"No, what do you mean?"

"Officer Cooper is what us girls call a free-rider. He expects to get his rides for free and if we don't give them for free, he busts us. Dirty pool if you ask me."

"So, by rides, you mean-"

"Sex acts. Mainly blow jobs but sometimes the other. Sometimes anal, which I always charge extra for, but he expects even that to come free of charge."

Aisha finally stood up. "Objection. I fail to see the relevance of this whole exchange, and, frankly, I find it offensive."

"Ms. Ross, what is the relevance? Please approach."

I approached the bench, and so did Aisha. "I remind you my theory of the case is that Officer Cooper killed Officer Parker because Officer Parker was investigating the murder of a girl Officer Cooper killed, and Officer Cooper wanted to be in charge of the investigation. As such, the fact that he harasses sex workers is relevant."

"That's a stretch, counselor," Judge Wright said. "How do you get from harassing sex workers to murdering a young girl?"

I really didn't have an answer for that.

"But her knowing Officer Cooper is relevant," I said.

"Then stick to what she knows about Officer Cooper without going into the sex acts she does for him and move on, counselor," Judge Wright said.

"I will, your honor."

Aisha sat down and I went back over to Ginger. "Now, Ginger, how long have you known Officer Cooper?"

"For about three years," she said.

"Okay. Now, take me back to the early morning hours of October 13 of last year," I said. "Where were you in those early morning hours?"

"I was with a john, James Whittier, and me and him were on the roof of a building right behind Church's Chicken. It's right next to the parking lot there."

"You were on the roof? What were you doing on the roof?"

"I was blowing him while he filmed me with his iPhone."

"How tall is the roof?"

"It's about five or six stories up."

"And it was dark, correct?"

"Right. The streetlights were turned out and the lights of the restaurant were turned out too."

"Could people on the ground see you?"

"The lights were out and we were high up, so no."

"What happened at around 12:20 that morning?"

"I heard a guy hollering at another guy. Then I realize the guy hollering was Officer Cooper. I don't know who the other guy was 'cause I never heard his voice."

"How long did they argue?"

"For about ten minutes and then I hear a gun shot. Only it didn't sound quite like a gun shot, but it sounded muffled. But I heard it."

"And what time did you hear this gun shot?"

"At 12:30," she said.

"How did you know what time it was when you heard it?"

"I took James' phone out of his hand, 'cause I wanted to call the cops. I looked at his phone and it read 12:30."

"Did you call the police?"

"No."

"And why not?"

"James said no. He says not to get involved in other people's problems. Plus I didn't want Officer Cooper harassing me again. He's been laying off me, in more ways than one."

"So you're sure you heard that gunshot at 12:30, not at 12:50, correct?"

"Right. 12:30, I'm positive of that, 'cause I looked at James' cell phone right when it happened."

"I have nothing further."

I sat down.

"Ms. Moran, your witness."

I sat back and waited for the onslaught.

Forty-Three

"Ms. Perry, or should I call you Ms. Cox, which is ironically one of your street names? Or perhaps I should call you Ms. Ellison or Ms. White or Ms. Chapman or Ms. Peters or Ms. Oliver? What should I call you, because you've gone by every one of those names in the past?"

"What are you getting at?" Ginger demanded. "Yeah, I have aliases, who don't have aliases?" She crossed her arms and looked at Aisha defensively.

"It's just that you seem to have those particular aliases for very specific reasons. Let's see, you opened up a bank account in Ms. Ellison's name. You know she died three years ago, don't you? When you were Ms. White, you married a very elderly gentleman suffering from Alzheimers who thought you were his wife. You tried to get his millions, but his family stopped you, didn't they?"

"Yeah," she said. "So what? What does all this stuff have to do with what I heard that night?"

"Let's see, when you were Ms. Cox, well, that wasn't a big deal, I guess, it's just a funny name you came up with for your street trade. Ginger Cox. How quaint."

"Yeah, because, see, it sounds like the word cocks. Like the word for more than one cock. That's why I took that name and I still don't know what that has to do with what I heard that night."

"And you took the name Ms. Chapman when you were-"

"Running from this wise guy named Sal. He was after me 'cause he thought I stole money from my boss and Sal was my bosses' boss, so he wanted to ice me. I hid out in a motel for a couple of months until Sal was iced himself." She shrugged. "What would you do if you had a wise guy after you? Just stand on the street and let him ice you?"

"And you became Ms. Oliver, who again was a deceased person, because you wanted to get her social security checks."

"Yeah, I did that. She wasn't using that money seeing as she's dead and all."

"And the name Ms. Peters was taken because-"

"Yeah, yeah, yeah, okay. You got me. Listen, I don't have all that schooling you got. I've been on the streets since I was 13 years old. I'm a survivor and the only way I've been a survivor is to do whatever I can to get by. Yeah, I took the name Peters 'cause I found her checkbook on the street and got my boss Vinnie to make an ID so I could cash her checks. She closed her account soon enough."

"But not before you wrote forged checks in the amount of $10,000, checks that cleared. The bank had to pay for that."

"So what? If you ask me, that crooked bank ain't gonna miss that $10,000. Not when it was making millions off ripping people off with shitty mortgages and throwing people out of their homes. Excuse me if I don't shed a single tear for that bank."

"Ms. Perry," Judge Wright said. "I'd like to remind you to not use profanity in this courtroom."

"What did I say?" Ginger asked. She was getting more and more defensive, not that I blamed her. As far as Ginger was concerned, she was doing what she could to survive. She didn't see herself as hurting people. So what if that old man with Alzheimers thought she was his wife? She made him happy, because he thought he had his wife back – shouldn't that be all that matters? She forged a few checks, so what? The woman who lost her checkbook didn't pay for it, the bank did. The bank never should've cleared the checks because the woman reported that checkbook stolen right away. The bank had to pay for those checks, but, as Ginger saw it, the bank was a bad actor so they deserved what they got. And she took the identity of a dead person – the government had to pay for that mistake, because she received social security checks made out in that person's name.

I knew Ginger's mindset and I had a ton of sympathy for her. She was the same as most of my clients – she didn't have skills to legitimately make it so she grifted and sold her body. She thought was that as long as nobody is really getting hurt, people should leave her alone. I didn't agree with her thinking – I thought forgery and identity theft were wrong, period, but it could've been worse. She could've taken the identity of an alive person which would've legitimately hurt somebody who couldn't afford it.

"Ms. Perry, you used a profane word to describe the mortgages made by that bank," Judge Wright reminded her.

"Oh, I'm sorry. Crappy mortgages, is that better?"

I heard members of the jury laugh. I hoped they were getting a kick out of her. I certainly was.

"Marginally," Judge Wright said, realizing he wouldn't necessarily rein Ginger in. He could very well hold Ginger in contempt for her language, but I got the feeling he would let her go. Everyone in the courtroom was an adult. The profane language wasn't something that hadn't been heard before.

"Well," Aisha said, desperately trying to retake control of the proceedings. "Now that we've gone through all the times when you were deceitful, let's get to the morning at hand, shall we?"

"Sure," Ginger said. "That's why I'm here. I didn't think I was coming here to be lectured by some high falutin' lawyer. I'd sure like to find a surgeon who could take that stick out of your butt."

At that, I heard more members of the jury laugh and even saw Judge Wright work to suppress a smile before he came down hard on her. "Ms. Perry, I'd like to remind you to not use profanity and please refrain from personal attacks on Ms. Moran. The next time you get out of line, I will have no choice but hold you in contempt."

She grimaced and looked at the judge. "Can I talk to my lawyer for just a second?"

"Ms. Perry, you are not represented by counsel in this proceeding."

"I'm not?" She looked bewildered. "But I thought Harper was my lawyer."

"You are a witness," Judge Wright said. "Witnesses are not represented by counsel. But I can let you briefly confer with Ms. Ross if that's what you're asking for."

"Thank you," she said, motioning me to the stand.

I went up and leaned down to hear her. "Harper, what is contempt?" she asked me.

"It's when the judge throws you in jail or fines you for getting out of line," I said. "Please try to behave."

She nodded. "I will."

I sat back down and motioned for Aisha to proceed.

"Okay, Ms. Perry," she said. "Now, you claim that on the morning of October 13 of last year you were with a client, is that correct?"

"No. I wasn't with a client. I was with a john."

"That's what I meant by client."

"We never use that term, client," she said. "That's why I didn't know what you were talking about."

"Okay, then," Aisha said, admitting defeat. Ginger was getting the best of her, I could tell – Aisha was showing frustration on her face. "You were with a john on the roof of the building right behind Church's Chicken, correct?"

"Yeah, that's right. That's where we were."

"And that building was closed, wasn't it?"

"Yeah. We broke in. James is real good at picking locks."

"Okay, so I guess we need to add trespassing to your list of transgressions," she said.

"We weren't trespassing," she said. "We were borrowing their roof, that's all. We weren't hurting nobody."

"You broke into a building after hours and went on the premises. That's the very definition of trespassing."

"But we weren't hurting nobody. We weren't hurting a thing."

"Under the law-" Aisha shook her head and took a deep breath. She *was* a bit of a tight-ass, come to think of it, and a girl like Ginger was her worst nightmare. "Never mind. So you were on the roof of the building when you heard a gun shot. Is that correct?"

"Yeah, that's correct."

"Let me back up here. Before the gunshot, you heard a man shouting, is that right?"

"Yeah."

"And you knew this voice belonged to Officer Cooper, is that right?"

"Yeah."

At that, Aisha got out the photo of the restaurant. She had shown this photo earlier to the jury to show where the body was. She pointed to the tall building that abutted the parking lot. "So," she said, "this is where you were, correct?"

"Yeah. That's where we were."

"So, you were some five stories above the parking lot and some fifty yards away from the dumpster where Officer Parker was found, yet you recognized a voice from that far away. Is that what you're telling the jury?"

"Yeah. Listen, I know Officer Cooper's voice. I hear it in my sleep. You know how they say a mother can tell her baby's cries when the baby is with fifty other babies? Well, I could tell Officer Cooper's voice like that. He could be with fifty other cops and I'd recognize his voice." She visibly cringed.

"So you're telling the jury you can recognize Officer Cooper's voice from fifty yards away and five stories up?"

"Yeah but that building wasn't no fifty yards away from that dumpster. More like 25 yards. Fifty yards is half the length of a football field."

At that, Aisha took the picture over to the jury and pointed to the building in question. "I'll let the jury determine how far away that building was from the dumpster."

"Go ahead," Ginger said. "But the dumpster wasn't no fifty yards away."

"Moving on," Aisha said with exasperation dripping from her voice. "Now, you heard the gunshot precisely at 12:30, is that right?"

"Yeah. I heard the gunshot, took James' phone out of his hand to call the cops, and saw the time. It clearly said 12:30."

"Were you under the influence that night, Ms. Perry?"

"No. I drank some boxed wine at a party earlier down the street, but I wasn't three sheets to the wind or nothing."

"Were you taking drugs?"

"I smoked a little weed, so what?"

"When did you drink that boxed wine?"

"I got out of that party around midnight," she said. "And I was drinking up until then."

"And when did you start drinking that night?"

"I guess at 10. I had three cups of wine from 10 to midnight. Big whoop."

"And when did you smoke the weed?"

"At the party."

"When did you get to the party?"

"At 10. I told you that."

"No, you didn't tell me that. You said you started drinking at 10."

"That means I got to the party at 10." Ginger rolled her eyes. She wasn't on Aisha's wavelength and Aisha definitely wasn't on hers. They were two ships passing in the night. "I always start drinking right when I get to the party. What, you think I got to the party at 9 or something and didn't start drinking until 10?"

"So, you started to smoke marijuana at 10, then?"

"Yeah."

"And how much marijuana did you smoke?"

"How am I supposed to know? They had a joint passing around in a circle and I took a hit every time it got to me. Share and share alike, you know?"

"And you have no idea how many times the marijuana cigarette was passed to you that night?"

At that, Ginger started to giggle.

"Ms. Perry, what is so funny?" Aisha demanded.

"Marijuana cigarette," she said before completely cracking up laughing. "Oh, my God, I've never heard it called that." She shook her head. "You're just too much."

"Judge Wright," Aisha said. "Can you please sanction this witness or something?"

Judge Wright was laughing, too, so I figured he didn't do much about Ginger's ad libs for the time being. He quickly composed himself and turned to Ginger. "Ms. Perry, please stick to answering Ms. Moran's questions."

Ginger crossed her arms and glared at Aisha. "Okay. What was the question again?"

"The question was, how many times did the-" She took a deep breath. "Joint get passed to you that night?"

Ginger shrugged her shoulders. "I guess five or six, I guess."

"So you're telling the jury you had three cups of wine and five or six hits of marijuana between the hours of 10 and midnight on the night of October 12, is that correct?"

"That about tells the story."

"I see." She nodded her head knowingly, thinking the point was no doubt made. "Now, it seems you don't particularly care for Officer Cooper, is that fair to say?"

"Yeah. That's fair to say, yes it is."

"In fact, you loathe him, isn't that right?"

"Well, yeah. I gotta eat, you know, and when I have to give him freebies all the time, I can't get to paying johns as much. It's not fair what he does. He should have to pay for it same as everybody else but every time I try to make him pay, he busts me. I can't win."

"So is it fair to say you'd do anything to make him stop harassing you on the street?"

"Yeah," she said. "That's fair."

"So, you would even, say, make a false accusation against him that would send him to prison, isn't that right?"

She shook her head. "No, that's not right. I don't care how much of a slime he is to me and the other girls. I wouldn't lie so he'd go to prison for something he didn't do. I wouldn't do that."

For my money, I thought Ginger was coming off as a credible witness. She was authentic, that was for sure.

"Oh, you wouldn't? Just think how much more money you could make if Officer Cooper isn't around to arrest you all the time. Fines, legal fees and all the rest adds up after awhile, don't they? Plus the downtime when you're in jail and in court and not working the streets. I'd think your business would be much better if Officer Cooper were off the streets, don't you?"

"Yeah, I guess, but I don't have to pay for a lawyer. Harper's my lawyer and she represents me for free."

I bit my lower lip and tried to give Ginger the *cool it* look, but the damage was done. Yes, I represented Ginger for free. She did me a huge favor in coming here and she was putting her life in danger by testifying. It seemed to be the least I could do, but I knew Aisha would twist our arrangement like a pretzel.

I was right.

"Oh, Ms. Ross represents you for free, how interesting." She nodded and smiled. "How interesting. What were the terms of your agreement with Ms. Ross? She represents you for free in exchange for you making up lies about what you heard on the night of the murder?"

I rose to my feet. "I object to that characterization. It's frankly offensive for Ms. Moran to insinuate that I suborn perjury let alone come right out and say it. Ms. Moran should know me better than that."

"Sustained," Judge Wright said. "Ms. Ross is correct, Ms. Moran. You should know better than to impugn and slander a fellow member of the Bar in open court." Judge Wright glared at Aisha and took a sip of water. "But you may continue."

"I apologize to Ms. Ross," Aisha said sweetly.

I knew her game. She threw me under the bus because she wanted the insinuation out there. She wanted the jury to suspect Ginger and I had a deal for her to lie on the stand for me. It was bullshit but Aisha played dirty sometimes.

"Let me rephrase my earlier question. What were the terms of your agreement with Ms. Ross?"

She shrugged. "I get in trouble and she gets me out of trouble for free. She said it was worth it to make sure I testify for her client. But she never asked me to lie. Harper wouldn't do that. She's a good egg."

Aisha finally just shook her head. "I have nothing further for this witness," she said and sat down.

"Ms. Ross, any rebuttal?"

I briefly considered asking Ginger a few rehabilitation questions, but I thought anything I asked would make things worse. "No, your honor."

"Ms. Perry, you may step down."

She nodded. She walked past my table and whispered to me. "How did I do?" she asked.

I gave her the thumbs up and she smiled as she sashayed out the door.

I looked over at the jury, and saw that, at the very least, they were entertained by Ginger. I had no clue if that was a good sign or not. It was a good thing that Ginger kept their interest. Then again, they might've thought she was a flake who wanted free legal representation to lie on the stand in exchange for my legal services.

Aisha certainly did an excellent job in showing that Ginger would do almost anything for money.

Forty-Four

We took our break and Aisha and I came back to give our closing arguments. This was my chance to shine. It was my chance to take all the pieces of the puzzle and put them all together in a neat package. My closing argument could make or break my case, so I had to make sure it was stellar. The last thing I wanted was for Darnell to go to prison, possibly even Death Row, because of something Officer Cooper did.

Aisha was first, of course. The prosecutor always went first. She had the option to do all of her closing arguments at once, or split it up – five minutes before I went, and five minutes after. If I were her, I'd definitely choose to split my time, because that way the jury can you see you first and last – the primacy and the recency effect would be in play. The primacy and the recency effect was that people remember the last thing they heard better than the things they heard before it and recall the first thing they heard more than they recall the middle things. In enabling the prosecutor to split up her argument, both effects work in tangent.

"Ladies and gentlemen of the jury," Aisha said. "You heard the evidence presented. You heard the defendant, Darnell Williams, is a known drug dealer."

I rolled my eyes when she said that. Just because she got Sally on the stand to lie about Darnell bragging about dealing drugs meant Aisha could characterize Darnell as a "known drug dealer" in her closing arguments. I'd have to hammer away again about how Sally was not a trustworthy witness, to say the least.

"A known drug dealer," Aisha continued. "He was bragging to his boss at Church's about how he could quit his job and move his brothers and sisters to a big apartment on The Plaza. Counsel for the defendant told you that Mr. Williams had big dreams. He had big dreams, alright – big dreams of selling enough drugs that he'd never have to dump another piece of chicken into a deep fryer again. Those were his dreams."

"Do you know what would stand in the way of those dreams? I'll tell you what would stand in the way of those dreams – going to prison. That's what would kill the defendant's dreams bigger than the state of Texas. And Mr. Williams wouldn't go to prison. He couldn't have that. So when Mr. Williams tried to sell drugs to Officer Parker in the dark parking lot of a closed chicken restaurant and Officer Parker showed him his badge, Mr. Williams saw his dreams go up in smoke. He walked out to the parking lot with a loaded pistol before he went to see Officer Parker and then shot him in cold blood."

"And how do I know Mr. Williams shot Officer Parker in cold blood after attempting to sell drugs to the decorated officer? The evidence shows this is what happened. Mr. Williams was standing next to the body. The murder weapon had Mr. Williams' prints on it including on the trigger. And when Officer Cooper asked Mr. Williams to get up against the wall to frisk him, the officer found a quarter kilo of cocaine in Mr. Williams' right coat pocket. A quarter kilo of cocaine. That has a street value of $12,000 ladies and gentlemen. Mr. Williams was looking for a big payday out of Officer Parker and didn't get it – he was threatened with arrest instead. So he killed Officer Parker in cold blood."

"Oh, Ms. Ross, the defendant's counsel, gamely tried to show that something else happened in that parking lot. She came up with this rather bizarre theory that Officer Cooper himself killed Officer

Parker for some unknown reason. She tried to show you that Officer Cooper was in the house of Leonard Jefferson before Leonard Jefferson's gun went missing, as if that's supposed to mean anything. Never mind the fact that Leonard Jefferson's roommate was shown to be a habitual drug user and a known criminal who is, in his own words, a 'wake and baker.' For my money, the roommate would be the much more likely candidate to have taken Leonard Jefferson's gun than Officer Cooper." She pointed at some of the jury members. "Occam's Razor, ladies and gentlemen. Occam's Razor. Usually the simplest answer is the right one, and in this case, the simple and logical answer is that Mr. Jefferson's own roommate stole that gun and pawned it to buy more marijuana. From there, it's simple – Mr. Williams bought the gun in a pawn shop and used it to kill Officer Parker."

"And then Ms. Ross brought in this ridiculous witness, Ginger Perry, who has been known by many different names because she's lived a life of grift and selling her body to the highest bidder. She was shown to have animus towards Officer Cooper – she admitted he harasses her and ends up costing her a lot of money because he's always arresting her. That means she has to pay a lawyer and pay court costs and fines, plus bail money to get out of jail all the time. Not to mention these arrests cause her downtime, time where she could be making money instead of dealing with the legal system."

"Oh, wait, wait, wait," she said, pointing her finger at the ceiling. "I did say she has to pay a lawyer, didn't I? My mistake. You see, Ginger doesn't pay a lawyer at all. She has Ms. Ross represent her for free." She put her finger to her cheek and shook her head. "Let's see here....Ginger is represented for free by Ms. Ross, and then Ginger helps out Ms. Ross by testifying in her case. Looks like a quid pro quo, and Ginger even admitted it was because Ginger admitted Ms. Ross represents her in exchange for her testimony. Now I won't say Ginger has the incentive to lie under this arrangement but you can draw your own conclusions."

"Plus, if Ginger lies and implicates Officer Cooper she gets Officer Cooper out of her hair. Everybody wins ladies and gentlemen! Everybody wins!" She clapped her hands and spread her arms out over her head.

"Everybody wins," she said in a more somber voice. "But the justice system and your community. I ask you to look at the evidence, which is incontrovertible, and find the Defendant guilty of killing a decorated and loyal cop in cold blood. And I urge you to do what's right and sentence the Defendant to the ultimate punishment, lethal injection. You must not let Mr. Williams get away with killing a police officer. If you send Mr. Williams to prison, you'll do your community a huge favor by getting one more murderer off the street. Thank you very much."

She sat down.

"Ms. Ross," Judge Wright said. "Your closing argument."

As I sat there for a few minutes, I remembered a *Twilight Zone* episode called "One for the Angels." A huckster salesman had to convince Death not to take a little girl so he had to give the pitch of his life to save her.

I'd have to give the pitch of my life to save Darnell.

"I'm ready, your honor," I said.

And I walked to the jury box.

Forty-Five

"Ladies and gentlemen of the jury," I said. "You heard what the prosecutor said about my client but let's take her points one by one, shall we? First of all, Ms. Moran talked about how Sally Monroe, Mr. Williams' boss, said my client, Mr. Williams, was a drug dealer because supposedly he bragged to her about all the money he was making in the drug trade. Well, let me remind you how much Ms. Monroe was shown to be lying. Not shading the truth. Not telling half-truths. Not prevaricating. No, she was straight-up lying. As in making it up as she goes along. She said Darnell was a terrible worker and then admitted on cross that he gets raises and he has had nothing but excellent reviews. She said she didn't like Mr. Williams to close because he does a terrible job cleaning up, but then on cross-examination admitted she had Mr. Williams close quite a bit. But the real kicker is that she said Mr. Williams admitted he deals drugs and is making all this money."

"Ladies and gentlemen, my client, Mr. Williams, doesn't even have a car. You heard him testify that he rides the bus to his job, and, if he can't make the late bus, he ends up walking five miles to his home. You heard the testimony of the bus driver, Suzanne Walker, who testified that Mr. Williams rides her bus regularly. You heard Mr. Williams testify that he lives in a two-bedroom apartment he shares with four of his siblings and his mother. His Aunt Violetta confirmed this. You heard all that. Now, I ask you - what kind of self-respecting drug dealer rides the bus everywhere? If Mr. Williams is making all this money, you'd think he could buy a car. You'd think a successful drug dealer wouldn't be share a bedroom with four siblings."

"Now let me take you back to the facts of the case. The undisputed facts of the case. My client was caught standing next to the body on the ground, his cell phone in his hand. Just standing there. Not trying to run. Just standing there." I shook my head. "Ms. Moran would have you believe that my client had dreams of being this big-time drug dealer so he killed Officer Parker in cold blood, but if that were so, don't you think Mr. Williams would've high-tailed it out of there? You've seen my client – he's a wiry 18-year-old boy in excellent shape. Plays basketball, runs. He could've outrun the police if he tried. Or he would've hid in the bushes, or something, anything, other than stand next to the body with his cell phone in his hand. I mean, really – the prosecutor talked to you about Occam's Razor, and I'll use that same theory. What is more logical and makes more sense – a guilty kid would run after he killed somebody, or a guilty kid would stand there with his cell phone in his hand? Seriously?"

"And then there's the issue of the silencer. You heard my expert testify the murder weapon had a silencer on it to make the noise softer. The silencer doesn't work like it does in the movies, in that the gun is still pretty loud but not as loud as a regular gun. But when the weapon was recovered, there was no silencer on it and no silencer found on the premises. Again I remind you my client was standing next to the body, so when could he have disposed of a silencer?"

"And let me take you back to Officer Cooper's testimony. You remember what he was saying on the stand – that, right before he allegedly heard a gunshot, he was attending a disturbance on Gillham Road. Then he mysteriously disappears for a good 25 minutes. He claims he was going down the road to check on another disturbance, but lo and behold, there's nobody to investigate anymore. Then he claimed he walked around for all of ten minutes, looking for two men, one of whom was holding the other at gunpoint. Ten minutes he's looking for an armed suspect. Then he gives up and goes back to the original disturbance. Does that make any damned sense that an officer would give up looking for an armed suspect after 10 minutes? If it doesn't make sense to you, you're not alone, because it makes no sense to me, either."

"And guess what restaurant is close to 3209 Gillham, where Officer Cooper was attending to that disturbance, and from where he disappeared for about 25 minutes. That's right, Church's Chicken. That restaurant is a three-minute walk from 3209 Gillham, ladies and gentlemen."

"So, here's how it all went down. Officer Cooper is at 3209 Gillham Road. He's having a problem with Officer Parker because Officer Parker is investigating the murder of a young girl, Alaina Morosky, and Officer Cooper doesn't want him to investigate this murder because he did it. Officer Cooper gets a call from his dirty dispatcher, who knows Officer Cooper wants to get rid of Officer Parker, and his dispatcher tells him Officer Parker is conveniently around the corner in a deserted chicken restaurant parking lot. Officer Cooper runs over to the restaurant, confronts Officer Parker, kills him and then runs back to 3209 Gillham Road. Then he goes over to the 7-11, makes sure he's on surveillance, makes sure his partner is in the store and then runs back over to Church's, claiming he heard a gun shot. He sees my client, makes him spread against the wall, plants drugs on him and arrests him for a murder he committed."

"You might think this is a tall tale, ladies and gentlemen, and that Officer Cooper wouldn't do that. But remember one thing – there was a witness to this whole altercation. Ginger Perry. She testified she heard the gunshot at 12:30, not 12:50, as Officer Cooper claimed on the stand. 12:30 was when Officer Cooper was conveniently missing from the 3209 Gillham Road disturbance. She testified she heard Officer Cooper yelling at somebody in the Church's parking lot. She testified she heard Officer Cooper yelling and then heard the gunshot at 12:30 AM."

"She heard a gunshot at 12:30 AM. Officer Cooper was adamant, adamant that he heard the gunshot at 12:50 AM. Somebody is lying, and the person lying is Officer Cooper. The other facts of the case point to Officer Cooper being the most likely liar in this situation, not my client. Yes, she's a working girl, and yes, she's done shady things for money, like forgery and identity theft. She's been getting by on the streets since she was 13 years old and she has to eat just like everyone else. Nobody has ever gotten hurt in her schemes. Two of her schemes involved stealing the identity of dead people, one involved forging a check the bank had to pay for and one scheme involved posing as a dead wife of an Alzheimer's patient. Nobody got hurt except that large bank, and Ginger felt like Robin Hood in that case, because she was stealing from the rich and greedy and giving to the poor."

"Yes, she's done shady things, but that doesn't mean she's lying in this case because she's not. She's not, and there's no way I'd put her on the stand if she were."

"Now, let me finally just tell you about the concept of Reasonable Doubt, because if you have reasonable doubt that my client did not murder Officer Parker and did not wittingly possess drugs, you must acquit. If you get this wrong, you'll be sending an innocent 18-year-old African-American boy to his death. That's serious business, folks. I always tell my juries that reasonable doubt doesn't mean you have to be 100% sure my client didn't do it before you vote to acquit. No, it just means you have doubt that he's guilty. It means that, if you have a nagging inner voice telling you there's the possibility Mr. Williams didn't do it, you must acquit. It means that, if you are in the jury room, talking with the other jurors, and you go over the evidence, and you say to your fellow jury members that 'there's the strong possibility he committed this crime but also a strong possibility he didn't,' you must acquit. You must in that case, because you have reasonable doubt."

"Thank you ladies and gentlemen for your valuable time and service. I look forward to hearing your verdict of not guilty."

At that, I sat down.

"Ms. Moran, do you have any rebuttal closing argument?" Judge Wright asked

"No, your honor."

"Okay," Judge Wright said. He then proceeded to give jury instructions and sent the jury off to deliberate.

I closed my eyes as the jury filed out of the box to deliberate.

I felt sick, because I always did whenever the jury went out, but I did the best I could. There wasn't much more I could do.

Darnell's fate was in their hands.

Forty-Six

I sat there with Darnell at the defense table, waiting for the jury to come back. I knew they would take awhile yet I was always so nervous waiting for them to come back. It was the most terrifying moments of my life, typically.

But it was made lighter by the appearance of Darnell's mother, Anita. She showed up in the empty courtroom while Darnell and I were sitting at the table and she called to Darnell.

"Darnell my baby," she said, and Darnell spun around.

"Mama?" he said and then stood up.

Anita walked through the little gate that separated the court area from the audience area, and I motioned to the guard, looking like he wanted to force Anita out of there, to stop. I got up and spoke with the guard. "Please let Anita see her son. She hasn't seen him in months because she's been recovering from a stroke. Please."

The guard nodded but kept his eye on Anita and Darnell.

Darnell was embracing his mother and sobbing like a little kid.

"There, there, Darnell," Anita said. "Mama's here. Mama's here. You're a good boy, and I know you are innocent. Lord, I've been praying on you every single night. Praying and praying and praying. I've got my whole church praying, Darnell, for you. I know you're going to beat this down, because I know you are innocent."

"Mama, what if that jury comes back that I'm guilty. What then? Will you still love me, mama? Will you come and see me in prison?"

"Shhhh," she said. "Don't you worry about that. I'm telling you you're going to beat this thing down. You are. But, yes, I'll always love you. You will always be my little boy. Okay?"

Darnell just nodded.

"I heard from MIT," she said, "I got that envelope right over there, in fact, from them. Let me go and get it."

Anita went into the audience area where she had her purse and a large manila envelope. I smiled as I recognized the large manila envelope was an excellent sign. It was my understanding that, when a school rejects you, you get a letter in a small envelope. But when they accept you, you get a large manila envelope, because the envelope contains a welcome packet of some sort. That was how it always worked for me, both for undergrad and law school.

She brought in the envelope, and she handed it to Darnell. "Open it," she said. "Let me see what it says."

He looked at the envelope for several minutes. He ran his hand over the back of the envelope and gripped it tightly. "Ms. Ross," he said to me. "Come over here while I open this letter."

I walked over to him and he handed me the envelope. "Open it," he asked. "Please. I can't look. I can't be disappointed again. I've had too many disappointments in my life."

I nodded and carefully opened the letter and read aloud.

"Dear Mr. Williams," I started. "We have reviewed your application, your test scores and your essay, and it is with great pleasure that we would like to extend an invitation to attend the Massachusetts Institute of Technology." I looked up and Darnell's eyes were filled to the brim with tears.

Anita whooped loudly. "Praise the Lord, praise the Lord," she said. "I knew it, I knew it. My boy will be a nuclear engineer. He'll follow his dream."

Darnell and Anita embraced each other tightly. "Go on, Ms. Ross," he said. "Go on with the rest of the letter."

I nodded. "Enclosed with this letter is a welcome packet that we would like for you to review before you attend orientation on August 12. Please allow us to congratulate you for all the hard work you put in to achieve your dream, and we know you will be a successful addition to our campus."

I took a deep breath, knowing this just made the stakes that much higher. It was one thing to go to prison. It was quite another knowing you are abandoning your dream and your dream was real.

"So, I guess MIT doesn't know about this court case," I said. "Either that, or they know Darnell is innocent until proven guilty. Okay, Darnell, let's-"

Darnell sat down. "Now I have something to look forward to," he said. "And something to deeply regret if that jury comes back finding me guilty. Something to lose." He looked at his mother. "I mean, of course I have something to lose – my family. But not getting to attend MIT would be-" He shook his head. "I can't even think about it."

"Darnell," I said. "You're half a semester behind right now, you can make it up in the summer, right?"

He nodded. "I'll have to," he said. "I can't let MIT go."

"Good. Now, don't think about that jury finding you guilty. We'll cross that bridge if we come to it, which we hopefully won't."

At some point, the bailiff came to the courtroom. "The jury is deadlocked," he said. "So the judge will send them home for the evening. We'll call you when there's a verdict."

I nodded. "Okay." I turned to Darnell. "Just go to your cell and pray," I said. "Pray hard."

"I will."

Anita hugged me. "Thank you for representing my boy," she said. "I know you did a good job. I wish I could've been here but I've been trying to reduce my stress and listening to people lie about my son would've sent my blood pressure through the roof."

"Oh, I know, I know. Don't worry, Ms. Williams. We'll get them."

I gathered my things and walked out the door hoping and praying my words were true. We had to get them. The jury had to find him innocent.

They just had to.

Forty-Seven

"Mate," Axel said when I got home. He was waiting for me on the porch. "I think I finally found a way to bring down that dirty Officer Cooper."

"Oh?" I asked him. "Come in the house and tell me. At the very least, if that jury finds Darnell guilty, and we can show for sure that Cooper did it, I can ask for a new trial. Hopefully it won't come to that, though. The kid got into MIT for the fall semester. He has to be found not guilty. He just has to be."

"Okay, here we go," he said. "I've been digging around Cooper and Facinelli's financial records. I got your girl, Anna, to find me these records. I'm seeing many off-shore accounts off the books. Nobody knows about these accounts. These two cops have millions in these off-shore accounts. I've been asking around the streets and I've discovered these two cops are running quite a racket. They're getting kickbacks from everyone on their beat. Every pimp, every drug dealer, every mobster, every illegal bookie on their beat gives them a cut in exchange for looking the other way. I've been shaking everybody down and nobody wants to talk. They all want their train to keep on running down the tracks so they won't testify. And these financial records were obtained illegally, so I can't use them to convince Internal Affairs to investigate Cooper."

"We're getting closer," I said. "But how can we get around the fact these people won't testify?"

He started to laugh. "I caught a break," he said. "That lady who lives next door to Officer Cooper, Lily Fuller? The one who told you she wouldn't testify? Well, she will now. She visited me today while you were in court and told me she wants to go to Internal Affairs to give her story. That'll give Internal Affairs probable cause to search that bastard's home, and, if they find something, they'll open a formal investigation."

I smiled. This was potentially good news, but I never liked to get my hopes up. "Why does she suddenly want to testify? I don't understand."

"She apparently went to the doctor and found out she has advanced pancreatic cancer. She has maybe a month to live. She's got nothing to lose now. She also said she's made a bucket list and getting Cooper is on the top of this list."

I had to laugh. Not because poor Lily Fuller was dying but that she made a bucket list and put Cooper on top. Seeing Cooper fry for the lives he destroyed and the people he killed was at the very top of my list, too. "Okay, so they search the house and find something related to Alaina. Maybe a hair, maybe an article of clothing. Then what?"

"Then they can investigate, and mate, get this. Anna also tracked down Facinelli's long-lost identical twin brother. Here's what I'll suggest Internal Affairs do. They get the twin brother to pose as Facinelli. He'll wear a wire and get Cooper talking about his crimes. Then we'll have positive proof to nail him completely."

I laughed. "This sounds very Hollywood, but if it works, I'll be the happiest person in the world. Seriously. That psychopath needs to fry somehow. Any way we can do that, I'll be all for."

The next day, I went to work, my mind on Darnell and on the plan Axel and I came up with. I had no idea if Luca Facinelli, the identical twin brother of Officer Salvatore Facinelli, would be willing to wear a wire to nail Cooper. First things first, though – we had to get the search warrant so Internal Affairs could investigate Cooper.

"How did it go?" Tammy asked when she came to see me.

"I think it went great," I said. "But the jury has been deliberating for 8 hours, so I don't know. They deliberated for four hours yesterday – they stayed and deliberated until 8 last night. They got into the jury room today at 9 and it's now 2, so that's another four hours of deliberation if you include lunch. Darnell is on pins and needles. He got accepted to MIT, so there's a lot riding on this jury verdict. There was a lot riding on it, anyhow, but now there really is."

"You think Officer Cooper is a psychopath?"

"Yep. 100%. All the evidence points to him killing Officer Parker because Officer Parker was investigating the murder of Alaina Morosky. Officer Cooper killed her, too. Then he arrested Stephen for Alaina's murder, with zero evidence, and had Stephen killed so the case could be closed." I shook my head. "He's a bad dude," I said. "A very bad dude."

"That's something, coming from you, saying somebody is a bad dude. Your heart is always bleeding for your criminals."

"That's because my criminals, as you call them, usually are innocent or have had heartbreaking lives. Who knows, I guess. Maybe Cooper has an excuse for his behavior. Maybe he was abused growing up. I don't know. But he's hurt far too many people I care about and he's going to pay. End of story."

"I hope you can get him. If he really did all you say, he needs to be off the street, at the very least."

"Yeah. At the very least. Hopefully he'll end up behind bars."

I went home that evening still not sure about Darnell's fate. What was taking that jury so long? I was getting little messages that Pearl was fielding from the court about the jury wanting to have another look at the picture of the restaurant – the one that showed the tall building right behind its parking lot. That cheered me because it showed they were taking Ginger's testimony seriously. Other messages were that the jury asked for the coroner's report. I had no idea why they asked for that. Still another report was that they asked for my ballistics expert analysis that showed a silencer was on the gun when the gun was shot.

I didn't know if these requests were good or bad. All I knew was that the waiting on this case was making me literally sick.

I got home and played video games with my two girls, and played fetch with Stella and Sue, but I wasn't into the games at all. However, I had to take my mind off Darnell's case, because there wasn't a thing that could be done about it.

I got a phone call at 9 that night to tell me the jury went home and would return in the morning.

Dammit, the verdict on the OJ Simpson case, with all those months worth of evidence, took four hours. Four hours. What was taking *this* jury so long?

I tossed and turned that night, worried the jury would hang. I imagined my blonde lady, the one who passionately spoke about Black Lives Matter, was voting to acquit and maybe the rest were voting guilty. I imagined her like Henry Fonda in the movie *Twelve Angry Men,* making arguments and trying to convince the others my client wasn't guilty. Maybe she was winning them over, one by one, but there was still a holdout. Maybe there was a racist guy or woman who wouldn't vote "not guilty" no matter what happened. Maybe there was a man or woman who would never vote "not guilty" because they were blinded by the victim being a cop and were determined to make *somebody* pay - might as well be my client. Maybe he or she couldn't be convinced and the jury would hang and I'd have to try the case again.

The good news was, by the time the trial came up again, I'd hopefully have all the evidence I'd need to show Cooper killed Parker and maybe Darnell would be set free after all.

But Darnell would miss his chance to go to MIT. They wouldn't hold a place for him – not a prestigious university like that. No way. Darnell wouldn't realize his dream. All because of that goddamned rat-bastard Cooper.

That bastard would fry for this if it was the last thing I did.

I went to work the next day, feeling more and more depressed. The jury would hang. I knew it. It wasn't a conviction, at least, but it wasn't an acquittal. Darnell would remain in jail for another six months to await another trial and maybe his mother would go back into the hospital because of all the stress. Maybe Lily Fuller would die before she could testify before the Internal Affairs Department and we'd never get the chance to bring Cooper down. Maybe when I tried Darnell's case again, the prosecutor would be better prepared, and the jury would convict.

I did all I could for this case. All I possibly could. If it still wasn't enough, could I ever win this case? If the jury hangs and the prosecutor offers LWOP, should I encourage Darnell to take it? Better that than to see him get the Death Penalty.

Then, at 5 PM, right before I prepared to go home for the day, the call came in.

The jury made a decision.

Forty-Eight

I raced down to the courthouse and sped up the steps, not even waiting for the elevator. Finally. There was a decision. That meant either a conviction or an acquittal, not a hung jury. My heart was pounding out of my chest.

Darnell was already there looking for me. He was dressed in a dark green suit with a white shirt underneath it and no tie. His pants were slightly too long. He smiled as I walked through the door and sat in the seat next to him. I grabbed his hand and squeezed.

The jury was sitting in the box waiting for everybody to get into the courtroom. Aisha came in five minutes later and took her seat at her table.

Then the judge spoke. "In the case of State v. Williams, has the jury reached a verdict?"

"We have your honor," the foreman announced.

"Will the Defendant please rise," Judge Wright said.

Darnell and I stood up and I held his hand tighter and tighter. I could barely breathe. My heart was pounding so loudly I could hear it in my ears.

"On Count 1, possession of a controlled substance with intent to distribute, how does the jury find?"

"Not guilty," the foreman said.

"On Count 2, murder in the first degree, how does the jury find?"

"Not guilty."

"Is this the unanimous verdict of the jury?"

"It is, your honor."

"The defendant is free to go," he said, and then thanked the jury for their service.

Darnell was standing and sobbing next to me. I put my arm around him and he embraced me tighter than anybody ever has. "Oh, Ms. Ross, thank you, thank you, thank you," he said. "Thank you."

I, too, was crying as much as Darnell was.

"You did it," he said. "You did it, you did it, you did it."

"No, *we* did it," I said. "We did it, Darnell. We did it."

We did it.

Forty-Nine

Three Weeks Later

"Okay, Luca," I said to Luca Facinelli. Lily Fuller came through for Axel and me and agreed to testify in front of Internal Affairs about Cooper's behavior and what she saw. That gave Internal Affairs probable cause to search Cooper's house, which they did one day when he was at work. They combed his entire house, looking for clues that Alaina Morosky had been in his house. They found her hairs all over the house and in his car.

Based upon that evidence, they obtained magisterial permission to wire-tap Cooper. Luca wouldn't tell Cooper he was Salvatore but wouldn't tell him he wasn't Salvatore, either. I had no idea if Cooper knew Salvatore had an identical twin brother, but, even if he did, I didn't think he'd think Luca wasn't Sal. I hoped and prayed this worked.

"Now, you go over to Cooper's house," I said to Luca. "You start drinking with him and get him talking. Get him talking about Alaina Morosky and about Officer Parker. Steer him to those subjects. He'll probably want to talk about these subjects because he's so damned proud he got away with their murders. I'll be with Axel and Agent Handler, the investigator assigned this case, listening in. Good luck."

I sent Luca over to Cooper's house with a six pack of beer and hoped and prayed he could get the necessary evidence to bring that bastard down. All we needed was Cooper confessing to these murders and we'd nail him.

The Internal Affairs investigators had already uncovered the off-shore account information, so Cooper was going down for corruption at the very least. At the very least. But I wanted his ass in prison for murder. I didn't want him serving time at Club Fed with the other guys caught with their hands in the cookie jar. I wanted him serving hard time with hardened felons. I wanted him as somebody's butt bitch. That's what I wanted.

I went into the van where Axel and Agent Handler were sitting with headphones on. Agent Handler was an African-American 40-year veteran cop and Internal Affairs investigator who said he'd suspected Cooper was dirty for a long time but never got the evidence to prove anything. He was just as anxious to bring Cooper down as I was, if that was even possible.

He was especially incensed when I told him about how Cooper tried to railroad Darnell. Darnell, for his part, was back at home, working double-time to get caught up in school so he could start his semester at MIT on time. He no longer worked at Church's – Sally tried to apologize, but he wasn't having it, so he got a job at the Costco close to his house. The pay was better and so was the environment. "And there's no chance I'll come up on a dead body there," he said with a smile.

Anita was fully recovered but she quit one of her jobs. Darnell was making four dollars more per hour at Costco, which added up and meant Anita only had to work one job.

Darnell said he was glad he went to jail. "I'll never take anything for granted again," he said. "And you have no idea how much I know that every day is a gift. Every second I spend on the outside means the world to me. I hated being in jail but now that I'm out, I'm glad I was in. Hardships make the good times seem even better."

Darnell would go far, of that I was sure.

Agent Handler had his head phones on and he snapped his fingers at me. I put on my headphones and listened.

The two men were laughing and I heard the sounds of beer bottles clinking together. "Man," Luca said. "I still can't get over how you beat that case down, man."

"I know, right? They never had anything on me anyhow, you know," Cooper said. "They'll never have anything on me, or you, either. I don't know how we get away with what we get away with. Nobody in our department has a clue. Not a fucking clue."

"Yeah."

A pause. "I only wish the jury would've put that nigger Darnell in prison. That case is active again. The case of who killed Parker. You haven't heard anything about that, have you?"

"No, man, I haven't heard. I hear they're investigating it hard though."

"That stupid cunt Ross put the spotlight on me at the nigger's trial," Cooper said. "If she didn't do that, I could've worked Parker's case. They'll never put me on that case now because that stupid cunt Harper Ross. Where does she get off, accusing me of killing Parker?"

"Well, you *did* kill Parker."

"I know I killed him but that's not the point. She had no proof of that yet she told the jury I did it. Fuck that bitch, man. Fuck her."

"You gonna take out Ross next?"

"No, I'm gonna take out Hammer next," he said, referring to the agent currently assigned to the Parker murder case. "Or maybe I'll offer him a cut of the money I got stored in the Caymans if he agrees to look the other way if he gets evidence I did it. I don't know. I'll burn that bridge when I come to it, man."

"And then take out Ross?"

"Yeah, she's definitely on my list," he said. "Fucking cunt. I'd like to gut her like a pig."

"Like you did to Alaina, right?"

"Nah. I didn't gut Alaina. I told you that. I strangled her." There was a pause. "That fucking Alaina would've ruined my life.

Fuck that bitch too. Threatening me with a paternity action. Threatening me with making me take a DNA test. I got your DNA test right here, you worthless piece of shit cunt."

I looked over at Handler, who looked back at me and smiled. He spoke into his microphone. "Okay, we got it. On my count, 1, 2, 3 go."

I couldn't quit laughing when I heard the SWAT team burst into Cooper's home.

"What the fuck is this bullshit?" I heard Cooper say.

"Morgan Cooper, you are under arrest for the murder of Officer Jake Parker and for Alaina Morosky," I heard one of the officers say. "You have the right to remain silent...."

Music to my ears.

Music to my fucking ears.

FIFTY

"Mate, you okay?" Axel said. He was standing next to me in the cemetery. I came to visit Stephen to tell him I finally got justice for him. That he didn't die in vain.

Stella the dog was lying beside the stone, whimpering softly. I think she knew.

I bent down and put a rose on his white stone in the ground. "Yes," I said, feeling my tears come. "I think so." I felt a huge lump in my throat, which subsided and then came right back up again. "Why do I feel so awful? I just feel like if I didn't bring him here, he-"

"He'd have still died, mate, but he'd have died miserable. At least this way he got to experience life again. It was too brief for him, and he should've gotten the chance to experience much more, but he got to experience happiness before he died. He had a job, a lady, and friends. If you would've left well enough alone, lass, he'd have lived on more years, but they would've been lonely years and not filled with love and joy. You gave him that for a brief time – love and joy. Be happy for that, mate."

The tears kept coming but I nodded and put my head on Axel's shoulder.

I bent down to the stone. "Stephen," I said softly. "I did it. I nailed that bastard who did this to you. Thank you for your bravery. I'm so sorry you died the way you did. All alone, stabbed in the shower by a psychopath. I'm so sorry, Stephen. I'm so sorry. But Cooper will go to prison for a long, long time."

"I got justice for you, Stephen. I got justice for you."

Axel and I walked slowly away from the grave. I realized I didn't really properly grieve for Stephen. I was angry for so long and then I was wound tight about Darnell's trial. It was only after Darnell was acquitted and Cooper was put into jail, awaiting his trial for two murders, maybe three if the investigators could throw Stephen's murder into the mix, that I let myself feel the sadness just below the surface. I no longer felt the burning and hunger for justice. Stephen was getting that justice, finally.

That burning was replaced by deep sadness.

It was then that I looked at my cell phone. I smiled as I recognized Ginger's phone number. She was apparently calling me from LA, where she moved to go into the adult film industry. I called her back.

"Hey Ginger," I said, wiping my eyes. "How are you?"

"Harper, you have to come out here, you just have to," she said, panic in her voice.

"Ginger, I can't-"

"You have to, Harper. You have to. I-I-I-I..."

"You what, Ginger? Ginger, talk to me."

"I've been charged with murder."

You know you wanna know what happens next with Ginger! *LA Defense* is available NOW!!!!!

Ginger Perry, Harper's star witness in her previous murder trial, left Kansas City for the greener pastures of the Los Angeles adult film scene. As soon as she gets out to the West Coast, however, she catches a case. A big case. A murder case.

The victim is a powerful studio head. Ginger insists she was framed. Harper's not so sure. She wants to give Ginger the benefit of the doubt, but Ginger's always been a little shady. Nevertheless, she agrees to take the case. After all, she hasn't had a vacation in years, and a trip to Los Angeles is as much of a vacation as she's ever going to get - even if it's not really a vacation, but another murder case. Harper knows that she needs another murder case like she needs a hole in the head, but she just can't resist a lost cause.

And Ginger's case seems to be as lost of a cause as you can get.

With the twists, turns and lightning-fast pace you've come to expect from a Harper Ross Legal Thriller, L.A. Defense is not to be missed!

For information about upcoming titles in the *Harper Ross Legal Thriller* series, sign up for my mailing list! You'll be the first to know about new releases and you'll be the first to know about any promotions!!!!http://eepurl.com/hBqhtr

Also by Rachel Sinclair

For information about upcoming titles in the *Harper Ross Legal Thriller* series, sign up for my mailing list! You'll be the first to know about new releases and you'll be the first to know about any promotions!!!! http://eepurl.com/hBqhtr

Johnson County Legal Thrillers (Kansas City, Missouri)

Bad Faith

Justice Denied

Hidden Defendant

Injustice for All

LA Defense

The Associate

The Alibi

Reasonable Doubt

The Accused

Secrets and Lies

Until Proven Guilty

Emerson Justice Legal Thrillers (Los Angeles)

Dark Justice

Blind Justice

Southern California Legal Thrillers (San Diego)

Presumption of Guilt

Justice Delayed

By Reason of Insanity

Wrongful Conviction

The Trial

Milton Keynes UK
Ingram Content Group UK Ltd.
UKHW040711201123
432908UK00001B/291